NIGHTHAWK

OTHER TITLES BY ARTEMIS OAKGROVE

The Raging Peace Volume One
of the Throne Trilogy

Dreams of Vengeance Volume Two
of the Throne Trilogy

Throne of Council Volume Three
of the Throne Trilogy

NIGHTHAWK

by

Artemis OakGrove

LACE PUBLICATIONS

LADY WINSTON SERIES

Library of Congress Cataloging-in-Publication Data

OakGrove, Artemis, date
  Nighthawk.

  (Lady Winston series)
  I. Title. II. Series.
PS3565.A4N5   1987   813'.54   87–26050
ISBN 0-917597-11-7

* * *

Printed in the United States of America.

First Edition.
First printing.

Cover design by Lambda Graphics, Denver
Cover illustration by Vicki

Lace Publications
POB 10037
Denver CO 80210-0037

All characters in this book are fictional and any resemblance to persons living or deceased is purely coincidental.

This book is dedicated to Karen Hays, my honey. She keeps on loving me and encouraging me to write. She has my heart.

The author wishes to thank Rachael, whose picture in *On Our Backs* inspired the creation of the character Nighthawk.

Moonyean for her skillful word proessing and lusty enthusiasm and meaningful insight.

Doris L. Harris for her valuable comments.

Chapter One

"Come on, Lori, meet me down at the Subway Club." Cloud's full, heavy voice rarely revealed her level of intoxication, but Lori suspected the big Indian on the other end of the line was near the falling down point. Why else would she be calling at one o'clock in the morning to make this unlikely request?

"Cloud, the Subway is a private club," Lori answered shakily. She had heard some scary stories about that place. Cloud went there often but had never invited Lori before.

"Aw, come on, baby, I miss you. I'll leave your name at the door so you can get in," Cloud pleaded sweetly, knowing Lori couldn't resist.

Lori felt her whole body heat up with the melt only Cloud could make her feel. "Okay," she consented softly. She would do *any*thing Cloud asked her to. "I'll get dressed and get a cab."

"Great, doll." Already the faint beginnings of disinterest could be detected in Cloud's words as she hung up the phone, leaving Lori silent, empty and hot with desire.

"Why do I *always* give in to her?" Lori asked herself helplessly. She didn't answer her own question. Instead she went to her bath to wash the sleep from her body, and put on the pretty floral-print dress that made Cloud smile wickedly every time she saw her in it.

For two years Lori had not known a moment when her thoughts did not congregate around her glamourized image of Cloud Three Eagles. Lori's neighbors in her building had questioned her with concern about the tall, broad-shouldered, fierce-looking Indian. They thought Cloud was trouble on the run and that Lori was too sweet to be mixed up with her. Lori dismissed their concern and went blindly about worshipping the woman.

So blindly that she was oblivious to the danger she placed herself in by going out alone in the core of a big city, at night, to a club in the ghetto. It wasn't until she walked in the door of the Subway and gave her name to the mean-looking black woman who confronted her that she thought she might be doing the wrong thing.

But the bouncer stepped aside for her, then pointed down the dark staircase. Lori descended gingerly and opened the steel door at the bottom. After her eyes adjusted to the murky atmosphere, she began to look around for Cloud. Surely she'd be easy to spot among these unwelcoming suspicious faces. Cloud's wild warrior look stood out everywhere. Lori wished that Cloud would spot her first; she didn't know if she could find the courage to actually *walk* through this bar alone.

Slowly she edged along a wall trying not to counter the glowering stares with the look of fear that was gathering in her heart. It didn't take long to realize that hers was the only white face there.

Lori noted with relief that a hush had not fallen over this angry group of women. The sound system still vibrated with heavy beat music and Lori took what comfort she could from the way it disguised the conversations going on around her.

The women let Lori by them easily enough. Still, her resolve was weakened by what sounded like hisses and growls in her wake. In her mind she was screaming for Cloud to *please* find her, make it all right for her to be there.

She spied the pool table and inched toward it. The women play-

2

ing there were too intent on their game to notice her; they were playing for money, lots of it, Lori decided. As she turned quickly away from the sight of someone shooting up, Lori was completely unaware that she was being watched — very closely — and had been since she first walked in the club's lower entrance.

She also wasn't paying attention to where she was walking. No matter. The woman who suddenly blocked her path would have stepped in Lori's way wherever she'd have headed.

Lori sucked in her breath, surprised. Her eyes were only chest-level with the very big, very black woman in her path.

"What's you doing in here, *white* girl?" the stranger demanded, making no attempt to hide the distaste with which she spoke the word "white".

Instantly trembling, Lori's mouth went dry. She tried to back away but was grabbed hard from behind by another woman who shook her back into place as if to say, Stay here and answer her, now.

"I . . . I . . . ," Lori stammered. Her heart was pounding but she knew she had to explain herself. It didn't take anything special to see she was trespassing. "Cloud asked me to meet her here," she replied meekly, lowering her eyes, praying fervently for Cloud to just *please* show up.

"Cloud!?" the booming voice of the tall woman erupted sneeringly. "Cloud left fifteen minutes ago . . ." she was enjoying the panic breaking out over the pale face, ". . . some friend of hers from . . . where was it?" She lifted a ring-studded hand and snapped her fingers for someone to provide the information.

"South Dakota," an anonymous voice declared.

The woman smiled devilishly. "Yeah, South Dakota," she pronounced the name as though the state had just won a contest. "Blew into town and Cloud acted like she was some long lost cousin or somethin'." She shook her head in mock sadness. "They took off, whitey, for god knows where and only the devil could care when she'll come back." A couple women enjoying the scene chuckled mysteriously. "Look to me like she forgot *all* about you." The woman poked her finger into Lori's chest for emphasis, then looked to the woman holding Lori for confirmation.

"Look that way, 'Hawk," Lori's captor chimed in.

'Hawk! Lori's mind cried out. The Nighthawk? God, no. Cloud, where are you? You can't have left me here alone! Lori had never met the Nighthawk but had heard of this friend of Cloud's.

'Hawk tipped the frightened girl's face up and looked directly into her eyes. Large, round, trusting brown eyes; it startled 'Hawk when Lori shut her lids because she had the most incredible eyelashes: thick, light brown fringes that seemed more like a clipping from a fur coat. And too, Lori's hair moved 'Hawk — soft layers of feathers with golden highlights; it was so clean and shiny, even in this dreary light. The girl wasn't beautiful with her button nose, round face and average mouth. But she certainly wasn't hard to look at. 'Hawk wasn't surprised the girl found it too difficult to look at her — face on. Not many people could cope with the sight which was why she pulled her motorcycle hat so the brim obscured her eyes from the casual glance.

They said that she'd been born that way. "The devil's eyes" they'd called them. Those haunting eyes had caused her mother to abandon her as an infant. She didn't know who had raised her — whores, mostly — women who had taken pity on her — not good Christian women like her natural mother — women without values to teach. And 'Hawk had learned only those values that would keep her and her ever-growing body alive. Everyone was relieved when 'Hawk had topped out at six-foot-one and didn't just go on to grow through the ceiling. And she had a street-wise, fearless face to match.

Lori waited breathlessly for 'Hawk to take her hand away — she was *not* going to look into those eyes again. She thought Cloud had the most dramatic face she'd ever seen, but this 'Hawk had one up on the Indian. Her face was beautifully unique — square chin, *sharp* angles on the jaw and cheekbones, skin the color of a ripe walnut shell, and that fascinating scar from the outside of her right eye down to the nostril of her wide nose.

'Hawk finally let go of her chin and Lori began to breathe once again and she opened her eyes. The smell of fine leather predominated as 'Hawk took a step closer. She wore all shiny black leather and silver studs and chains except for the black net muscle shirt under her creaking jacket.

"Check out these knockers, will ya?" 'Hawk invited generally to those of her friends close by. 'Hawk loved big tits — the bigger, the better and this girl's tits were as big as most women she'd played with. Their full generosity filled out the cotton wrap-around dress almost to the point of straining. She noticed how nicely they moved when the girl's chest heaved with fear.

Lori flinched when 'Hawk's big hand reached for the bow at her hip. They were nice hands actually—long, squared fingers — but the rings, they were another matter. Lori saw one in silver of a skull with ruby eyes and stopped looking. Something told her to keep her mouth shut unless she was told to speak. Not hard for Lori since she wasn't much of a talker anyway, except with Cloud who sometimes genuinely seemed to care about what she had to say. 'Hawk knew her way around women's clothes and in an instant she had Lori's dress open in the front.

"Fu-uck," 'Hawk uttered hoarsely drawing attention to herself and her obvious surprise at what she saw. She'd seen pierced nipples before; they all had. Only once before had she seen a woman with both nipples pierced but it had been an unattractive butch woman and the sight had done nothing for her. What was before her now was glorious. These beautifully huge breasts, each pointing its own direction now that it was free of the garment, had large, dark brown areola. And, as if God had planned it, through each hardened tip was a thick gold ring. Each ring had a knob on it and was big enough around to slip a finger through to the first knuckle.

Cool whistles of appreciation covered 'Hawk's brief loss of composure. In a way some of the women witnessing this rare scene were glad to see that 'Hawk could still *be* moved. It made her a little more like them: human.

Lori was stunned. No one had ever reacted to her in that way before. A brief thrill of electricity rushed through her, followed by a deep blush. No matter how exciting it was that her physical body had just shaken the unshakable, she was still partly naked in front of a room full of strangers. In the last two years only her doctor and Cloud had seen her breasts (and the woman who had pierced her nipples).

She was a shy, private, small-town girl and mostly naive. Everything she'd learned about life, she'd learned from Cloud. The women she'd been with prior to Cloud were about as unknowing as she. So how was she supposed to just stand there and let someone ogle her bare breasts? Still, even the most foolish girl knew when to set aside morals and decency in favor of survival. These women carried knives — and guns. Lori knew *that* much. If one of them decided she wasn't worthwhile and killed her, who would know? Who would tell? No one. She'd just become another statistic on the police blotter . . . if anyone even found her body. Lori didn't have much in the way of fine attributes but she was nothing if not able to keep her wits in a crisis. This was definitely a crisis. Completely embarrassed or not, she maintained a quiet, yielding attitude.

Man, 'Hawk thought, something is really different here. She had never been with a white woman — it was practically against her religion. She wanted to explain the growing pressure in her abdomen on the nipple rings and wasn't succeeding. There was something about this white girl that drew her, something she couldn't explain. Why try? It felt *good* to get this turned on. And wasn't she the cool customer who could always look unaffected even when she was burning up with need? But she had better get her shit under control, right now. She did. To everyone she was once more the Nighthawk — undisputed leader of a large range of turf. Top dog. King of the hill.

But it took everything she had to stay reasonable when she reached for the rings and took a tight hold of them with her thumbs and forefingers. The *feel* of them as they strained between her grip and the weight of the breasts was unreal. She lifted the rings up to stretch the nipples.

"Who made you do this?" she asked gruffly.

Lori was confused. "No one," she supplied cautiously.

'Hawk turned the rings to fold the nipples to the side. She was mildly pleased when the action didn't seem to faze the girl. The piercing was clearly well healed.

"What?" 'Hawk growled. If this bitch was lying she'd be in for some stuff.

"I did it for Cloud," Lori added quickly sensing she'd better tell. "Cloud said she liked . . ." her voice lowered to a whisper because actually saying the term embarrassed her further, "pierced nipples. So I did it to make her happy." She must have said the right thing because she was rewarded with a beautiful toothy grin. Then laughter.

"Well, I'll be damned," 'Hawk roared. She let go of Lori and stepped back to rest her haunches on a stool. With one hand she took a cigarette from her jacket and her other hand lowered to her crotch to adjust herself. It was a calculated move designed to draw Lori's attention to the long, low bulge in her black leather pants. She took a match and sparked it with her thumbnail. Casually she lit her cigarette while savoring the widening of Lori's eyes.

Her comrades shifted restlessly waiting to see which way the wind was going to blow.

"Hear that, guys? Cloud's been holding out on us," she announced to show she wasn't at all displeased with this situation. In fact, she was very pleased. This was about as ideal as if she'd planned it. She *had* planned to ask what Cloud had seen in this girl but forgot all about *that* concern.

A murmur of assent and chuckling rustled through the crowd. It was clear that Cloud had been seeing this little tart for some time and had been hoarding her. That was against the rules. Being head honcho was a lot of work requiring constant vigilance, perfected fighting skills and cunning. But the benefits made it worthwhile. One of those benefits was that whoever could stay at the top got a piece of any broad she wanted. No one there that night who had a girl of her own could say that girl hadn't been banged by the Nighthawk. 'Hawk took her share whether she wanted the bitch or not, strictly on principle. And nobody *ever* stood in her way.

So now here was Cloud's woman, right in front of her, in about as vulnerable a position as possible. 'Hawk was going to take more than her share — she was going to take it *all*. And she'd also put the word on the street that the 'Hawk was *lookin'* for Cloud Three Eagles. Cloud was gonna *pay* for this bit of treachery.

"It seems big chief Three Eagles had herself a squaw all this time and hasn't paid the 'Hawk for the privilege. . . ." She let her statement disintegrate into the smoke for a moment, watching horror transform Lori's face.

"Castle," 'Hawk called loudly to be heard over the music.

"Hey," Castle replied quickly.

"Your old lady's about this girl's size, isn't she?" 'Hawk had an impeccable memory for women.

"Yes, sir!" Castle agreed smartly, ever aware of her position.

"Tell her the 'Hawk sends her a gift — this pretty dress." For the first time Lori put up a struggle. She tried to fight against the dress being stripped from her. Not because she realized the significance of being deprived of it but because the dress was special. It made Cloud smile at her *that* way.

Her struggle was amusing. The dress came off easily and was draped over Castle's shoulder. Likewise the half-slip. The panties 'Hawk pocketed. What remained was a helpless piece of white tail in thigh-high nylons and black heels. Her hands were tied with rope behind her and she was suddenly picked up by the upper arms and thighs and spread wide. These women had presented unwilling women to 'Hawk before and they knew what she expected.

Silently, 'Hawk unzipped her pants and reached inside for the long, black dildo strapped to her. She pulled the fat tip free and worked the shaft with her hand.

Lori froze. She knew what a big stick like that could do if she fought against it — it could rip her wide open. She knew only too well. Lori was only twenty-one years old but she had already lost her uterus because Cloud had gone crazy one night and wouldn't listen when she begged her to stop.

If 'Hawk had known how traumatized and used this sweet girl already was she might not have enjoyed herself as much. As it was she lost herself in the idea that she was defiling this virginal-looking cunt for the first time and it was driving her wild.

She paused to tease the pink lips with the tip of her thing, momentarily mesmerized by the contrast of her black prick and this white pussy. She diddled it over the girl's clitoris and smiled when it stiffened for her.

Lori was alarmed that 'Hawk's attention felt good. But she was relieved, too, because she *had* to relax if she was going to survive this. She focused her attention on her pelvic muscles and succeeded in letting the pole glide into her. Slow and easy — to the hilt.

Watching her cock disappear into the pussy shut off reality for 'Hawk. From there, there was nothing but her cock and that cunt. The grunting, moaning and cries went unheard. 'Hawk was only aware of the slipping, sliding wet sounds of this white piece of tail.

She had *never* cared about pleasing a woman she was raping but the draw of Lori's pulsing clitoris was too much. Almost without her permission 'Hawk's own thumb gravitated to it and jiggled it as only an expert like 'Hawk could. Had she known her fellows were availing themselves of Lori's mouth and abundant breasts she would have been even more seriously out of her mind. But she wasn't aware and they went on yanking on the rings and grinding their fingers into Lori's tits and shoving their hard tongues down her throat. 'Hawk went on stabbing the receptive hole and pounding her thumb on the clit.

Lori just went. She had no idea how many hands pawed her, pinched her or pulled at her. Mouth after vicious mouth gagged her. Furious moans assailed her. She was being relentlessly fucked — hard — so hard, and fast. It hurt. It felt good. It frightened her. It excited her. She dared not cry out for fear of being misunderstood or slapped silly to shut her up. Despite the frenzy, she felt her thighs and buttocks tighten. She was building for an orgasm and couldn't keep it from happening.

'Hawk was fast approaching her boiling point; she rapped the accomplice closest to her on the arm to signal her condition. The-woman took the warning and stopped working on Lori, then made certain everyone else left off so their leader could finish her business without distraction.

By now everyone in the club knew what was going down and, to one degree or another, was enjoying the activity whether she was participating, watching or just listening in. Among the spectators were women who had themselves been raped by the Nighthawk; women who looked upon this act as a kind of initiation rite they all had survived to become members of an elite sisterhood.

To a woman, everyone in the club looked forward to that wonderful moment in time when the Nighthawk climaxed. The crowd and the music were silenced in anticipation.

The two women supporting Lori's weight closed their grip against the strain of her tightening body. The rigidness of her torso made her breasts all the more responsive to the merciless humping movements 'Hawk pushed through her.

The giant tits jiggled and bobbed rhythmically. 'Hawk focused on the helpless breasts as she quickened the pace of her hips. The fingers of her free hand dug into Lori's thigh for support. Sweat began to drip from 'Hawk's glistening face; her lips parted and a gurgling moan passed through them. While actually in the clutches of her own orgasm, 'Hawk stopped working Lori's clit. The once occupied hand dug meanly into Lori's other thigh as 'Hawk made the final cruel thrusts that would break off her last fragment of reason to reveal the pure essence of her animalistic state of madness.

Head tipped slightly back, lips snarling, eyes squeezed shut, back taut, 'Hawk was breathless for a second, then let forth a screaming groan of seeming anguish worthy of any birthing room.

Lori was overwhelmed by this display of conquest and passion. For as fearsome as 'Hawk was, it was impossible not to look at her. 'Hawk bound people to her by allowing them to observe her in this vulnerable position of uncontrol. She was sharing something deep and meaningful to her with each of them. In return these women gave their unfailing loyalty to 'Hawk.

Had Lori known enough about herself and life in general, she would have been aware of the beginnings of that same attaching loyalty growing within her. With more self-knowledge Lori may have been able to understand why she found women like Cloud and 'Hawk so exciting and appealing. She would have also known that this activity had ceased to be rape and had begun to be sex. And her body was screaming for it to continue.

Lured by Lori's tangible, unspoken need, 'Hawk listened for the collective sigh of relief that came to her from all sides and soothed her back to a frame of mind where she could resume normal functions. She was surprised that it didn't feel awkward to find a nearly orgasmic woman mounted on her rod after what had begun as an act of violation.

Lori's voluptuous body was flushed and shimmering. Her face was vibrant with longing. Those eyes! Christ almighty, the look in them shot through 'Hawk like well-aimed arrows, lodging somewhere in a core of her being she had never before discovered.

'Hawk alone was aware of the interchange. If Lori had had the courage to look into the leader's eyes, she would have seen it, too. And known. Instead, the moment was discharged when 'Hawk returned her thumb to the energized peak of desire between Lori's swollen lips. Her other hand reached for a gold ring, grabbed it and dragged the nipple and its burden of womanflesh to meet its twin where she took the second ring and pulled them together. Lori's eyes enlarged as she saw the dextrous black hand start to tug on them, increasing the tempo of her yanks to match the furious pace of her clitoral massage.

As able to silence herself as Lori was, she was in over her head now. The sensations were simply too incredible to concentrate on anything but what 'Hawk was making her feel. The full scope of being completely taken, used, mastered, forced and overpowered engulfed her. She was utterly at 'Hawk's mercy, an instrument of 'Hawk's whim. Her cries were plaintive, urgent . . . moans at first. Then, as 'Hawk put the full force of her will behind her work, screams came. She was held securely as she bucked and bucked. When she came her body folded and collapsed.

'Hawk's smile was the image of triumph. She watched Lori's abdominal muscles flex over and over. The dildo moved in and out independently as Lori's vagina pumped it with deep contractions that left her heaving and sighing with delicious relief.

A small butch woman fell to her knees next to 'Hawk with the hope of being allowed to lick the remains of Lori's come from the black pole gliding luxuriously out of Lori's soaking pussy. The woman watched it eagerly as it dangled in front of her. Her disappointment was obvious when the object of her desire was tucked neatly back into the dark embrace of 'Hawk's leather pants.

'Hawk ignored the offer to clean her cock. She wanted the wet and smell and taste to stay with *her*. (Had she known herself more completely, she might have realized that she felt there was something precious about it that she wasn't willing to give away.)

This unusual behavior did not go unnoticed by her comrades. First she pleased this woman, then she didn't have her prick cleaned, they thought in unison. They would have understood this turn of events if the woman who had inspired this new behavior had been black. But this was a *white* cunt . . . .

'Hawk didn't get to the top by being slow on the draw. She knew exactly where she was going with this apparent new twist. She reached between Lori's spread legs for the balance of the rope that secured the girl's wrists. Holding the length of cord loosely in her hand, she motioned for Lori to be let go to stand. While waiting for the girl to regain enough stability to walk 'Hawk built her case.

"Kramer," she addressed one of the women who had been holding Lori.

"Yeah, 'Hawk," Kramer replied attentively.

"Have I ever made a play for one of your bitches?"

Kramer knew 'Hawk meant: In all these years have I ever tried to take a woman away from you? "Not once, 'Hawk," she answered confidently.

"What about you, Shirl?" 'Hawk only addressed people who she considered friends by their first name. (From now on, Cloud would be Three Eagles.)

Shirl didn't hesitate to answer. She was a friend and could speak freely. "No, 'Hawk. You always take your share, but after that we've all always had the right to turn you down if you wanted more." No one ever did turn 'Hawk down if she expressed a desire to use someone's girl. It was thought of as an honor to possess a woman who occasionally caught 'Hawk's fancy. Shirl was glad 'Hawk had never wavered from that policy because the Nighthawk liked her woman a lot.

"That's right," 'Hawk confirmed as she purposely looked Lori up and down. "And now I'm gonna show you what happens when you try to keep a bitch a secret the way Three Eagles has."

Lori's heart pounded faster. She was just sure she was in for a beating. But 'Hawk grew distant and cold. She yanked the rope so that it pulled Lori's wrists against her spine and the rope cut into her crack and cunt. 'Hawk turned around, raising the rope over her shoulder and walked slowly through the bar. Lori followed helplessly, struggling to keep her balance.

"If you don't play by the rules," 'Hawk announced loudly, "your woman will become the property of the Subway Club. And we all know that everything that belongs to the Subway Club belongs to the Nighthawk."

The women in the bar were laughing mockingly but they were afraid. The Nighthawk was not temperate in her reprisals. To cover for their fear they began to torment Lori by grasping at her breasts, swatting her backside and abusing her verbally with taunts of racial hatred.

The bartender, a pretty but street-hardened Puerto Rican woman, walked over to the scene of the rape and picked up the small purse Lori had dropped. After putting it in a cupboard under the bar she watched 'Hawk and waited. She knew 'Hawk would look her way and when she did, Magdalene or Maggie as everyone called her, answered with a stern, unforgiving stare. She disapproved of what 'Hawk was doing. She didn't say so openly; she didn't have to. 'Hawk countered with a stubborn, resolved expression, and went on dragging the innocent girl behind her.

As 'Hawk made the circuit of the bar everyone realized that their harassment of Lori was appeasing their leader. The cruelties intensified as she neared a dirty black door at the rear of the club.

Lori was mortified and paralyzed with fear. Women were spitting on her and the femmes were clawing her with long, sharp fingernails. Suddenly she was pushed, alone, through the opened black door into a dark room and the door was closed and locked after her.

Lori stumbled and nearly fell but she caught herself. She'd never known a place could be so dark. Once her eyes grew accustomed to the absence of light she saw it wasn't totally dark after all. From under the door she'd been shoved through came a faint sliver of light. Wanting to cry but more curious than afraid, Lori reached out with all her senses to find something that could tell her where she was. It was the smell of the place that gave it away: it smelled dirty certainly, but it smelled lived-in. Stale cooking odors, trash that needed taking out, body odor—Lori picked each smell out and knew she wasn't in a storeroom or closet as she first feared.

If this were a place where someone lived there would be a light, if she could just find it. Warily she stepped to the side of the door where she hoped to locate a switch. It was there; she nudged it with her upper arm. She knew it was too much to ask that it be a simple lever she could move up with her shoulder. The switch would have to be turned and Lori's hands were still secured behind her back. After some concentrated effort, Lori was rewarded and the room was now glaringly bright after the near complete darkness. How much less frightening it was now to be able to *see*.

Lori was right—someone did live there. The room where she stood served as a living, dining room and kitchen. She noted a mattress-like couch, a table with one chair, an old refrigerator and an even older sink. The sparse counter top and cupboards were overtaken by dirty dishes, rotten food and bugs which hadn't bothered to scatter when the light came on. Even though Lori didn't have a queasy stomach, she preferred clean.

To her right was a door to an equally dirty bathroom that had another door to a bedroom she discovered as she walked part way into it. A second door to the bedroom led back to the kitchen andthe light from there showed a mussed bed, a footlocker, night-stand and a weight bench which was surrounded by free weights.

Lori's best guess was that this "apartment" was occupied by 'Hawk. Suddenly, Lori's adrenalin stopped fueling her courage and she felt empty and frightened and alone. She sat on the couch in the main room and cried. Before long, Lori had cried herself to sleep.

* * *

'Hawk couldn't remember the last time she'd seen the sun; she was a creature of darkness; she only lived at night. After she'd dispensed with Lori, 'Hawk had left the bar to do her "rounds". She kept a kind of law and order in her neighborhood using an effec-tive, elaborate system of communication and justice. While her upbringing had been patchy and inconsistent, 'Hawk had managed to carve out an education for herself. She could read and write quite adequately and figures came easily to her. So did business and human nature. She was really very intelligent, a fact she kept hid-den because she was too proud to admit she hated being denied the opportunities she could have capitalized on to get her out of the ghetto that trapped her. She didn't know any other life but she made the most of what she knew. She ruled her turf with an iron hand, dealt out justice according to her own standards, and brooked no defiance.

'Hawk had two causes: homeless children and women of the night. Hate was not a strong enough word for what she felt for pimps. 'Hawk didn't allow them to operate on her turf. All the hookers in her domain belonged to houses, with madams. A couple pimps had tried once to defy 'Hawk and had been found dead with bullets through their skulls fired at point blank range. The police sort of "looked the other way" and were glad of the free housekeep-ing.

Homeless children were protected by a system of "parents" and-"grandparents" who, while not adopting the children outright, saw to it that no one did without.

'Hawk had learned early that most people were basically good and if you made it easy for them to help, they'd do it. She knew how to instill a sense of pride in her "community" and its constituents were glad for 'Hawk's vigilance, and that she genuinely cared about them. Her ruthless leadership was tempered by altruism.

What then was she doing with this helpless white girl curled up on her crash couch (a place where she was more used to seeing an occasional stray sleeping)? 'Hawk suspected the only thing this girl had ever done wrong was fall for a big, dumb Indian. She untied Lori's wrists stopping her own hand short of smoothing the girl's hair. After placing an old blanket over Lori's desirable body she stood tall and shook her head sadly. She knew she had to play this hand out to the end but a part of her wished she could find a way to punish Three Eagles, spare the girl and still preserve the respect of those beneath her. She couldn't budge a millimeter from her stance and that knowledge drew a deep sigh from her. Then, as though she'd forgotten all about her problem, she turned toward her bedroom and shut both doors. It was dawn.

Lori stirred at mid-day. Absently she used the bathroom before she realized she wasn't in her own apartment. She checked the front door and found it locked from the inside. Looking around her, glad her hands were free, Lori saw only one way to cope.

She was the oldest child of a large family from a small town. Doing dishes and cleaning house and cooking were what she'd done since she was tall enough to reach things. She and Cinderella had a thing or two in common. But Lori knew better than to believe any fairy godmother was going to help *her* out. There were days when she wondered if anyone in her family had noticed that she'd saved enough money as a waitress to pack her bag and strike out for the big city. She'd been so invisible. She was glad actually because her father had never noticed her as he had a younger sister who wasn't smart enough to stay out of his way. Or maybe the sister liked it, Lori couldn't decide, or even really care. Nobody in her family knew anything about loving or caring.

How she came to realize she had no interest in men Lori couldn't say. All she knew was that she'd found herself in bed with a woman one night and it didn't seem odd or out of place. She just accepted it and found ways to keep making it happen because it felt good . . . felt better than anything she'd known prior to that. Admitting she was desperately searching for love and acceptance wasn't something Lori knew how to do.

But she knew how to make a home and somewhere in the disarray and filth she found soap and something to scrub with. She had to fill the time somehow. Looking at the closed bedroom door she told herself it *had* to be Nighthawk on the other side of that door. At some point someone would emerge from the room and maybe tell her what was going on. Or at least where she could find some-food that hadn't already perished.

It didn't occur to Lori that there was no way to tell what time of day it was until she was startled from her work by the closing of the bathroom door. The one window, well above the sink, was painted over. No light or air from outside found a way into this subterra-nean haunt.

'Hawk did finally come out of the bedroom, through the kitchen and out the front door. Lori's heart sank when she heard the dead-bolt lock from the outside. 'Hawk hadn't even looked at her, much less spoken to her.

It wasn't all *that* long before Lori heard a key in the door again. It was Maggie (although Lori didn't know who she was). She left a white styrofoam box on the table and took away the trash Lori had stacked by the door.

When she realized Lori didn't know the food was for her, Maggie pointed to the table and said, "Eat." Lori waited until Maggie left to eat the greasy ribs and heavy biscuits that had been left. Re-stored, she kept up her work until 'Hawk returned with a calm-looking woman who was carrying a case with strange instruments in it.

'Hawk moved Lori to the couch, made the girl sit on it and handed a key to the new woman. The woman locked the door after 'Hawk when she left and sat down to her work. Lori next noticed the music in the bar began to play as the woman swabbed her right breast with alcohol. She watched silently, curiously and was sub-missively cooperative. But Lori would not forget the next two hours of pain if she lived to be a hundred.

At last the woman unlocked the door and signaled to 'Hawk.

"Have any trouble?" 'Hawk asked when she closed the door.

"Not a peep," the woman replied as she started to put her instru-ments away.

'Hawk inspected the work earnestly. PROPERTY OF THE NIGHTHAWK the tattoo on Lori's right breast proclaimed in clear black lettering. Below the words was the 'Hawk's unusual device of an "N" with wings. The seal could be seen anywhere in 'Hawk's range. The whole tattoo measured less than two square inches. Then, just above Lori's triangle of sex hair, the tattoo artist had affixed two words using the sharp-angled street writing with a small arrow pointing downward. The tattoo said: FUCK HOLE. 'Hawk parted the lips of Lori's cunt to find the two gold rings that now pierced those lips then turned the girl around to inspect the last tattoo: a purple and black emblem resembling a government stamp on meat hanging at a butcher shop that said GRADE A WHITE MEAT. It was blazoned on the girl's right buttock.

"Man, you do nice work," 'Hawk congratulated the tattoo artist.

"Thanks, 'Hawk." The artist put her hand up to keep 'Hawk from paying her. "You've sent plenty of business my way and got my bike back when it was ripped off . . . this one's on me, pal." She creamed and bandaged her handiwork, then left written instructions and more bandages for its care. She slipped a pain pill into Lori's palm when 'Hawk wasn't looking and left. 'Hawk followed her out and locked the door.

Lori's mind was blank. She took the pill, cried, and once again fell asleep from sheer exhaustion.

The next few nights passed quietly. Lori was usually always alone with her work and her thoughts which mostly settled around Cloud Three Eagles. Lori knew not to look for the Indian to show up any time soon—she'd disappeared like this before. A friend would come into town and Cloud would take off on her motorcycle for weeks at a time. ("It's family, Lori," Cloud would insist emphatically whenever Lori tried to get an explanation for the long absences.) Cloud didn't think Lori had a right to question any of her activities. That didn't stop it from hurting any less.

Lori had no friends to speak of—only people around her who took a casual interest in her life. They all questioned why Lori put up with such shabby treatment. She dodged their concern with silence because she couldn't explain how good it was when Cloud was nice to her—how thoroughly special she felt when that big carved face opened with a warm smile. Or when those dark eyes bored into her with spears of desire that stabbed into her heart and belly like brands drawn from the fire. Would they understand what it was to have Cloud's huge square hands tear at her clothing to get at the body she needed? To feel the feathers from Cloud's armband

17

tickling her stomach while Cloud's mouth and fingers worked her nipples? To watch the patina of sweat glisten on her hard, muscular arms as she pulled her big poker from her chamois pants? To have a mouth and cunt so filled with tongue and cock she saw stars? Would any of them ever know what it was like to be so proud of having aroused, endured and satisfied such a powerful woman? No, Lori just did what she always did: kept to herself. She couldn't explain why she put up with Cloud's erratic behavior. Glory had a price and she was willing to pay it.

Yet here she was, cooking, cleaning and being invisible again. She still didn't know who Maggie was but she was always glad to see the older woman. Maggie had taken a liking to Lori although she was careful not to show it. She kept her contact with the captive as business-like as possible. By the second or third night of Lori's stay Maggie realized that some serious housework was being accomplished with the most rudimentary tools. If the girl was determined to be useful, she ought to have some help, Maggie decided. Without any exchange of words cleaning supplies and groceries began to appear, then little personal items such as nice bath soap and a comb.

Lori didn't take this special treatment for granted—every time Maggie entered the apartment Lori favored her with a warm smile. Maggie figured it was as close to a hello or thank you as she would get from the girl and replied with a knowing nod of approval. Lori was, after all, being held against her will. She didn't *have* to do *anything*. That she not only didn't complain or try to escape but was making the best of her situation genuinely impressed Maggie.

One evening after 'Hawk had gone Maggie walked into the apartment with some index cards in her hand. She found Lori scrubbing the walls in the bathroom. She'd never uttered more than a word or two to the girl and wasn't surprised when Lori was startled by a full sentence.

"Can you cook?" Maggie asked carefully. Silly question, Maggie, she told herself. I'll bet a round of drinks this girl has cooked since she was old enough to reach the stove. Something about Lori's willingness made Maggie want to get the girl to trust her.

Lori stopped cleaning and turned slowly toward Maggie. Eyes enlarged warily she nodded her head with a tiny, faraway movement that made her look all the more like the scared, trapped animal she was.

Maggie pressed on, ignoring the ache in her heart. She handed the cards to Lori who took them guardedly.

"These are recipes for food 'Hawk likes. 'Hawk will eat anything you put in front of her but she favors these."

Maggie's last sentence was colored with such obvious affection that Lori's heart warmed. Holding the cards reverently she read through them. Finding nothing beyond her ability in the instructions Lori smiled and nodded her agreement to prepare the dishes for her captor.

"Good," Maggie said gratefully. "'Hawk's had a tough time these last few nights . . . fighting off a new gang that's been trying to move in on her turf. Some good food would help her keep her strength up. I'll send somebody out to get what you'll need."

Lori was astonished by the unexpected confidence; it took her outside her own problems to recognize that someone had harder things to face than she did. Now she understood the disturbances she heard coming from the bar, 'Hawk's unusual hours, the bloody rag around 'Hawk's hand and the intense preoccupation with things other than her home base.

Maggie had slipped out leaving Lori alone again. She looked at herself in the mirror. Finally she began to see the tattoo on her breast. It was real and it wasn't going to wash off. Was that really what she was? Property? Something 'Hawk paid no more attention to than her weights? What would Cloud say or do when she discovered the brand? Lori fantasized about a dramatic rescue but it seemed as unlikely as a fairy godmother.

Lori *could* draw logical conclusions: if 'Hawk were tough enough to fight an entire gang, what chance would Cloud have? That was it, then. She *belonged* to the Nighthawk. Possession was nine-tenths of the law, wasn't it? And 'Hawk had stolen her, rustled her like cattle, the moment the Indian had turned her back. Lori would have much preferred to have been taken because she was desirable rather than as an example to demonstrate 'Hawk's dominion.

What if 'Hawk lost this battle she was waging against outsiders? Would Lori be passed on as spoils of war? That frightening thought got packed away in a dark corner of Lori's mind. But it was clear her very life was dependent upon 'Hawk and any good feelings

'Hawk might develop toward her. It would not do to have 'Hawk tire of you, Lori reminded herself.

She had spent some real effort trying to figure out what the other tattoos said. She had been humiliated by them, ashamed and insulted. While she wasn't proud of them, accepting their presence and meaning was obviously a matter of survival. That viewpoint meant she didn't have to accept responsibility for them.She hadn't asked to be marked, nor had she fought their application. Lori's helplessness was beginning to sink in.

Someone like Cloud could have fought her way out of getting caught in this situation. The only self-affirming act Lori had had the strength to do was leave her family. She wasn't sure what she was but the word fighter didn't qualify for describing her. Lori didn't see much when she looked inside herself, and attached no significance to labels like patient, generous, tenacious, durable.

Maybe that was why she so easily drew her identity from the first interesting thing to come into her dull, sleepy life: Cloud Three Eagles. Now there was strength, will, fire, courage and fascination. She conveniently ignored selfish, irresponsible and mean. She had been "Cloud's woman" for the last two years. That fantasy was crumbling in the face of hard reality. Was being a Fuck Hole above or below being totally invisible? Was she worse off now than when she lived with her family?

If 'Hawk would just acknowledge her, somehow, even *notice* her, it would make her situation bearable. Belonging to 'Hawk was better than not belonging to anyone though, Lori convinced herself as she began washing the wall in front of her with a small bit of purpose that hadn't been there before.

* * *

Around midnight of the tenth night of Lori's captivity, 'Hawk let herself into her apartment. Lori continued scrubbing the floor of the living room area, not stopping to notice the liveliness in 'Hawk's step.

'Hawk tossed the studded arm band she was holding into the air then caught it smartly in mid-descent. She was proud, triumphant and relieved. The armband had been worn by the leader of the rival gang. Now he was dead and the armband was hers. For as bloody and intense as the fighting had been the losses were surprisingly low. Only two of her own were injured seriously and three of his (one of whom wasn't expected to make it through the night).

'Hawk had just come from the hospital where her members, a man and a woman, were recovering from their battle wounds. Each had brightened with the news of the victory and reassured their conquering leader they were mending nicely.

Of the remaining vanquished gang fully half had crossed over to 'Hawk's ranks: followers who attached to whoever was the strongest. The others, unable to follow a female warrior no matter how strong, clever and battlewise, dispersed to join other warlords elsewhere in the city.

'Hawk was confident that it would be some time before she'd have to concern herself with a similar problem. She'd seen to that. The ruthless, sadistic fashion in which she had executed the rival leader served notice far and wide that the Nighthawk was not to be taken lightly.

After tossing the armband onto her bed, she poured a cup of coffee for herself, and sat down at the small table to relax.

When she stretched her hard body against the chairback she noticed Lori. The sight of the girl nearly startled her because she had completely forgotten about her captive.

Absently she moved her coffee cup away from her mouth to the table as she took in the stirring sight of Lori on her hands and knees scouring the linoleum. As Lori vigorously applied soapy water to the floor her dangling breasts joggled and jerked as she moved the brush in a circular motion. If she put both hands on the brush and moved forward and back her womanly burdens slapped from her arms and back close to her large pillowy thighs. Her plentiful buttocks were spread open and quaking, drawing attention to her unprotected crotch which gaped invitingly.

'Hawk reached into an inner pocket of her leather jacket for a cigarette and a match to light it. The plan was to sit back and watch this little show. But by the second tug on her cigarette 'Hawk's hand had unknowingly begun to massage and stroke the dildo she always wore under her sleek leather pants. In all these nights of war she had been careful not to dissipate her energies by screwing any women. She hadn't even thought about sex — she hadn't had time to. She was thinking about it now.

21

Her eyes were fixed on Lori's massive tits swaying under the sturdy torso. Her finger pads ached from wanting to touch the firm pierced nubs. The memory of how Lori's cunt had swallowed her cock tugged at her spraying sparks through her belly that started fires between her legs.

Lori moved sideways, taking the bucket along and 'Hawk pulled her thing from its warm, dark den and continued to squeeze and pull on it. Once more her white prisoner began the back and forth motion of scrubbing and 'Hawk forgot about her cigarette.

It had required all of her concentration but Lori was succeeding in her attempt to ignore 'Hawk's interest in her naked,quivering vulnerable flesh. She knew better than to let it show she knew she was being paid attention. If her captor could go for over a week and not so much as see her, then it followed she wasn't likely to have much use for a girl who might make even the slightest attempt to get noticed. The unseeableness she'd cultivated during her youth appeared to be her best ally.

Lori was jolted from that place inside herself where she hid at such times by 'Hawk's stiff rod at the entrance of her pussy. Precisely as 'Hawk had calculated, the busy action of scrubbing had impaled Lori on the black pole. Lori was suddenly aware that the Nighthawk was kneeling behind her! And was taking advantage of her back and forth movements to work her way inside Lori's private self! What a well-devised predicament Lori found herself in. She didn't *dare* move away, or stop her work. As she pushed forward on the brush her pussy was almost emptied of its invader except for its large head. When she pulled back on the brush her hips moved toward 'Hawk's pelvis and stuck the cock deep inside her vagina.

Lori was shamed by this trap she found herself in. It was one thing to remain passive and quiet and not fight against getting fucked. It was quite another to not only participate actively but do all the work herself. Lori knew what all of this looked like to 'Hawk: her possession, her "fuck-hole" was going for a ride on her rod.

That was *exactly* what it looked like to 'Hawk. Her mind was reeling with excitement. What a thrill it was to use this piece of white meat this way. To make it fuck itself! But her hands were dying to get at those dancing nipples. She lowered her torso onto

Lori's back so she could let the ringed nubs skate across her tingling palms and pads.

To adjust to 'Hawk's solid weight on her back, Lori had to stop working but her captor's fierce command seared frighteningly through her body.

"Keep scrubbing, white meat," 'Hawk barked. The body under her braced itself with one hand and made fast circular motions with the other to comply with the order. A deep, barreling moan escaped 'Hawk when she felt the nipples jerk and rub over her opened hands. Indescribable pleasure burned through her as she moaned again, loudly and with full unrestraint.

Just when Lori thought she could hold up no longer 'Hawk straightened up and dug her fingers into Lori's pelvis. Lori had been fucked from behind before and knew what to expect. What she didn't know was how she was going to keep cleaning the floor during this attack. 'Hawk had made it perfectly clear that screwing the drudge while she went about her chores was a significant part of the pleasure she was deriving from this act of exploitation. And that drudge had best keep at her chores if she knew what was good for her. She'd read in a dime novel once about plantation slaves who were taken advantage of by their overseers. ("Keep pickin' that *cotton*, gal. Don't you pay me no nevermind back hehr.") Lori gritted her teeth and held on as best she could.

'Hawk plunged into the white pussy with lightning speed. She both rocked her own hips and push-pulled on Lori's. The sound of Lori's buttocks slapping against her leathered pelvis and the sight of her bone-jarring fornication making great rippling waves through this plush body unraveled all the stress of the past few nights. Long before she normally would have, 'Hawk peaked, sparing the girl the ordeal she might have faced. Great heaving grunts accompanied 'Hawk's orgasmic releases as her final jabs pummeled Lori's cunt.

Relieved and in pain, Lori dipped her brush into the bucket and stayed cleaning the floor as 'Hawk's weapon moved out of her violated cunt. She wasn't sure this had been what she'd meant when she hoped to be noticed by 'Hawk. Instinctively she knew the battle 'Hawk had been fighting had been won and she was glad not to have been passed to some other leader as booty. A more realistic possibility of a future existed now. Lori was determined to rise above the status of a fuck-hole. She wanted to mean more to the leader than a convenient way to relieve tension.

Saying nothing, 'Hawk stood, tucked her cock into her pants then fastened them. Remaining a moment longer to get the full effect of what she'd just done, 'Hawk watched Lori for signs of distress or desire. But Lori played her part perfectly by going about her work as though nothing at all had happened. Pleased and content, 'Hawk joined the victory party going on in the bar without giving her captive another thought.

Chapter Two

Lori was beginning to get used to sleeping during what her body called day. She was learning to count nights and there had been fourteen of them. The apartment was hopelessly clean! She'd even managed to show Maggie that 'Hawk needed a better mattress for her sparkling bed. There were times when she longed for a razor to shave with but she was afraid to ask for one. It wouldn't be long before she had everything mended including her own shabby blanket which she was working on. Then she would be *looking* for activities to occupy her time. She was growing less and less uncomfortable with her constant nakedness. She *did* wish 'Hawk were a little more predictable so she wouldn't be so startled every time she heard a key in the lock.

The door opened and through it walked the tattoo artist! Lori's heartbeat quickened as she eyed the box the artist held in her hands.

Her eyes darted nervously from the box to 'Hawk who followed the artist into the apartment.

'Hawk leaned against the wall, arms folded across her chest, legs crossed at the ankles. Lori searched the dark face for anger but the expression reminded her of a boss she'd once had in a restaurant. He always watched to make sure everything was going according to plan. Were the contents of the box part of 'Hawk's *plan*?

The artist brought Lori to her feet in full view of the leader and inspected the tattoos and piercings. All were healed or healing fine so she opened the box to take out C-shaped silver bands that she began putting on Lori in the way they were designed.

Lori's mouth went dry when the first two C-shaped bands fit together around her neck with a solid clicking sound. She remembered, then, the odd measurement-taking session after her tattoos had been done. Coldly the artist banded her upper arms, wrists and ankles. Lori was curious about these silver affairs and looked at the one on her left wrist. The barest hints of seams showed where the C's had become ovals but there was no latch! No way to take these things *off*! And the rings imbedded in the sides, what were they for?! Everything fit perfectly, too. Had they been made specially for her?

"Stand up straight," the artist ordered. Lori did. "Put your arms above your head and pull in your stomach." Lori obeyed with large eyes as she watched the artist take two bands, much larger than the others, from the box and start to fit them around her waist. "Suck it in. More," she shouted as she struggled to get the bands to join. When at last they did click together Lori let her breath out with relief.

'Hawk was very pleased. The two inch wide belt of silver-coated steel took in Lori's waist like a corset and made her already voluptuous body seem even more so. The hourglass look was very becoming on the girl. Next the artist fastened chains from the collar ring to the nipples, from the armband rings to the nipples, and from one nipple to the other. 'Hawk looked forward to the day the cunt piercings were healed enough to use. The final installment to all this body decoration was a stout chain from one ankle to the other which the artist padlocked then handed the keys to 'Hawk.

'Hawk inspected the bands. "You're sure these won't come off?" Hawk asked.

"The only way you're gonna get those off, 'Hawk, is to cut them off," the artist reassured blandly. Her mind had wandered from 'Hawk's concerns to one of her own. 'Hawk had promised her that she could play with this little toy and it was all she could do to keep from pawing it until she'd been given permission.

The artist's disinterested statement reverberated in Lori's mind: only way . . . cut them off! Like the tattoos, the collar, bracelets and belt were permanent reminders of her condition. It would be some time before Lori would learn to accept these devices as 'Hawk's way of paying attention to her. Or see that she had been noticed and thought about.

Lori would probably never know that she, or rather her compliant presence and ideal figure, had uncovered a whole new realm of sexuality for 'Hawk. The fierce leader had never been conscious of a desire to own, brand and restrain a female of her own. 'Hawk never questioned or analyzed her sexuality. She acted on her needs and desires. Lori hadn't been hers for more than an hour when the idea for the tattoos, piercing and permanent fetters came to her. Now the picture was almost complete. She went into her bedroom, unlocked her trunk and took Lori's shoes out. There was no need to keep them from her or keep the front door locked when she wasn't around. Lori *couldn't* get away now.

She set the pretty black heels on the floor before Lori. When the girl slipped the shoes on, 'Hawk knew that, apart from being able to use the cunt rings, *this* was what she wanted.

"Pretty fuckin' hot, 'Hawk," the artist acknowledged passionately.

As promised, and because the artist had been instrumental in making the intoxicating sight possible, 'Hawk granted her the right to use it first. She placed her hands firmly on the artist's shoulders leaning down to talk into her ear. "Go for it, man. I got to make my rounds."

The artist's voice shook with need. "Yeah?"

'Hawk squeezed her shoulder. "Yeah," she answered with a low, hot whisper.

Lori's eyes were wide with panic as she watched 'Hawk leaving then turned her frightened gaze on the light brown-skinned woman closing in on her. She tried to step away but the chain between her legs impeded her progress. The artist wrestled her to the couch-bed kissing her violently and moaning in waves.

Without warning, the artist raised up and bruised Lori's face with a mean backhand slap. She stood, grabbing the chain between the nipples forcing Lori to stand also. She produced a smallish padlock from her pocket and, using the rings in the wrist cuffs, fastened Lori's hands behind her back. She then proceeded to pound her fists into the great cushions of Lori's breasts. She socked them over and over from every direction: side to side, up from underneath, and crashing down from above. With each blow she moaned and breathed as though she were working herself into some kind of crazed trance.

Lori was stunned almost senseless at first. This was the beating she thought would have come long before now. But she hadn't done anything wrong! Very few products of negligent or abusive homes grew up thinking that running from a beating would lessen its severity. Run and pay, it was simple as that. When she tried to spread her legs to improve her balance she realized how absurd the notion of running was. She wasn't going anywhere.

Be tough, Lori, she thought. Be glad it's your tits and not your face. But as soon as she thought that a blow to her face sent her tumbling to the floor. Against her will and her clenched teeth she whimpered. Now her poor breasts were being kicked by metal-edged boots and she was moaning and trying to roll under the couch-bed. When the beating stopped, it was for seemingly as little reason as it had begun.

Lori looked around to see the artist peeling her jeans off over her boots. Then she was standing over her with a boot to either side of her stomach.

"Move and I'll open you up," the artist threatened. She bent her knees some pulling her own pussy lips apart. Breathing hard she focused on the purpling breasts below her and began to piss on them, aiming her hard stream from one to the other. The yellow water splattered on her nipples and sprayed Lori's face. The artist dropped to her knees and smeared her throbbing pussy over the luscious mounds then moved up toward the moist face. She felt the girl shift under her to get the weight off her pinned wrists. Grabbing her by the hair she forced Lori's face into her needy cunt. "Lick it, cunt!" she demanded loudly. "Yeah. There you go. Do me good, fuck-hole. Yeah." She settled in to enjoy the soft mouth as it cleaned her pee and come and tickled her hardened clit. Somebody has trained this one *right*, she thought. Before long she was crushing the face between her thighs while screamed with delight as Lori brought her to orgasm.

The artist stood and walked about a foot beyond Lori's head ordering, "You gotta lick my boots clean now, fuck-hole. Get over here." She knew Lori would have to wriggle through the puddle to get to her. Once she was satisfied with Lori's work she dressed, put the key to the padlock on the table and left.

In the bar, Maggie was keeping half an eye on the door to 'Hawk's apartment. When the tattoo artist exited through it without locking it before leaving the bar, Maggie decided to investigate.

She found Lori still lying on the floor where her attacker had left her. When the girl saw her, she tried to stop crying, closing her eyes to hide from the shame she felt. Maggie's heart went out to Lori. Mentally she was shaking her fist at 'Hawk for allowing this to happen.

Leaning over to touch Lori's arm and seeing the locked wrists, she clucked with disgust. Lori hadn't had a *chance*. "Did Tattoo do this to you?" she asked gently.

Lori had never heard the artist called by name before. She nodded yes but couldn't look at Maggie.

So, the rumors about Tattoo were true, Maggie thought. "Mary, Mother of God what *was* 'Hawk thinking of when she left you alone with her?" Maggie stood to look for the key, missing the look of surprise on Lori's face.

Lori had just assumed anything 'Hawk did was all right with everyone around her. It shocked her to realize that somebody might not sanction 'Hawk's actions. And actually say so, out loud! She didn't feel so humiliated now that someone seemed to think of her as a victim and not a willing participant.

Maggie unlocked her wrists and swore when the key didn't fit the lock on the ankles. "Does 'Hawk have the key for this?" Lori nodded yes. Wasn't this girl *ever* going to talk? she wondered.

Maggie had been beaten her share in her life, by pimps and johns alike. 'Hawk had grown up watching those beatings, too. That's why 'Hawk made sure it didn't happen to the women working in her territory. Why, then, did she allow it in her own home? Was 'Hawk so concerned with what went on outside that she couldn't see what went on in front of her? The possible answers to those questions made Maggie worry about 'Hawk, who was as close to being her daughter as anyone would ever be.

"Do you think you can get in and out of the tub to take a shower with those on?" Maggie asked with great concern. Apparently 'Hawk hadn't thought of any of the practical problems these bonds might create for their wearer. 'Hawk really *didn't* care about this girl. That worried Maggie, too. Another nod and the girl went into the bath.

When Lori finished with her shower she was amazed to see that-Maggie had cleaned the urine off the floor before she'd gone back to the bar. Lori was so completely touched by that act of compassion, she wept.

The passing of the next few nights saw Lori becoming decidedly depressed and listless. Maggie watched as the apartment became unkempt and Lori not only stopped cooking but stopped eating as well. Maggie was resigned to the fact that Lori wasn't a fleeting fancy of 'Hawk's. The girl was there to stay, for good or bad. She saw no reason for it to be any worse than it had to be. Something had to be done to make Lori feel a part of what was going on around her. Even if only an insignificant part. Lori needed a sense of purpose. Besides, Maggie thought, the girl had a sweetness and strength about her that 'Hawk was killing off with her callous attitude. Maggie wondered what she would have been like if someone had intervened earlier in her own life. Lori's sensible goodness reached out to what had been good and kind in Maggie. She couldn't stand by and watch another loving spirit ruined the way hers had been.

Resolved, she went early to the bar and coaxed Lori out of the apartment to sit with her while she drank some coffee. Lori looked around her like a child in a museum for the first time: overwhelmed by the vast, grownupness of the place.

Lori studied Maggie. The older woman wore jeans, a tight, brightly colored sweater, and a red scarf that pulled her shoulder-length black hair away from her face.

The bartender was of predominantly Spanish descent. Her eyeswere brick-hard and icy, her tiger-eye coloring softened what otherwise might have been an impenetrable toughness. Only when she smiled did her oval-shaped face reveal the true beauty within.

Lori thought Maggie could have been a model if life had been kinder to her. Maggie still had the figure to qualify even if she-wasn't tall. The high cheekbones, contoured mouth and full eye-brows made for a dramatically elegant face.

Maggie brought a broom to Lori and asked her to sweep up. The girl needed something to do to get her outside herself for awhile. She countered the wary, unsure expression of Lori's with, "It's okay. 'Hawk won't mind."

For several nights after that Lori helped Maggie clean the bar. Maggie's strategy worked. Lori settled in to her life as 'Hawk's captive with something akin to pride. The apartment was clean again. She almost smiled when she was cooking. There was peace.

* * *

Rain had been falling for two days and nights. 'Hawk *hated* the rain. It was okay if it rained during the day but when it continued through the late night, 'Hawk could get pretty foul-tempered if people didn't step lightly around her. For that very reason Maggie had warned Lori to stay out of 'Hawk's way.

Early into the third night of ceaseless rain Maggie was being extra careful around her friend. The bar was empty (word got around quickly when 'Hawk's temper was flammable). 'Hawk was concentrating on cleaning her gun.

"The weatherman said this shit's supposed to let up in a couple hours," Maggie supplied encouragingly.

'Hawk grunted and looked through the barrel of her gun for nicks.

Unexpectedly they heard a high-pitched scream coming from the apartment. 'Hawk was at the door instantly throwing it open, fol-lowed closely by Maggie. Lori was standing on the couch-bed plas-tered to the wall with fear. 'Hawk's lightning eyes and reflexes spotted and eliminated the problem with a flash of shining vio-lence.

Lori barely saw the knife come from 'Hawk's sleeve. Flawlessly aimed, 'Hawk's knife had speared the large rat scuttling across the floor by the stove. Death was immediate. Lori turned toward the wall to keep from looking at the gruesome sight. Maggie took the knife out, wrapped the carcass in paper and handed them both to 'Hawk who walked into the bar shaking her head, confused and angry. Maggie persuaded Lori to sit down, reassuring her the thing was gone and followed 'Hawk into the bar.

'Hawk dumped the rat in the trash and cleaned her knife with a bar rag before putting it back in her sleeve. "Fuckin' A, you'd think she'd never seen a rat before," 'Hawk remarked disgustedly.

Sitting on the bar stool next to her, Maggie placed a soothing hand on 'Hawk's arm venturing softly, "I don't think she has, 'Hawk." She was the only person who knew how to handle 'Hawk's redoubtable temper.

'Hawk turned sharply toward her friend, eyes ablaze. She tipped her cap up to let her eyes bore directly into Maggie's softening, wise, brown ones.

Knowing 'Hawk wouldn't hurt her made it no easier for Maggie to hold the menacing gaze with her own. "Honest, 'Hawk. That girl's not from the city. I *know* city when I see it."

Understanding could be read in 'Hawk's eyes as they moved to look in the direction of her apartment. "Jesus, why didn't *I* see that?"

Relieved, Maggie chuckled to defuse the explosive situation. "She's to be forgiven a scream, 'Hawk. She's been here a month and it *is* the first sound she's made."

'Hawk turned sharply toward Maggie. "Month?" she repeated, amazed. She hadn't known how long the girl had been there.

Maggie laughed. "Oh, 'Hawk. I'll bet a week's pay you don't know what that girl's been doing all that time."

Genuinely puzzled 'Hawk shook her head.

"She's completely transformed your apartment into a decent place to live. Who do you think's been cooking all that food you been eating?"

"And never talks?" 'Hawk asked incredulously.

"*Not one peep*, mister," Maggie emphasized. She watched 'Hawk take it in for a couple minutes, not surprised she hadn't noticed. She moved her fingers in a fork-it-up motion in response to the smug smile cracking 'Hawk's serious expression. "Okay, smartass. . . ."

"I do recall her scrubbing the floor, though," 'Hawk provided-teasingly.

"Why?"

"Because," 'Hawk slid off the stool to move right into Maggie's face, "I *fucked* her while she was doing it." Grinning, she winked and pulled her hat cockily over her eyes again. After sharing a good laugh she went back to cleaning her gun in a much-improved mood.

Maggie began setting up the bar. Now was the time, she felt, to say something. "Hey?" she called.

'Hawk looked halfway in her direction.

"Do me a favor?"

"Anything for you, Mag," 'Hawk agreed.

"Don't leave her alone with Tattoo again?" Maggie asked carefully.

Looking like she was remembering something, 'Hawk thought about Maggie's request. She had heard the artist slapped women around some, but Lori's bruises had surprised her. They reminded her of how Maggie used to look before she'd gotten out of the profession. It seemed the bruises reminded Maggie, too. Reassembling her gun, she replied quietly, "Yeah, sure."

Maggie smiled. Maybe 'Hawk was doing better than she thought. Later the door-guard stepped inside the bar to say it had stopped raining.

* * *

The city was dry, the bar was crowded, and the Nighthawk was horny. There were times when she thought about how nice it would be if Shirl would get tired of her bitch. It wasn't likely anybody would become bored with *that* bitch, 'Hawk thought. She was one foxy piece of tail. But 'Hawk had heard Shirl complain that her woman was a pain in the ass to live with and 'Hawk didn't think she could abide by fighting with someone all the time. No, maybe she was better off borrowing the wench when the urge came. Like now. The bitch had seen 'Hawk watching her and was shamelessly flashing beaver by letting her leather miniskirt ride up as she spread her legs open.

Shirl was pretending to ignore her bitch's nasty behavior because it turned her on to see 'Hawk become interested in her woman. Other women tried regularly to attract the leader's interest. None of them *ever* succeeded the way this cunt consistently did. But it was

Shirl who reaped the rewards of 'Hawk's sexual contact with her lover because the bitch became a true nymphomaniac after a turn with 'Hawk. Once 'Hawk had stirred her, she would always be willing to try new things, and go for hours on end until they both collapsed from exhaustion.

Now the bitch had peeled off her tight jacket to show all she wore under it was a leather bra that had holes where her black nipples poked through. She had 'Hawk's full attention now (not to mention several others who were enjoying the free peep show). Her heart raced as 'Hawk walked smoothly and confidently toward her.

"Hey, buddy," Hawk addressed Shirl.

"What's happing, 'Hawk?" Shirl answered in a friendly way.

"It's cool, man. It's cool." 'Hawk offered her handshake which was accepted soundly. "Need to borrow your bitch for a while so she can show white meat how to give head without gagging."

Shirl laughed good-naturedly. The whole transaction was taking place while ignoring the object of the conversation. She liked the idea of her bitch showing 'Hawk's possession how to give head since nobody did it better. Plus nobody had seen the white girl since she'd been shoved through that door several weeks before. Rumors abounded. 'Hawk had been oddly silent on the subject and all Maggie would say was, "She's in there," and point to the apartment. The natives were getting a little restless to see the captive, maybe even play with it.

'Hawk was all too aware of how her comrades felt about the white girl, and their grumbling was beginning to get on her nerves. She wasn't ready to turn the skittish lamb out for slaughter yet. She knew she'd have to soon because she had said the girl was part of the bar. That it ought to be available for use in the same fashion as the pool table. Lori's silence and innocence made it hard to think of her in those terms. Maybe she was waiting for the piercings to heal; she didn't know. It didn't matter now because she was throbbing with need; a need Shirl's bitch could take care of quite satisfactorily.

"Take her," Shirl said casually.

'Hawk patted Shirl's leathered and chained shoulder then took the bitch by the hand. Shirl watched proudly and smiled when 'Hawk lifted up her bitch's skirt to fondle her naked ass as they walked into the apartment.

34

'Hawk leaned her back against the closed door grabbing the bitch's ample buttocks and spreading them apart so the woman would fall against her vibrant body. Even with her five inch, spiked platform heels the woman was still not as tall as 'Hawk in boots. 'Hawk tilted her head and thrust her tongue into the bitch's deep, wide mouth. 'Hawk began moaning heavily as the dark sex queen responded perfectly to her rhythms and chemistry. The bitch loved the feel of 'Hawk's net muscle shirt roughing up her nipples. How it excited her to feel the leader's gun and holster next to her arm as it wriggled into 'Hawk's bulky leather jacket. And the sharp studs of her belt dented the skin of her bare midriff. And that hard rod bruising the bone of her pussy as 'Hawk's hips began to work against her. Nobody kissed like 'Hawk did. She swallowed a woman, she fucked the throat with her tongue. She worked a mouth with such skill a woman's toes felt the need and desire.

Few women had opened 'Hawk's pants as often as this bitch had. She performed the feat so well 'Hawk could barely tell the thing was done until she felt her cock pull free and tug to the maneuverings of the bitch's masterful hands. 'Hawk let go of the kiss long enough to show she approved, "*Work* it, bitch, *work* it," then resumed consuming the mouth.

Lori looked on, unsure if she was permitted, but unable to turn away from the compelling sight. She'd been mixing cornbread batter when the couple had appeared. Now she was feeling very insecure. What if this woman was what 'Hawk really wanted? What would happen to her? The more she watched the more she became involved in the saturating arousal. To see 'Hawk kiss someone made her more accessible sexually. Lori had wondered if 'Hawk ever did kiss women. It alarmed Lori that 'Hawk was so similar to Cloud when aroused. It alarmed her because she was becoming equally charged with need; she hadn't believed she could feel this way about anyone but Cloud. Then she remembered the rape and how intense 'Hawk had been and how she had responded to that intensity.

This new woman's sexual entrance was frothy with white creamy-evidence of 'Hawk's prowess. The sight made Lori's own cunt ache.Then she saw 'Hawk looking at her and her heart did a flip-flop in her chest. 'Hawk's finger was pointing to the floor in front of where she stood. Lori walked quickly to that spot. 'Hawk's large, ringed hand grabbed her shoulder and pushed her down to her knees. The bitch was watching her now and it embarrassed her.

The bitch whistled under her breath at the sight of the complex body adornment. "Ain't that something?" she admired passionately.

"Get to it, bitch," 'Hawk ordered impatiently.

The bitch leaned over to instruct Lori. She was amused by the patchy sex-flush on Lori's chest and neck. She knew her own kind when she saw it: pure cunt. "You got to suck 'Hawk off, whitey, and I'm going to show you how to do it so you don't choke." She took 'Hawk's cock lovingly and fondled it in front of the girl's eyes. She ran the tip over the mouth, telling her to kiss it and lick it and squeeze it so 'Hawk would moan and rock her hips. She taught Lori how to open her mouth right and how to relax against the gagging reflex so the cockhead could go down her throat. "It's got a good throat, 'Hawk. Soft and ready. You're in all the way now, 'Hawk," the bitch announced triumphantly. She stood to let the leader see the red, straining face filled with her black thing.

Moaning, 'Hawk moved in and out of Lori's mouth, up and down the throat. "Yeah, take it, white meat. Suck it." Lori moved her head back and forth in an effort to please the leader. "Yeah, suck it. Keep suckin' it."

To reward the bitch for a job well done she began to tug and pinch the bared nipples. The bitch flowed and rocked and whimpered passionately, needing it as hard as 'Hawk gave it. "Yeah, please," she begged happily. One hand lifted her skirt to probe her sopping pussy. The fingers dug in, then pulled meanly on the slippery lips producing louder and louder cries. The other hand grabbed the back of her head to lock it into a kiss, then lowered to do something it had wanted to do for weeks! Run its fingers through this white girl's soft hair.

The feel of Lori's hair made 'Hawk moan loudly. It was incredible to feel it tickling her palm. Then, because she could stand all this no more, she forced Lori's head into her pelvis and began to fuck the throat mercilessly while her other hand jerked over the bitch's clit at breakneck speed. A barrage of cries and moans rained over Lori so loudly she didn't know some of them were her own.

Bursts of rapture exploded in 'Hawk's mind. The mixture of this black bitch she'd borrowed being overtaken by a mindless orgasm and the white meat she owned struggling to survive the assault on her throat was excitement at its finest. She was filled with her own virility.

The bitch fell off 'Hawk's hand to land against the door for support to recover from the debilitating release 'Hawk had given her.

'Hawk wove her sticky fingers into Lori's whispy hair locking the skull in a vice grip as she finished having her way with the helpless receptacle.

Lori tried in vain to see what this ground-shaking, bone-rocking spasm looked like. She could hear it, though, and it was excruciatingly satisfying. Cloud had been this difficult to please, too, but oh, when Lori succeeded there was nothing to compare with it. Her throat would be raw for days but she didn't care. The gurgling, gasping wails of pleasure would keep her happy and feeling worthwhile for some time. Remaining still she kept the pole in her mouth. She waited patiently for 'Hawk to pull it out.

The bitch was electric and ready to screw again. She knew the Nighthawk wouldn't give her another turn whether she was satisfied or not. Taking a bitch twice in one night came under the heading of "making a play for someone else's woman", and 'Hawk didn't do that. So while she waited for her heroic sex partner to come back to earth she looked around. She was impressed by how nice the apartment looked. As punishment she had had to clean the place herself a time or two. But all anybody had ever done before was shovel it out and wash the dishes. This was the kind of clean only a true homemaker could produce.

She looked at the placid white girl hanging from 'Hawk's thing. This was the girl Cloud had kept secret all this time, eh?She had always wondered why the dynamic and appealing Indian had never shown any interest in her. Now she knew Cloud had all she wanted to keep her content. Selfishly, the bitch hoped 'Hawk wouldn't discover this girl's inborn talent or she might become as content as Cloud must have been. Then 'Hawk might lose interest in her and that would be a big loss. Yes, the bitch knew her own kind and this white tail had all the makings of a perfect sex partner, able to learn and do anything required of it. She wondered if the girl knew how dangerous she was. Examining 'Hawk's facial expression, the bitch watched carefully for signs the leader might be responding to her possession's magic.

'Hawk *was* responding to Lori but her face showed nothing of it because she was refusing to see it herself. Something deep within her stirred when she looked down on the impaled white face.Lori's eyes were closed showing the imperious captor her remarkable eyelashes. Unconsciously 'Hawk wanted to create this scene again because it *did* something to her.

The bitch concluded that 'Hawk was immune to her little toy and relaxed, confident that her place as her leader's favorite was secure. She began to pant over the fantasy 'Hawk might stick that thing in her snatch after taking it from the white mouth. She wouldn't tell. But the beautiful black prong withdrew into the pants once more to lie in wait for its next conquest.

Before she could wonder any more, the bitch found herself in the bar getting a pat on the rump and sent on her way. 'Hawk smiled and nodded at Shirl as she left the bar for the night.

Chapter Three

Lori had slept well and was feeling rested. She cooked breakfast while listening to the reassuring sounds of 'Hawk lifting her weights and showering. 'Hawk emerged from her room dressed and fit, ready for the good meal of eggs and bacon. Lori washed the dishes quietly while 'Hawk drank coffee and smoked a cigarette.

Something told Lori that 'Hawk was watching her. Still she dropped a plate in the sink when 'Hawk spoke.

"Are you pregnant?" 'Hawk questioned sternly. She didn't like the idea of paying for an abortion and was getting cross just thinking about it.

Lori turned the water off and picked the pieces of broken plate from the sink. She shook her head emphatically, praying 'Hawk would be satisfied.

But 'Hawk didn't believe her and the nervousness she was displaying didn't help Lori's case any. "Maggie says you been here nine weeks and ain't got your bloods the whole time." 'Hawk was determined to get at the truth.

And Lori could tell 'Hawk was serious. She had to be because this was the first time she'd ever spoken directly to her when she wasn't in the throes of passion. Maggie had already asked if she were pregnant, and Lori had believed the subject was closed because the bartender hadn't pressed beyond the initial negative reply. She dropped the dish fragments in the trash, purposely ignoring 'Hawk.

Which was the *wrong thing to do*. 'Hawk stood abruptly grabbing Lori by the arm and yanking her around to face her inquisition. "You expect me to believe you ain't pregnant!" she yelled meanly. "Why haven't you had your bloods?" She shook Lori sharply meaning she had to answer.

Lori was extremely frightened but managed to answer, "I can't."

"Can't what?" 'Hawk pressed.

Lori's voice quivered. "Have periods." She was so afraid that 'Hawk was going to keep asking questions that she defeated her own purpose by showing her fear.

'Hawk was seething. This girl's fear looked to her like she was protecting somebody. If it was a man, 'Hawk would reach up inside the girl and rip that baby out herself.

Lori was protecting someone but not who 'Hawk imagined. 'Hawk's grip tightened around her arm and it hurt. A lot.

"You got ten seconds to start explaining why . . ." 'Hawk didn't have to say what would happen if the girl didn't start talking. Right now she'd just as soon kill her as look at her.

The girl came unhinged before her eyes. "Please don't make me tell, 'Hawk. Please," she begged through her tears. "Please, she said she'd kill me if I ever told. God, please," Lori pleaded with genuine fear.

'Hawk could tell when someone was more afraid of an unpresent danger than a present one. Somebody had put the fear of *God* into this girl. She knew how to turn *this* around. She held Lori's face and forced her to meet her eyes.

"Who said she'd kill you?" 'Hawk demanded, locking the girl hypnotically with her demonic stare.

The potent effect of 'Hawk's eyes made Lori realize just where she was, and with whom. What were Cloud's threats when measured against this very real situation she found herself in? Lori wasn't completely sure if Cloud had ever killed anyone but Maggie had assured her that 'Hawk *had* killed before and would again without overmuch provocation.

"Cloud," she said, giving in to 'Hawk. She knew that the whole story would have to follow to get 'Hawk to believe her.

"I can handle Three Eagles," 'Hawk confirmed confidently. "Now suppose you stop playing games and tell me what Three Eagles don't want nobody to find out." 'Hawk was looking forward to getting some of the goods on Three Eagles.

Lori didn't doubt 'Hawk could deal with Cloud. Cloud didn't have to know she'd told, did she? Tentatively she tried to recount that awful night. "Cloud went . . . crazy on me one night. I begged her to stop but she wouldn't listen."

'Hawk's temper cooled a bit once she saw she was going to get the story. "Stop what?"

Lori looked down shyly and tried to say what. "You know," she said quietly, "taking me."

"Taking you?" 'Hawk was puzzled. Then it occurred to her that the girl was too embarrassed to say the word. Completely fascinated that someone as sexy as this girl could be too inhibited to talk about sex, 'Hawk asked, "You mean *fucking* you?" It was almost laughable until she saw where the girl was going with her tale.

Lori's head nodded sadly. 'Hawk spared the girl having to say with what. She'd recognized the telltale signs of a dildo under the Indian's chamois pants.

"What happened?" 'Hawk asked, almost compassionately.

"When she was finished she rolled over and fell asleep. I tried to sleep but the cramps hurt too much. I thought my period had come but the flow was too hard. My bed was all wet and I saw blood all over Cloud's . . . you know," she murmured.

"Yeah," 'Hawk verified.

"I wanted to clean up but when I stood up, the pain . . ." Lori took a deep breath before going on. It was hard to talk about. "I screamed. I couldn't help it," she looked up at 'Hawk apologetically. 'Hawk's face was becoming grim. She knew the girl wouldn't make up a story about Cloud that would make the Indian look bad. It was clear the girl idolized Cloud.

"I didn't mean to wake her up . . . she saw the blood going down my legs and got up . . . I passed out. I don't know about anything more until the doctor came into my room in the hospital. He told me that they had performed emergency surgery on me because I'd been bleeding to death." Her voice was low and tiny. She wasn't aware that 'Hawk had let go of her arm and was clenching the side of the sink instead. Lori's fingers locked prayerfully as though she could make it all go away somehow.

"He said he had saved my ovaries but my cervix had been completely ruined and there was no way to save my uterus. That's how I got this scar on my abdomen." She pointed to it but having it seen shamed her.

'Hawk had never noticed it. She'd never looked that carefully at the girl. But there it was, plainer than life. If Cloud Three Eagles had been standing there at that moment, 'Hawk would have cheerfully slit her throat.

For her own part, having children was out of the question. But this girl might have wanted children and would have made a decent mother, too. The fact that, moments before, 'Hawk was ready to murder any unborn thing living inside this girl was overlooked by the leader. What Cloud had done sickened her because the act had been one of purposeless, selfish meanness. That was how 'Hawk tried to view it. At the *very* least it was unjust. Why couldn't 'Hawk just say, "It hurt this innocent girl who is beginning to mean something to me."?

Instead her heavily ringed hand struck the inside of the metal sink to signal her disgust making Lori jump. Saying nothing 'Hawk turned and left, slamming the door behind her.

Suddenly *filled* with panic Lori dropped to her knees and began to sob. All she could see was 'Hawk — killing Cloud. And it was about the time Cloud was due back, too. Cloud, she prayed, stay away, please. Lori still loved the big Indian with all her heart and secretly wished Cloud might rescue her. Wished for it even though Cloud's chances were slim to none.

Maggie opened the door slowly expecting to see Lori in a crumbled heap of half-dead flesh. She was greatly relieved when the girl stood, wiping away her tears, showing no signs of a beating. "Are you okay?" Maggie asked. Lori nodded and Maggie left the girl alone, shaking her head in amazement.

It was nearly dawn before word got back to the Subway Club that 'Hawk had been seen in another bar, *drinking*. Part of what made 'Hawk seem so fearsome was that her fierce, callous ways were in no way aided by artificial means. She didn't drink or take drugs. Maggie closed up and struck out to find 'Hawk. She finally convinced 'Hawk to sleep through the day at her place but the next night 'Hawk started drinking again. It wouldn't be until the third night that 'Hawk willingly resumed her normal activities.

Maggie was seriously worried. She had never seen 'Hawk drunk before. It was very frightening to see, and Maggie wasn't easily frightened. Despite her best efforts she couldn't get 'Hawk to speak of what had happened. She heard on the street that 'Hawk had made it a high priority to find Cloud Three Eagles but beyond that she couldn't figure a reason for the odd behavior.

* * *

Maggie scoured the bar counter restlessly. She had two problems and they both required getting Lori to talk as part of their solutions. She watched the girl going about her work with the quiet patience she applied to everything. It was fascinating to watch her compensate for the chain between her ankles as she walked, or swept the floor. Maggie admired Lori's ability to carry herself gracefully in spite of her high heels and ponderous breasts. How could she get a person like that to talk when she so doggedly endured all that befell her? Threaten her? Maggie didn't think so. If this girl had *willingly* stayed with the likes of Cloud Three Eagles, it wasn't likely she was afraid of much beyond rats and death.

Maggie thought about the times she *had* gotten through to this girl on some level—when she believed the girl might have talked if she'd been the sort to speak up for herself. Those had been the times when she'd been gentle and warm like she would with a stray kitten or lost child. That was what had worked with this girl. Call her, Maggie thought. Call her what? White meat? She shuddered. Surely she has a name. Then Maggie remembered the purse she'd rescued from the rape scene on Lori's first night. She opened the cupboard to find the small bag and looked inside it.

The driver's license was the only item that could tell her anything about 'Hawk's captive. Lori Smith. Her name was as plain as she was. At least Maggie had judged the age right: 21, barely. She guessed Lori had been with Cloud for as long as two years from what she knew of Cloud's history. She could then surmise Lori hadn't been in the city long before she'd met Cloud. Knowing most girls who left home for the big city did so a lot younger than Lori made Lori seem even more like a "good girl" who had done what was expected, *then* left.

Maggie looked at the address on the license: not a good one but certainly better than the one she had now. Would anybody be looking for Lori? Probably not, Maggie decided, or this girl would have been worried about causing someone concern.

Since Cloud was gone, anyone who might have looked for Lori would have thought the girl had vanished with the Indian. Still she would wander by the building Lori lived in someday to see just what was the prevailing belief.   She put the license away and motioned to the girl to join her at the bar. Lori sat on a stool and drank from the glass of orange juice Maggie had given her.

Lori enjoyed seeing the bartender smile. She was pretty, and kind in her own careful way. Lori had grown to admire Maggie because she worked hard and was loyal. She could tell the older woman was close to 'Hawk. That 'Hawk didn't trust just anybody was a given, therefore Maggie must be special to have earned the leader's trust. Lori admired 'Hawk, too, although she would have been hard-pressed to admit it. Strength, courage, individuality and leadership were qualities Lori unconsciously looked for in people she chose to admire. Cloud seemed to have those characteristics, too. Although from her unique vantage point Lori was beginning to see 'Hawk's traits were more well-developed than Cloud's, were more than potentials to be encouraged, were already in use.

Maggie was hopeful, the girl might trust her enough now. "Feeling okay tonight?" she opened.   Lori nodded and smiled.

"Your name is Lori, isn't it?" Maggie asked carefully. Don't frighten her, Maggie, she cautioned herself. She watched the girl sit straighter, eyes blinking. Offended? she wondered. No, surprised and confused. "I found your purse the first night you were here. Your license was in it," she reassured quickly.

Shocked was more like it. Lori had almost forgotten she had a name and had despaired of anyone ever caring, much less using it. 'Hawk's approach to her made it extremely hard to follow through with her determination to elevate her status. The leader was so thorough at ignoring her, having only touched her the three times, Lori was beginning to become invisible even to herself. Had it not been for Maggie's nightly attention, Lori would have begun to waver from her goal to become more than a thing that went about its chores through a robot-like grind of endless nights.

But a *name*. Did that mean she meant something? Absently she nodded her head. Yes . . . Lori. That was her name.

"I've been real patient with you, Lori. You've got a right not to talk if that's what you want." Maggie was frustrated. She couldn't make Lori talk but she had to. She sighed from discouragement. "I need your help, Lori. You've *got* to talk to me."

As if she said the magic words Lori reached out, touched Maggie's arm gently and spoke. "What's wrong?" she questioned softly. Lori didn't think any of these strong women *needed* her, but she was born to help others and her heart opened the moment she was asked.

Finally, Maggie thought, greatly relieved. She scarcely knew how to proceed beyond the initial hurdle. "It's 'Hawk," she began, "something's eating at her. I've never seen her act like she has the last couple nights."

Lori had been curious about the leader's absence, too. She prayed that the angry woman hadn't found Cloud.

"Didn't you wonder why 'Hawk hasn't gotten up yet tonight?"

"Yes."

"She has a hangover. She doesn't know it yet because she has never been drunk before. 'Hawk doesn't drink, Lori," Maggie furnished, "and she's just spent the last two nights drinking herself into a stupor. It hasn't caught up with her before but it will tonight. Now I want to know why, Lori." Maggie knew the girl was amazed by the revelation and that the girl knew why 'Hawk had been behaving so completely out of character. She was glad no one else suspected that Lori was the catalyst for the drinking binge.

"Listen, kid," Maggie continued in answer to Lori's look of concern, "if 'Hawk trusts me, then so can you. I'd never do *anything* to hurt 'Hawk."

"She was mad about something Cloud had done to me," Lori provided weakly.

Maggie leaned against the sink, studying the girl thoughtfully.

What could have made the girl say a thing like that, she puzzled? Certainly not ego. The girl didn't think for a minute that she was important to 'Hawk.

"You talked to 'Hawk?" Maggie asked curiously.

"I had to. She thought I was pregnant and made me prove I wasn't." Lori's voice began to quiver. "When I told her what Cloud did to me so I can't have periods, she got real angry and left."

And those are very real tears forming in those eyes, too, Maggie, the bartender told herself. This girl is telling the truth. If 'Hawk had been that angry at Lori, she would have beaten her. But 'Hawk hadn't laid a hand on the girl. So now why all of a sudden was finding Cloud 'Hawk's number one priority? If she had found Cloud, she wouldn't have gotten drunk. She would have taken her anger out on Cloud.

There was only one answer to this puzzle and discovering it almost brought a smile to Maggie's lovely face but for the realization of what had brought about her *other* problem.

That was it, then. 'Hawk was beginning to care about this girl and couldn't handle it. Caring about a white girl went against everything 'Hawk was and believed in. It went beyond caring, though. 'Hawk *cared* about the residents of her turf, too, but she didn't go on two-night drinking sprees when some one of her people was hurt or wronged. She did kill from time to time, however. Would she have killed Cloud? Maybe. Then what? Come home and say it was, "Time for white meat to start working in the bar when it's busy". Which was precisely what she had said to her. Sure, Maggie, she told herself, to get some room between her and this girl because if she can make the girl even more like a thing and less like a person, then she can stop feeling this way about her.

Now she understood it all. She was itching to know just what Cloud had done but she thought better of asking the girl to repeat it. If it was bad enough to make 'Hawk that angry, it was better forgotten.

"Thank you, Lori. It helps to know what went down between you two."

"May I ask a question?" Lori asked smally. She *had* to know but was afraid to find out.

"What?"

"Did 'Hawk kill Cloud?" There, it was asked.

Maggie, you *are* a fool. Why didn't it occur to you that this child is still in love with that damn Indian? she scolded mentally. 'Hawk had to have seen it, too, and wasn't taking it lightly. All the more reason to wipe out her feelings for this innocent thing.

"No. She couldn't find her," Maggie replied unfeelingly.

The girl looked so relieved Maggie saw it was a waste of time to ask if Lori knew where Cloud was. She wouldn't tell if she did know. None of this changed the fact that Lori was going to have to start working in the bar.

"Do you know how to bus tables?" Maggie asked in her most business-like manner.

"Yes," Lori replied, nonplussed.

"Well, 'Hawk said you have to start helping out when it gets busy." She watched Lori digest the bad news while she leaned over to answer the phone. "Subway Club." She stood up suddenly, surprised by the welcomed voice of the caller. "Tiên Le," she almost whispered in disbelief. "Where are you calling from?" "Here, now?!" "When did you get back?" "Welcome *home*. Are you coming down tonight?" she asked excitedly. "Great. 'Hawk will be so surprised. I can't wait to see you again. Was your trip a success?" Maggie purred contentedly when she received her answer. "Wonderful, I'll see you then." She hung the phone up gently then turned her broad smile on Lori.

"What luck! Oh, Lori, this is so much better than I could have hoped for. That was Tiên Le, 'Hawk's right-hand-woman, if there is such a thing. She just got back from Vietnam. She went over there to get her younger sister and now they're back together. God, 'Hawk hasn't been right since Tiên Le left four months ago. But now," Maggie met Lori's fascinated expression with a hopeful one, "*now* she'll be okay. Listen," she took Lori's hand between hers, "do you trust me?"

"Yes," Lori answered with wide-eyed faith. She *had* to trust Maggie or cease to exist.

"You're gonna *have* to come into the bar. And get pawed and used and probably abused. I can't stop that. But I can make it easier on you if you do exactly as I tell you. Promise me you will."

"I promise," Lori said confidently.

"Make Tiên Le happy tonight. Do *anything* she wants."

"Okay," Lori agreed somewhat unsurely.

"If you make Tiên Le happy, Lori, you'll make 'Hawk proud. . ." Maggie offered the statement like a cookie to a starving child.

Lori took the bribe readily, almost greedily. She knew what making 'Hawk proud could lead to. "I will," she promised.

"Yeah, good," Maggie accepted. She made an odd-looking drink and wrote a note to accompany it. "'Hawk will be up soon. Put this on the table for her and then finish sweeping."

Lori read the note and smiled. "Maggie's Miracle Cure. 'Hawk — Never thought I'd be making this stuff for you. Love, Maggie."

* * *

'Hawk was grateful for Maggie's Miracle Cure; she felt like hell when she got up. She couldn't understand how people could do that to themselves every night. Having a strong, healthy, agile body was important to her, and ruining it with alcohol didn't make sense.

The kind of escape she was paying for with this hangover wasn't worth it. Besides, drinking hadn't solved the problem. She still didn't know where Three Eagles was and she couldn't undo the damage the Indian had done. Her line of reasoning didn't conclude with: and drinking hadn't changed her feelings about the girl. Her thoughts bumped into a wall of inner resistance and retreated. Not one for internal struggles, 'Hawk finished Maggie's liquid, swore never to drink again and took a shower.

Hearing the water run, Lori crept back into the apartment to disappear into the shadows where 'Hawk would not notice her. From there she could assimilate her conversation with Maggie. It felt good to talk with someone. Having her name used again restored Lori's hope for her limited future. Even the idea of working in the bar when there were people in it didn't seem so terrifying if she could talk with Maggie once in awhile. Maggie actually wanted to help her. Which she'd been doing all along in one way or another. She would work hard to make Maggie glad she'd gone to the trouble.

Then, as was often the case, Lori's thoughts turned to Cloud, who was still alive, for the moment. She wished there were some way she could warn Cloud of the danger that awaited her.

During all her musings and struggles to understand what was

going on around her, Lori never once thought she might mean a thing to 'Hawk.

* * *

Reluctantly, 'Hawk had agreed to let Maggie be the judge of when she could use help in the bar. To take 'Hawk's mind off the subject, Maggie started taking bets on a nine-ball challenge skillfully drawing the leader into the action by giving inviting odds on 'Hawk's favorite player.

By the time the match was winding down and 'Hawk had handily supplemented her gun-running income, the bar was filling up with customers. 'Hawk had already given Maggie one dirty look and was near sending a visual warning signal when a stir near the front door of the bar drew her attention. Shoving the folded money in her pocket she leaned back against the pillar to get a look at what or who was causing the commotion. As if by unspoken command, the crowd moved away from the newcomer.

'Hawk's heart skipped a beat when she saw the dark-clad figure. A wide grin opened her face to shine like a lighthouse beacon to show the long-gone traveler the way home. A sense of peace flowed through her mighty body as she spoke the name with quiet reverence, "Tiên Le."

Here was the perfect complement to her sometimes restless, always vigilant warrior soul. Alexander had his Hephaiston, Cheon had her Brodca, and the Nighthawk had Tiên Le. The alliance was the same. A full-blooded sister could not have been closer or more loved than this Vietnamese woman was by 'Hawk.

The sparkle in Tiên Le's black eyes was authentic. All her life Tiên Le had been needed by someone: a family member, a movement, a country, but being needed never felt as good as it did at this moment. Seeing the deep and real relief written in 'Hawk's underworld eyes brought Tiên Le *home*. This was home: 'Hawk's turf, not the seething jungles and rank cities she'd just come from. The weeks and months of traveling and struggling were completely forgotten when she felt 'Hawk's powerful arms gather her in a heartfelt hug that lifted her from the ground.

'Hawk let the smaller woman down but wouldn't take her hands from the narrow shoulders. She had to keep the contact to prove to herself Tiên Le was really there. "Fuckin' A. *Man*, it's good to see you."

"It's good to be back, 'Hawk." Tiên Le squeezed 'Hawk's hand firmly. Yes, I'm here, the touch conveyed. (Tiên Le had never been able to break 'Hawk of touching her shoulders. She'd explained the superstition about the genie who lived there but 'Hawk couldn't grasp the concept of a genie. Tiên Le made an unseen sign against bad luck without thinking anyway.)

"When did you get in?"

"During the day. I got my sister settled in. She's pretty overwhelmed by American culture but glad to be here." Tiên Le related with an accent that revealed an intriguing blend of Asian, French and American that was pleasant to the ears.

"Was it hard getting her out?" 'Hawk asked intently. She'd seldom left her own part of town and thrived on Tiên Le's exciting stories about the world she'd seen so much of. A part of 'Hawk worried that the world and its vast variety of life would one day capture Tiên Le's attention and hold it forever. Only now did she realize how hard these last four months had been without her good friend.

"Tough. It was real touch and go for awhile but we caught some bureaucrat with his pants down and slipped through a loophole. That forged visa your contact made for her worked like a charm. She's safe now, 'Hawk. Thanks."

The two comrades clapped hands together in a solid, bond-reaffirming handshake that produced murmurs of approval from those gathered to share in the welcome.

"It was nothing, Tiên Le," 'Hawk replied. "I'm just glad you're home."

"Home late from what I hear. Missed a pretty good war they tell me," she laughed.

Before 'Hawk could get revved up Maggie broke in. "Save your war stories . . . ."

"Maggie! How's my girl?" Tiên Le kissed the bartender soundly.

Maggie had gone sour on sex years ago. She hadn't had a lover in over a decade and didn't seem to mind. Still, if anyone were ever going to renew her interest, it would be Tiên Le. "Better now that you're home, Tiên Le," Maggie answered affectionately. She let the woman's strong hand roam over her still well-shaped backside for a

50

moment then took it away just at the point when a tremor of arousal tickled along her belly. No one else had even gotten *that* far with Maggie.

"I take it 'Hawk hasn't told you about the new bar fixture she acquired but hasn't let anyone use yet?" Maggie introduced the subject of Lori as lightly as she knew how.

"Yeah. Hey, 'Hawk, bring it out here. Let us see it, too, 'Hawk," came the chorus of encouragement. Tiên Le's curiosity was aroused and one of her slender eyebrows lifted under the black headband tied around her forehead.

'Hawk's expression read to Maggie as, touché, bitch. She walked calmly into her apartment to get Lori. Before taking the girl out she decided she didn't care if the cunt piercings were healed or not. She affixed the small padlock to the rings anyway.Grasping the girl by the elbow she led her into a bar filled with waiting vultures.

Whistles and calls of approval heralded the unceremonious entrance. The girl was much changed from when last she'd been seen by this crowd. The tattoos and chains and fetters were objects of wonder and spawned an immediate atmosphere of sexuality that only the coldest among them could ignore.

Lori kept her eyes lowered until she was brought to stand before Tiên Le. She'd expected some huge presence in the person of 'Hawk's right-hand woman. But Tiên Le was no taller than she was. Dressed in loose black cotton gauze slacks and tunic, soft black leather, flat-soled boots and a black silk sash that hugged her middle, Tiên Le's look was almost casual. Her hair was short and shone with a blue cast that measured its blackness. Large piercing eyes gazed at her with calm hardness. Lori thought: If steel had life, it would look like this. The calloused hands had strange, frightening tattoos on them. Later Lori would learn that Tiên Le was a martial arts master but now all she cared about was what it would take to please this woman.

From the corner of her eye, Lori spotted a small black butch-looking woman kneeling to 'Hawk's right, dressed in black denim, head bowed and hands neatly folded in her lap. She remembered the docile woman from the night of her rape and wondered if the woman belonged to 'Hawk, too.

She kept her breathing steady and her demeanor meek as Tiên Le examined the tattoo on her breast, then ran her fingers through and over the chains and bands. She read the tattoo above Lori's cunt. "Fuck hole, eh?" She fondled the little padlock dangling from the rings in the lips. "But it's locked!" she said, pretending to be surprised. She was really quite tickled by 'Hawk's little message.

Lori had been relieved by the padlock until Tiên Le's rough hand wandered around her backside followed by Tiên Le herself. "But this isn't," she jeered loudly. "What's this?" She checked the purple mark on Lori's rump. "Grade A White Meat," she read aloud and roared with laughter. The crowd joined her. 'Hawk was perched casually on her stool, leaning against the pillar, arms folded over her chest, smugness rippling over her every feature. She was enjoying their enjoyment.

Tiên Le spit on her finger and pushed it inside Lori's ass. Lori swallowed a gasp.

"How is it?" 'Hawk inquired.

"It's pretty tight back here, 'Hawk. Haven't you used it?" Tiên Le asked flatly. She knew assholes didn't appeal to her leader the way they did to her.

"I don't recall, good buddy," 'Hawk stated. Hisses and grumblings came back at her from the restless population who would have used this thing a hundred times over if given the chance. Questions about 'Hawk's sex drive went unspoken but heard. "Need some help?"

Tiên Le's attention was seriously focused on this virginal opening. It's lack of pliant response told her it had never been addressed before. She guessed that what was up front had been distracting enough to keep this little rosebud safe from intruders. But no more. "Yeah. You want to work its titties to get it loose?" she asked of her friend.

"Happy to," 'Hawk agreed enthusiastically. It was easier to touch Lori when it wasn't her idea. That way she didn't have to own her desire for this delectable body. She took each nipple between her fingers and began to tease them. "Shirl, get these hands out of the way," she commanded. Shirl was an expert on bondage. Silently she took a chain from her epaulet and hooked it through the rings on Lori's wristbands and quickly had them behind the girl's back and dangling from the collar.

Lori truly was a virgin from the back and knew nothing of what to expect. She caught a brief glimpse of Maggie nodding her head toward her. The wordless sign said, This is what I was talking about — do it right. Lori conquered her fear and gave into the feeling of 'Hawk's skilled fingers playing with her nipples. In a very short time her chest was heaving and her body was responding. Tiên Le's finger moved in further and began a circular motion that felt wonderful.

'Hawk grabbed her nipple rings and shook her teats back and forth making her tits jiggle and chains jingle. Lori's mouth fell open to let out soft sounds of delight as a second and third finger entered her hole.

Sounds of pleasure were all around. This crowd had never seen 'Hawk and Tiên Le work a woman together before. It was a duet worth paying to see.

Tiên Le reached into the folds of her billowy pants and whipped out her thing. Like a sleight-of-hand artist she replaced her probing fingers with the smooth, solid instrument, jamming it into the girl's bunghole.

Lori's eyes opened wide and she clamped her teeth over a squeal of surprise. She was given no time to think as Tiên Le began to pound her bucking hips into Lori's soft ass. 'Hawk released the tits to watch them bounce in time with Tiên Le's reckless sodomy.

It seemed Tiên Le would never be satisfied but the combination of taking a virgin, that belonged to 'Hawk, in front of all these voyeurs was enough to do it for her sooner than it normally would have. Her cries of pleasure, though not as dramatic as 'Hawk's sometimes were, were still exciting to hear. Her eyes were glazed and her breathing erratic as she pulled free of the hole letting her dildo dangle below her crotch.

Of those in the bar that night, none were more relieved to see Tiên Le again than her little black slave. Quickly the small butch woman crawled to kneel before her Master and lavishly licked the light-colored prick clean, ending the four month hell Tiên Le's absence had caused her. Her face was radiant with joy.

Satisfied with the job her slave had done, Tiên Le flipped her cock back into her pants and walked around to see what Lori looked like in front. Unlike 'Hawk, Tiên Le had fucked white women before and knew what to look for. Just as she had hoped, this one was the type that got a noticeable sex rash. "I want to see what it looks like when it comes, 'Hawk."

"Do it," 'Hawk agreed throatily. This scene had been hot up to now. Why not have still more fun?

Tiên Le grabbed her slave by the hair and forced its mouth into Lori's asshole. She didn't have to instruct the slave, it knew what to do and did it beautifully. Tiên Le smoothed a finger into the locked lips and began to massage the erect, wet clit. 'Hawk went back to the nipples. The trio brought Lori to the edge — the slave rimming, Tiên Le diddling and the Nighthawk yanking. Lori screamed and shook and wrenched with ecstasy. When she could bear no more she fell to her knees breaking all contact. If her hands had been free she would have hugged herself. She prayed this was all Tiên Le wanted because in pleasure or pain, she did have her limits.

Tiên Le patted her slave's head fondly and let it rest against her firm thigh. This was the lowest, cruelest thing her Master had ever done to her — making her rim a white asshole, the asshole of a lowly piece of white meat. But she didn't mind one bit because she was with her Master again. The endless nights of feeling lost and abandoned were over. Her eyes closed contentedly and she smiled.

Tiên Le looked down at the crumbled mass of used flesh and smiled. "Very nice, 'Hawk. Where'd you find it?"

'Hawk snorted. "It used to belong to Three Eagles but she got careless and I found it." She was dangerously close to becoming angered anew by the Indian's betrayal.

Tiên Le read carefully between the lines. Three Eagles, eh? That meant the Indian no longer enjoyed the status of friend then. "Yeah?" she said bending over and grabbing the chain between Lori's collar and penned wrists to lift the girl to her feet. She looked it over with new interest. "So, was this a new acquisition of Three Eagles'?"

"Couldn't say," 'Hawk admitted. "Hey, white meat. How long did Three Eagles have you?"

Lori could almost hear Maggie thinking, Don't screw it up now, answer her. "Two years," Lori revealed clearly. After all, could 'Hawk be any angrier with Cloud? Did she have to risk her own hard work in a feeble attempt to cover for Cloud? They'd get it out of her anyway. If 'Hawk was proud of her, she wanted to keep it that way.

"I'll kill 'er," Lori heard 'Hawk say under her breath.

"Well, that sly dog," Tiên Le said with admiration. "All this time we thought she wasn't interested in women and she's had this hot little piece stashed away all along." She pointed to the brand on Lori's breast and claimed, "You did right taking it, 'Hawk. She cheated you and lied to you. Can't stand for that." Abruptly Tiên Le dropped the subject and hopped onto the stool to 'Hawk's right, lodging her slave's head between her knees. She looked around and smiled like she was ready to hold court. "So, tell me about the war with the Imperials," she quieried cheerfully, extracting 'Hawk's attention from the scene. She'd just backed her leader up and now there would be no question that the white girl was both a hot number and irrefutably a possession of the Nighthawk.

What followed was what Maggie had hoped for: most of the women in the bar turned their interest to 'Hawk and Tiên Le as they rehashed the war 'Hawk and her tribe had recently fought. She moved Lori out of the way, whispering carefully in the girl's ear as she undid the chain to the wrists.

"You were beautiful, kid," she praised Lori. "Now work the tables on the other side of the bar first. In a few minutes most of them will forget you're here."

True to Maggie's word, most of the women did forget about her. But not all of them. One woman in particular could think of nothing but Lori. The scene she'd just witnessed had her so fired up that even the war stories couldn't distract her. She watched the girl clean the first three deserted tables before walking up behind her and grabbing the object of her desire.

Lori was jarred by this unexpected approach. The woman behind her must have weighed 250 pounds and had the power in her hands to match. Acting on blind impulse, Lori put the glasses and bottles she'd collected on the table next to her along with her rag and butt can. This woman didn't care if she was working or not. Before she could gauge this woman's intentions Lori's front was forced against the wall. Massive black hands brutally mauled her breasts and a great solid bulk crushed her from the rear. The woman's breath was raspy and thick with the smell of alcohol.

Lori struggled to find a way to breathe. She had a feeling this attack wasn't going to last long and it didn't. The woman stuck a wet tongue in her ear and humped her with fast, even stabs then came, groaning ferociously and panting rapidly. She slid off Lori's back onto a bench and passed out.

This was the kind of thing she would have to get used to from now on. Her body was a thing to play with, fuck, hump, tease and torment. If anything were done to her to purposely give her an orgasm it was not for her benefit or enjoyment. Rather the degree with which she responded to sexual advances indicated the sexual prowess of those who sought to force her to those limits.

The bottom line was: no matter what the cost to her physically or emotionally, her future depended on her ability to please everyone who required her services.

Lori was beginning to learn that sex didn't always feel good. It hadn't felt good with Tattoo, but it felt good with 'Hawk and Tiên Le. She couldn't judge whether 'Hawk was proud of her or not, but Maggie was pleased.

Lori found it difficult to understand what it meant to trade her sexual ability and compliance for her very existence. She didn't know if it were possible to define herself in those terms. She felt she had nothing more than that to offer. Wasn't that all Cloud had ever wanted from her? Cloud hadn't wanted to build a life with her. She just wanted dinner, sex and occasional conversation. Maybe that was all anybody like Lori could expect out of life. Well then, she told herself, if that is all there is, then you'd better give the best you have. She wasn't going to get old and look back at her life and say, You only had three things to do: fuck, cook and clean, and you did it half-assed. She wanted to look back at her life and be able to say, And you made the Nighthawk proud of you. *That* was worth work- ing for. What she really wanted to be able to say was, The Night- hawk desired you. Another pipe dream, she told herself. She de- cided she would just have to settle for having been a woman Cloud Three Eagles had kept "stashed" for two years, and let it go at that.

The only other woman who caught Lori before Maggie put her back in the apartment was a very attractive Hispanic woman with copper-red hair. Lori noted how different this woman looked from the other customers with her well-pressed tan slacks and neat white shirt that she wore with the collar up to frame her striking features and slicked-back hair. When Lori wasn't looking the woman had clamped her key fob around the chain between Lori's nipples. As Lori finished wiping the small table and tried to straighten she sucked in her breath against the painful tearing sensation in her nipples.

"Going somewhere?" the woman asked arrogantly.

Lori indicated acquiescently that she clearly wasn't going any-where by shaking her head fearfully and adjusting her weight to bow helplessly before this woman. The woman took a cigarette from her shirt pocket, put it between her well-shaped lips and handed a matchbook to Lori.

Lori struck a match and held it before the cigarette end but the woman didn't attempt to light her cigarette until the flame was close to burning Lori's fingers. Her laugh was low and cruel when Lori had to drop the match into an ashtray to keep from being burned. She exhaled a stream of smoke into Lori's face but the girl didn't back away.

"Gutsy little shit, aren't you?" she taunted. "I've watched you get done," she declared as she unzipped her slacks, "now let's see how well you can do." She took Lori's hand and pushed it into her wet cunt. "Whack me off, white meat," she ordered smoothly.

Lori's fingers worked into the moist folds, easily locating the blood-congested mound. Her movements were slow and circular until the woman grabbed her head with the hand that held the cigarette and brought it to her to kiss her roughly. Lori was drawn into this woman's passion; she returned the kisses ardently,moving her hand in jerky up and down movements that were answered by rocking hips and stuttering moans. Suddenly the woman's head pulled away, her hands came down to brace her against the bench as her body stiffened. Her mouth opened to let free silent exhales of elation as she grabbed Lori's hand to make it stop pleasuring her. She made Lori stand there in her humbled position as she panted and heaved her way to relaxed bliss. Saying nothing to acknowl-edge the girl or dismiss her, the woman didn't even open her eyes. She simply squeezed the clasp of her key fob until it opened enough for Lori to pull free and go about her work.

Chapter Four

Nightfall was coming earlier as winter approached. Maggie held her collar close as she stepped smartly toward the address she'd seen on Lori's driver's license. She had to get there before dark or no one in the apartment building would talk to her, a stranger.

A middle-aged woman sat on the front stoop, petting a calico cat and drinking from a mug of steaming coffee. The woman smiled at Maggie as she walked up the steps.

"Lookin' for somebody?" the landlady asked kindly but seriously. She liked to think she took pretty good care of her tenants, but in truth she was just a busy-body who liked to know what each one was up to.

Maggie knew the type and relaxed. This one wouldn't be hard to get to talk. "Yes, would you help me?" she asked innocently. "I'm looking for Lori Smith. Have you seen her?"

The landlady looked Maggie over, judging her quickly. She looked harmless enough. "Haven't seen her in about three months. Had to clean out her things from her apartment and rent it to somebody else. Things being what they are, I couldn't afford to keep it for her. She didn't have much, just some clothes and kitchen stuff. I put 'em in the storeroom in case she ever comes back for 'em. Although I'm beginnin' to wonder if she ever will."

"Has something happened to her?" Maggie asked, feigning concern.

"I was hopin' *you* knew," the landlady answered half-suspiciously. "What's she to you?"

"My brother owns a restaurant downtown. Lori told me she was looking for another job. I told her if he ever needed any help I'd look her up," Maggie lied.

The landlady cocked her head and narrowed her eyes slightly. She didn't remember Lori ever saying she was unhappy with her job. But then the girl never said much of anything anyway, so maybe she was looking for a new place to work.

"Wish I could help you." The landlady paused making Maggie worry she might get the brush off. The woman looked into space and shook her head sadly. "Lori was such a nice girl — quiet, sweet, clean — never could figure out why she kept company with that crazy Indian, though." She shrugged her shoulders. "We all thought she'd run off with the Indian until she got that letter from some place in South Dakota. I remembered Lori telling me her friend was Sioux so I ain't ashamed to tell you, I opened that letter. Now we're *really* worried about her 'cuz she *ain't* with that Indian nor has she been," the woman pronounced self-importantly.

"Oh, dear," Maggie exclaimed. "Have you gone to the police?"

"Huh," the landlady huffed. "Don't have to, they won't do nothin' about it even though the girl's clearly missing." She put the cat down and got to her feet. "Come out of the cold, Miss. I'll show the letter to you if you think you can make anything out of it."

Maggie followed the woman into her apartment and thanked her for being so kind. She memorized the return address before reading the letter.

So, Cloud was in a county jail, for drugs, and wanted Lori to send money to her. Maggie shook her head pretending to be shocked.

"Hell of a note, isn't it. Fine thing asking that poor girl for money. Drugs," the woman spat disgustedly, "I say let her rot in jail. In a way I'm kinda glad Lori isn't here to get this letter. She'd send every penny she could spare to that jailbird and wouldn't get so much as a 'Thank you, ma'am' from her. Well," the woman sighed, "if you see Lori tell her I've got her things and she can come back for them any time. I'd like to have her back as a tenant, too, if she stops seeing that fool Indian."

The woman started to mumble something and Maggie decided it was time to go. "I'll tell her. I wish I could tell you where she was. I can see why you can't go to the police," Maggie agreed to keep the woman from following through with the idea. "Good night."

Maggie wrote the address down her first chance. She handed the piece of paper to 'Hawk later that night when Lori wasn't around.

"I think I found out where Three Eagles is," Maggie said.

"Where?" 'Hawk asked impatiently.

"She's doing time for drugs in a county jail. That's the mailing address of the jail probably."

'Hawk smiled maliciously. "In the joint, eh. Good. I'll have this checked out and find out how long she's in for. Nice work, Mag," 'Hawk congratulated her while pocketing the slip of paper. She didn't care how her friend had found out; she always trusted Maggie to have done the right thing.

* * *

'Hawk and Tiên Le leaned against the cool brick of the building that provided ample shadows to blend into. It was a weeknight and fairly quiet because it was cold. Tiên Le had been home a month; her presence had produced visible positive effects on her leader. 'Hawk was calmer for the most part, and easier to get along with. Still, Tiên Le could sense an uneasiness building in her friend that showed in the way the woman continuously twisted the big diamond ring on her left hand. She was trying not to notice the nervous habit, focusing her attention instead on the street they were watching.

'Hawk didn't "lean on cars" like some night people did, insisting the practice was "for kids and fools who wanted to get their shit blown away." She clung to the shadows and kept alert knowing that anyone driving down a street or alley might be somebody with a gun and a score to settle. When 'Hawk did her rounds she always varied her routines and paths. No one *ever* knew when to expect the Nighthawk to appear except to say, "After the sun goes down and before it comes back up again."

Cars drove by slowly if they belonged there and quickly if they didn't. Only rarely did one carrying cops cruise by. This was a neighborhood that the police didn't spend much time in unless they had to or could be sure they were going to make a collar. 'Hawk was very proud of the fact that she'd never been collared. She had an understanding with the precinct cops who were eminently bribable: she sometimes provided them with information via informants and they pretended not to see when she stepped outside the law.

They knew she ran guns but her operation was small time compared to the outfits who dealt in military arms sales to foreign countries. Her whorehouses were rousted from time to time to make appearances look good but the charges against her girls never seemed to hold up. The official policies against vigilantes somehow failed to apply to 'Hawk's activities. It was a nice arrangement.

Newspaper skidded along the pavement carried by a biting wind. The pair kept their eyes moving, scanning the rooftops, windows, street and the drunk who snored loudly from the doorway a few feet from where they stood. A sudden movement caught their attention. 'Hawk glanced down the street and spotted a short figure running in their direction. She judged the runner to be a small boy and when he tried to run by her she snatched him up by the collar of his coat.

He was a young black boy who couldn't have been older than eight. He fought against being caught by flailing his fists and kicking his feet, swearing fouly and loudly. 'Hawk held the boy at arms length, patiently enduring the onslaught in the way a lioness endures the play-fight of her cub. When she'd had enough she cuffed his head with an open-handed blow that wouldn't injure him, just get his attention.

Tiên Le watched their surroundings even more carefully as 'Hawk dealt with the ferocious child. "Hold up, little man. Who you running from?" 'Hawk asked sternly as she reached into the boy's coat to relieve him of the small handgun he was carrying.

"I ain't running from nobody," he stated loudly but the affect of being called "little man" was beginning to work on him. Being treated with respect by an adult was both complimentary and soothing to his ego and cause for suspicion. Weren't adults always getting in his way? Adults were suckers. "Gimmie back my gun!" he yelled indignantly.

'Hawk handed the weapon to Tiên Le who emptied the bullets from it and stashed them and the weapon in her coat lining. There was no way of knowing how worthy the weapon was without dismounting it. For all they knew the thing might blow a hand apart instead of discharging a bullet.

"What gun?" 'Hawk asked while checking the boy for more weapons.

"The one she just put in her coat," he insisted, pointing to 'Hawk's partner.

"Tiên Le, you got a gun?"

"No way, 'Hawk. I never carry guns," Tiên Le stated matter-of-factly.

"Oh, man," the boy whined, stamping his foot.

'Hawk finished her search, checked the area to see if anyone were chasing the boy then looked him over more closely. If the gun had been fired, she would have heard it so she suspected the boy had just been frightened away from a burglary. 'Hawk didn't know the boy, and he clearly didn't know her; she knew *all* the children on her turf.

"When was the last time you had something to eat?" 'Hawk quizzed sincerely.

"What's it to you? What do you care?" the boy shot back defiantly.

'Hawk changed her grip on the boy and lifted him with one arm bringing him level with her disquieting eyes. It wasn't so dark that he couldn't see what he was up against. "I *care*," she stated with an intensity that cut through the boy's hard defenses.

"I stole something from the market this morning," he provided proudly but angrily. He was ready to fight the world that made him ache with hunger on a daily basis.

"Where are your folks?"

"Got none," he flung back at her, challenging her to do something about his situation.

'Hawk let him down to the ground while tightening her grip on him. "You're coming with us, little man. I'm taking you to get a meal and a place to sleep. You don't have to stay . . ." she added to show her intention was not to take the only thing the boy had from him: his freedom. "You're on the 'Hawk's turf now and the law around here is: you make trouble on 'Hawk's turf and you pay. You got to pay by staying for one meal and one night's sleep, then you can go if you want. You can stay, too. Nobody makes the decision but you, hear?"

Nighthawk and Tiên Le ignored the boy's barrage of questions and demands as they walked around the next corner and carefully up the littered stairs of a dank apartment house.

On the third floor 'Hawk rapped on the door with four sharp raps and one small one. She spoke clearly to the voice on the other side of the door.

"Sophia, it's 'Hawk and Tiên Le."

"Lord be praised," the bulky woman shouted happily as she flung the door open in a gesture of hearty welcome. "What you got here? Come in, come in," she offered, looking the boy over. He had that lean, tough, wary look of the hard case child she knew how to handle better than anyone. She'd turned 'Hawk into something besides a wildcat, hadn't she? Surely this boy couldn't cause her half the grief. Or give her half the satisfaction. Or pleasure, she thought as she accepted a hug from the fearless leader.

It had been Sophia who had given 'Hawk her taste for big breasted women. 'Hawk had learned many a lesson at Sophia's metal kitchen table, but it was what she'd learned in the sagging old bed she was most proud of. Furtively she let her hand explore one of the familiar breasts and tweaked the nipple. It stood up under the worn woolen fabric aching for more. Male or female, child or adult, 'Hawk was the best partner Sophia had ever had.

"Okay, little man, this is Sophia. You eat here and you sleep here, understand?" 'Hawk asked patiently. "In the morning, you talk to Sophia about staying on if you want and you'll get a good breakfast. Or else you can go. Get it?"

The boy nodded carefully, not exactly trusting but that spaghetti smelled awfully good and his stomach suddenly hurt.

"I'll take good care of him, 'Hawk," Sophia assured as she followed 'Hawk and the ever-silent Tiên Le to the hall. "And you *know* what I want in return," she whispered.

'Hawk smiled and patted the woman's backside fondly. "And you'll get it, too, mama," she promised, looking forward to losing herself in that ample body again.

Back on the street, 'Hawk realized that the unnamed agitation she'd been feeling for the last few weeks had just come to a head. Seeing Sophia again had been the catalyst for a new train of thought which she wasted no time in pursuing.

"Do you think if I'd had a better education I could have done something better with my life?" she asked Tiên Le, casually abandoning the tone and language she used on the street.

Tiên Le recognized the shift in attitude and relaxed. It was conference time now and she was finally going to learn what was bothering her leader. She knew 'Hawk had avoided school more than most, but she'd also *learned* more than most. Tiên Le admired 'Hawk's mind, and thought it was a tragedy that no one had gotten her to apply it. "You mean go legit?" she asked, drawing 'Hawk out.

Striding along thoughtfully, 'Hawk replied, "Yeah, I guess."

Tiên Le chuckled. "Man, who'd hire somebody as ugly as you?"

'Hawk stopped sharply. "I'm serious."

Tiên Le walked back to 'Hawk and looked up at her. "So am I," she said forcefully. The team moved into a doorway to talk more comfortably. Tiên Le knew Americans took not looking into their eyes as a sign of submission or dishonesty and had learned how to override her native courtesies. Still, it took some doing to hold eye contact with 'Hawk for more than a minute. It was worth the effort, she found, because 'Hawk truly listened to her and that made her feel honored.

"Think about it, 'Hawk. If you *had* finished high school and gone on to college, what would you have done with a degree? No way you could have gotten along with someone being your boss, right?" She knew 'Hawk pretty well.

"Right," 'Hawk verified soberly.

"So if you'd gone into business on your own, you couldn't have built a paying clientele."

"Why?"

"Because . . . they'd take one look at that big, black, amazon body of yours, that ugly scar and those eyes that speak to the devil's own soul and run the other fuckin' way. That's why. So then you'd end up down here, and these people can't pay anyway and you'd be no better off than you are now. Worse, probably," Tiên Le added, "because then you'd think you were a failure and have to pay off your college loans to boot.

"Don't you see, 'Hawk? You're already doing what you're most qualified to do." Even in the dim light from a faltering street lamp nearby Tiên Le could see the question on 'Hawk's incredible face. One of the traits she admired most about the big woman was that she never pretended she knew things she didn't, nor was she ashamed to want to learn more.

"I never told you this before, 'Hawk, because I never thought you needed to know but I heard about you years ago from somebody in a bar in L.A. Do you remember when I showed you on the map how fuckin' far away L.A. is from here?"

Intrigued, 'Hawk nodded her head.

"*You're* the reason I moved here, 'Hawk," Tiên Le revealed. She waited while 'Hawk's eyes bored through her, looking for a lie or an angle. But none was there to be found. Tiên Le was telling the truth. "I'm not the only one who has, either. I've talked to several women who've said they did the same thing I did: heard about you and decided that if you were for real I had to be by your side. I've been here all these years because you are for real. Have you ever met anyone else who could take care of the people of this neighborhood the way you do?"

"You," 'Hawk disclosed candidly.

Tiên Le seemed a little shaken by the comment. "I'm flattered that you think so 'Hawk. If that's true it's only because I've learned from you how to be tough and strong and still care about people. What do you think the people in your neighborhood really feel about you?"

"I never thought about it," 'Hawk told her truthfully.

"They respect you because you're a self-made person. They're afraid of you but there's nobody else they'd rather have looking out for them. They come to you for help and are more than glad to help you if you ever need it. You're like a father to everybody, even the old men. You're fearless and devoted, streetwise and just." She wanted to add, compassionate, but didn't think 'Hawk was ready for that. "They appreciate you and know they live in a neighborhood with someone who looks after them. You're a village elder, 'Hawk, and it's sad that you don't think your life means anything." It was thrilling to see that 'Hawk had been genuinely listening to her. It was about time someone told 'Hawk what she just had. "Is that why you've been so nervous lately, you thought your life was meaningless?" Tiên Le was surprised and only then realized how little appreciation 'Hawk received for her tireless efforts. Perhaps the people in her neighborhood were afraid to approach their intrepid protector.

"It's the eyes, 'Hawk. They're the reason you grew up the way you did, but they're also the reason nobody can look directly at you and tell you how much you mean to them," Tiên Le said sadly.

'Hawk looked out toward the street; she grew distant then. Tiên Le saw the big lids open and close rapidly and thought that if 'Hawk had known how, she'd have cried.

"Let's go down to Beniña's for some coffee, 'Hawk." Tiên Le urged her friend onto the street again where the chill wind froze the moment, shutting Tiên Le out of her leader's heart for the rest of the night.

They found Shirl at Beniña's restaurant and joined her at the back table. Tiên Le hoped that Shirl would improve their brooding friend's mood with her easy-going charm.

Shirl and Tiên Le exchanged concerned looks out of 'Hawk's field of vision. Standing to excuse herself, Tiên Le said she was going to look in on "em gái" (the younger sister). Tiên Le was extremely protective of her charge who she wouldn't even call by name to her friends. Only 'Hawk understood why her foreign friend couldn't break the habit of hiding her sister. Tiên Le's village had been destroyed by the North Vietnamese when she was a young girl and her sister just a newborn. Tiên Le had rescued the infant and fled to the mountains knowing the rest of her family had perished. Now the "em gái" was a young woman in a new country-staying with yet another Vietnamese family Tiên Le had persuaded to guard her against "the enemy".

'Hawk considered the hardships Tiên Le had faced in *her* life. As hard as her own life had been, it had never been as difficult as her friend's who had suffered through the horrors of war and spent her entire life looking over her shoulder. If this dynamo of a woman had traveled the miles to be by her side, then maybe her life had meaning after all. "How is she doing?" 'Hawk asked softly.

Tiên Le stopped and turned to answer the tender question. "Okay, 'Hawk. English is a hard language to learn but she has lots of determination. She's very smart," Tiên Le revealed with a sense of awe. She was just getting acquainted with the girl she'd only written letters to and seen pictures of for so many years. It seemed to 'Hawk and Shirl that Tiên Le was really enjoying the company of her only living relative. They were happy for her.

"If there is anything I can do. . . ." 'Hawk offered sincerely.

A brief look passed between them — both saying the thanks with their eyes that neither woman could say with her voice. TiênLe left quietly.

Beniña stood behind the counter taking in this rare scene. She told herself that it wouldn't be good to let 'Hawk grow uncomfortable with her own humanness because she might find it hard to be that way again. She distracted 'Hawk deftly. "So the Nighthawk finally comes around for some of Beniña's ribs. I see you haven't been starving to death," she commented abruptly with her heavy Spanish accent.

"Beni! Hey, what's happning?" 'Hawk asked happily, not realizing how long it had been since she'd seen the energetic woman.

"You get tired of my cooking?" Beniña asked, almost hurt by 'Hawk's absence.

"No way, you Cuban wench, you make the best goddamn ribs I ever had."

"Then why you ain't been here for months?"

'Hawk stared at the woman in disbelief. The other patrons in the establishment shifted restlessly as the air between 'Hawk and Beniña grew chilly. Shirl cleared her throat to get 'Hawk's attention. She whispered out of the side of her mouth, "You been eatin' at home, 'Hawk."

'Hawk turned to look at Shirl, thinking about what she'd said. "By god, you're right. I have, haven't I?" She started laughing as she got up to lean across the counter and kiss the cook. "Now that I think of it, Beni, I *have* been eating someone else's cooking. Do you remember the big Indian used to hang out around here?" To Beniña's affirmative reply, 'Hawk said, "Well, I took her woman and been keeping her at my place and, yeah, she cooks, and cleans, too. A pretty little piece of *young* white meat, ain't that right, Shirl?"

Shirl whistled and confirmed, "She is that, 'Hawk."

"And when Three Eagles gets out of the joint she's gonna have to find something *else* to fuck because I got her piece working for me now."

Beniña understood the situation clearly. "You eat some of my ribs, anyway."

"Just a bite, wench, I'm on edge tonight," 'Hawk told her.

'Hawk dutifully tasted the woman's offering, praised it, and promised to get back in more often. Shirl followed 'Hawk out of the restaurant to accompany her on the balance of her rounds. She was glad 'Hawk had found Three Eagles and settled down about wanting to kill the Indian. Shirl didn't think the white girl was worth a murder. Taking the cunt was enough to exact revenge for the betrayal. 'Hawk seemed to be growing comfortable with the idea, especially now that she could talk about it without being angry.

They went "on top" for awhile, traversing rooftops, using their keen eyesight to observe the activities below. They checked with their lookouts for their nightly reports. Satisfied that all was well, the two women went down a ladder and through a secret door into a building that buzzed with activity. This was one of 'Hawk's whorehouses. The people who worked here never knew when to expect "the boss" and had to keep things in order against the event of a surprise visit. She and Shirl strolled casually through the hallways and down the stairs where they came upon the "parlor" and its madam.

The woman was mean and ugly and kept her girls in line. 'Hawk wouldn't allow any beatings but the girls got slapped around enough to keep them scared of disobeying or getting too smart-mouthed. This was a business and they were employees. They worked, ate and slept in the "house" and were free to go any time they wished. None left because they all knew they had it better as 'Hawk's whores than they would anywhere else in town.

'Hawk had a gift for stealth; she stood behind the madam, waiting to be noticed.

The woman jumped, putting her hands over her heart. "*Jesus,* 'Hawk. Fuck, why can't you come through the front door like everybody else?" she asked, annoyed, knowing she wouldn't get an answer from her mysterious boss. She handed the ledger book to her employer and went back to filing her nails.

'Hawk scanned the entries quickly, not realizing other people-didn't work figures as rapidly as she did. She stopped at an inordinately large amount. Pointing to it she leaned the open book toward the madam who scowled at it and said passively, "We had a little accident around here," meaning a girl had had an abortion.

'Hawk frowned but kept on reading. That was the third "accident" this house had had so far this year. She began to suspect the madam of skimming funds and decided to start having the surly woman watched.

'Hawk always knew when someone's eyes were on her. She turned around to see who was looking at her. It was one of her girls, curled up on a couch, sulking. "What's wrong with Angel?"

"She got company," the madam replied loudly. She hated it when one of the workers was doubled up with menstrual cramps. Shirl smiled; she liked it when a woman had her bloods.

"Yeah, and I just got my clean card, too," Angel bitched from the connecting room. She was mad because she'd been to the VD clinic that afternoon and checked out okay and then her damn period came, stopping her from having any fun. Unless, of course,a customer came who *wanted* a bleeding cunt to fuck.

'Hawk walked over to the coffee-colored woman. "Let me see," she said, holding her hand out for the proof. Angel grinned wickedly and reached into her skirt for the clinic card. 'Hawk looked at it carefully. She could spot a forgery easily. This one was real but she didn't give it back to the woman. Shirl walked in and stood next to her friend when she saw 'Hawk holding the valued card out of Angel's reach.

"'Hawk, let me have my card back. Please," she begged sweetly.

'Hawk shoved the card down the front of Shirl's pants. "What are you going to do to get it back, whore?" she asked teasingly. She knew how to get a working girl out of a bad, non-productive mood.

Angel began to sit up and take interest. Her body moved fluidly and seductively toward Shirl. Her hand reached up to caress Shirl's bulge. "I could suck off your friend . . ." she suggested musically.

"Stop talking and start sucking, whore," 'Hawk directed preemptively.

Angel expertly unfastened Shirl's pants and took out the big,black tool. She loved women who always wore dildos like some of 'Hawk's clan did. It excited her to make a woman come this way. She took the whole of it into her mouth and throat effortlessly. Shirl was quick to respond. Moaning and clamping her hands over Angel's head, she fucked this new face with a hard driving motion.

'Hawk sat down next to Angel encircling her with long arms that held probing hands. She yanked the tube top off the breasts and pulled meanly on the taut nipples. Two other girls looked on enviously. 'Hawk slid her lap underneath Angel letting one of her hands pull back the tiny skirt to find the whore's hard clit. Massaging and pinching she played the woman like an instrument while Shirl had her way with the well-trained mouth.

"Ohn fuck!" Shirl exclaimed as her body snapped, releasing the sexual tension in gripping waves. 'Hawk pulled the mouth off the stick and stepped up the pace of her attentions. Angel squirmed and writhed, greedily taking all she could bear. Getting done by the Nighthawk was something to make last as long as possible. When 'Hawk bit her ear, her resolve collapsed, then her body followed. Her screams were like hisses as one seizure after another plunged through her. 'Hawk let her rest on her lap for a moment before standing with her. Shirl returned her card and the team left as quietly as they arrived.

The northern border of 'Hawk's turf was delineated by a set of elevated railroad tracks. The border had not been disputed in several years owing to a bond of mutual respect between 'Hawk and her neighboring warlord, a tall, charming Puerto Rican man whom 'Hawk had known since she was a teenager. Along this carefully but inconspicuously guarded line 'Hawk and Shirl met two men who were confirmed followers of the Nighthawk. Sid, a young Hispanic man 'Hawk had looked after since he'd grown too old for youth gangs, approached casually to make the meeting appear chance and of no significance. Bad Man, a lanky, defensive teen, hung back. Bad Man admired 'Hawk intensely and wanted to be like her — tough, cool and indestructible — but he got tongue-tied around her and couldn't speak directly to his hero. Sid always did the talking during these encounters.

"Got a buyer who wants a couple .45's," he entered softly.

"What'd you tell him?" 'Hawk quizzed.

"What you always say: No .45's, just .38 specials, UZI's and .38 rifles. He said he wants .45's, and I said I'd ask anyway but the 'Hawk never sells .45's," Sid reported.

"Who is this man?" 'Hawk asked, concerned. Buyers who insisted on getting cannons like the one she carried were usually trouble of one sort: undercover agents, ex-cons or head cases. 'Hawk didn't like arming people with guns that were as accurate and deadly as her own.

"Says his name is Franklin. Bad Man don't like him," Sid said looking his partner's way for confirmation. The teen shook his head meaningfully.

"It's been awhile since we busted the Imperials up, 'Hawk. Could be they're arming for a war," Shirl suggested edgily. The people who'd survived the last war had been too quiet, were laying too low.

'Hawk thought the same way. "Sid, break off, go south and start listening. Bad Man, go south with Sid and west. Stay up top as much as you can. I'll meet you at the pool hall on Haverson in ten days," 'Hawk instructed cryptically. The men touched their hats by way of a salute and dispersed. 'Hawk had just told them to stop running guns and start spying along the disputed borders of her turf.

'Hawk and Shirl turned to walk quietly along the one border she didn't have to worry about, the river that flanked her turf's easternmost limit.

During this quiet part of their tour Shirl kept up her vigilant guard while 'Hawk withdrew into herself to think and plan. This was the coldest, darkest hour of the night, the hour just before dawn would begin to lighten the sky on the horizon.

They came upon a small all night grocery store and Shirl mentioned that her old lady needed a couple items. 'Hawk was low on cigarettes so she agreed to stop in with her friend.

Walking into the store, 'Hawk's hair tingled on the back of her neck. She stood still and cocked her head as if to smell or taste the air for trouble. Shirl recognized the gesture for one of warning. The confirming nudge on her arm told her that it wasn't wise for them to be together. She walked two aisles further down, eyes jumping, hand steady and poised, senses extended to test each individual within close range.

Almost as though on cue, a rangy, bearded black man entered the store calmly and pulled a gun on the portly clerk behind the cash register counter yelling, "Everybody drop and nobody gets hurt. Give me the money, old man."

'Hawk and Shirl had dropped a second before everyone else, turning on their heels toward the robber and pulling their guns from their holsters as one. 'Hawk assessed the intruder quickly as an experienced if somewhat careless thief. She attributed the over-confidence and impatience he displayed to drugs. 'Hawk had lived as long as she had by trusting her instincts. After checking about for accomplices in the small crowd of shoppers and seeing that no one was making any foolish moves or bids to become heroes, she stole silently up behind the man.

The grocery clerk was blanched with fear but gave no hint that he saw 'Hawk approaching. He fumbled with the cash register to buy time hoping the man wasn't reckless enough to try to get the money himself.

'Hawk put the barrel of her gun into the robber's hair and spoke to him, quite deliberately, "All right, asshole, there is a Colt .45 pointed at your head. If you look in the round mirror you can see an Army vet sharpshooter who doesn't miss, aiming a .38 special at your ribs. Now if you don't give up, I'm gonna splatter what little brains you got all over this nice man's apron. Get it?" 'Hawk warned darkly.

The man's eyes darted up to the convex mirror mounted on the wall above the cash register and saw that the person who claimed to have a gun at his head had something anyway and two aisles down-someone was on one knee aiming a gun at his body. His confidence began to waver but his pride persisted in motivating him to do harm.

"I ain't afraid of you," he insisted, "you ain't going to kill me."

Hisses and gasps flew through the frightened, cowering shoppers. The grocery clerk was emboldened some now that 'Hawk appeared to have the situation in hand. "Son, don't be a fool. The Nighthawk has a gun at your head and she's trigger happy." He didn't think that 'Hawk would mind the exaggeration.

The man faltered and his gun shook. He'd heard of the Nighthawk. Was this really her? He tried to pick out the facial scar on her reflection in the mirror but couldn't.

"Patience is not my strong suit," 'Hawk cautioned.

"I'm thinking, man, I'm thinking," he shouted desperately. He was in a real jam and didn't know what to do. His survival instincts won out over his macho in the end.

"Time for thinking was over before you walked through that door," 'Hawk said angrily. "Now move the gun back over your head so I can take it without hurting somebody."

The man obeyed her. Once 'Hawk had his gun, Shirl stood up to search him. "He's clean, 'Hawk," she said and took the new gun from her friend. She thrived on this kind of excitement and knew 'Hawk did too.

'Hawk escorted the man out of the store and returned alone, completely unruffled. She had *given* the man the money he needed for his fix, told him to get some help and to stay away from her turf. Relieved and grateful, the man took the money and disappeared. 'Hawk was confident he wouldn't bother her again.

In the store everyone came up to thank her. She was embarrassed but pleased by the outpouring of gratitude from the people she was devoting her life to. The incident relieved the gritty uneasiness she'd been feeling the past weeks. The clerk wouldn't let 'Hawk or Shirl pay for their purchases and thanked them again before they left.

Chapter Five

Lori looked down at the woman sucking her nipple. She couldn't get used to how different the handsome woman was from the others. She knew her name now — Carla — and knew what she wanted, too. Carla's visits had become almost nightly. On the nights when Lori was brought out to help in the bar Carla was always there and always demanding Lori perform sexually for her in some way. Lori both dreaded the encounters and looked forward to them. Carla paid attention to her. Not positive attention, but Lori was hungry for any sort and was growing hungrier with each day that brought no news of Cloud Three Eagles. Cloud had never been gone for such a long time and Lori was beginning to feel forsaken and lost. She had misgivings about her contacts with Carla because she feared 'Hawk might notice and become angered by them.

Lori couldn't afford to make 'Hawk angry, for any reason. Little by little she had learned enough about 'Hawk's life and the complex social structure of her world to see that she was utterly helpless without 'Hawk's protection. Her owner was very much like the tribal chiefs Cloud had described to her, a woman with great power and leadership ability. Lori knew now that if 'Hawk were to fall, then Tiên Le, who was second in command, was her chosen successor. She had made a point of listening for information that would assure her that Tiên Le would even want to assume 'Hawk's awesome position as warlord. It was Lori's feeling the mysterious Vietnamese woman was fully prepared to take over. In which case Lori doubted her status as a well-guarded plaything was terribly safe, but there was an outside chance the woman would, in some way, honor 'Hawk's arrangement.

Lori's brief encounters with Tiên Le's slave did little to boost her confidence. The small woman was openly hostile to Lori, perceiving 'Hawk's property as a rival who could threaten her own tenuous position as Tiên Le's possession. To make matters worse, Tiên Le's slave's behavior was condescending toward Lori. Not only had the slave belonged to Tiên Le for several years, giving her seniority, her skin wasn't white, which in *this* world gave her more rank.

But the larger fear was that Lori might lose even this lowest status if 'Hawk were to become so angered with her that she simply turned Lori out onto the street for the first passer-by to claim.

On the nights when she wasn't trying to save her selfhood, she struggled to save her life. 'Hawk's indifference gnawed away at Lori's strength. It was no small wonder Lori was learning how to enjoy the notice of women like Carla. The slender woman's looks were cool, detached and sculpted; her bronze complexion and copper-tinted hair fascinated people, especially Lori who was naturally attracted to interesting-looking women. Since the first night Lori had been made to work in the bar, Carla had seen to it that the exceptional body was willing even if its occupant wasn't.

Carla played with the padlock securing Lori's cunt. The girl had become quite accustomed to all her sexual adornments; the padlock was no exception. The small silver thing dangled and sparkled between her legs like an irresistible temptation, the little apple hanging before dozens of eyes making them desire the forbidden fruit more with each exposure to it.

Lori was completely aware of what the lock had come to represent to these women: something 'Hawk had said she would share and hadn't. Carla tugged on it because she liked to see Lori's mouth open and lids lower when she did. The pierced cunt lips were terribly sensitive to touch.

What Lori knew, Carla also knew: 'Hawk was watching them. Lori had been resistive and tense at first because of the leader's observation. Carla was patient and persistent and soon Lori's breathing pattern was interrupted by a sigh, then a low gasp as Carla thumped her other nipple. Again. And again. Then a steady barrage of finger-thwacking on one nipple, bites on the other and tugs on the lock tormented the girl's able body.

Maggie rang up a purchase and gave a customer her change. She tried not to watch when someone was taking advantage of Lori but 'Hawk's determined stride toward the helpless girl caught and held her interest.

'Hawk grabbed Lori by the arm and pulled her away, ripping her nipple unceremoniously from the grip of Carla's mouth. Taken aback by the jolting action Carla didn't react to the situation immediately. Upon realizing who had taken the treat from her, she thought better of her angry desire to beat a head in, and sat up to see what was amiss.

Lori nearly stumbled trying to keep up with 'Hawk's long stride given the reach of the chain between her legs. She didn't go far, stopping at the pool table against which she was shoved. She toppled onto the green felt scattering the balls remaining from an in-progress game of nine-ball. The players stifled their complaints but their faces were pinched with anger. Anyone but the Nighthawk would have started a fight with such an action. As it was the players retrieved their bets and wordlessly agreed to a rematch.

One of the object balls was pinned painfully under Lori's breast. She was given no chance to stand to alleviate her problem; 'Hawk forced her chest back onto the table. Lori at once complied. To her and everyone watching, this scene had the makings of an about-to-be-dealt-out-punishment. If 'Hawk were angry at her for responding to Carla, then so be it. She only prayed that she would not find herself abandoned afterwards.

Maggie was confused by 'Hawk's actions. Surely 'Hawk didn't expect the girl to know when to and when not to respond sexually, and with whom, she thought. Yet Lori's stance—feet spread on the floor to the length of the chain, buttocks up, bent at the hips and splayed over the table — looked like a preparation for a spanking if she ever saw one.

'Hawk unlocked the padlock and took it from Lori's cunt rings. She produced two lengths of small linked chain and used them to open Lori's lips by threading each ring then fastening each chain to a leather corner pocket of the pool table. The padlock was used to bring Lori's wrists together behind her back. The brilliantly simple bondage left the girl defenseless and exposed. The only way she could move away would rip the rings through her skin. The left-over sexual lubrication glistened on her lewdly stretched lips.

The entire crowd gazed expectantly at the fascinating sight. Maggie looked away when she saw 'Hawk take her dildo out. She knew what was coming next and couldn't watch.

Lori *didn't* know and was surprised when she felt the large probe enter her vagina. Lori could see nothing of what was being done to her, even how her lips were held open. She managed to cope with 'Hawk's brutal rutting and was relieved when it was over because it had never taken that long to please the leader before. She could feel the restlessness of the crowd of women and wondered why they all seemed so fidgety. It got very quiet when 'Hawk backed away. Lori held her breath.

'Hawk motioned unfeelingly to Tiên Le and a sigh of pleasure and anticipation rolled through the bar. This was what they had been waiting for. Tiên Le stepped behind Lori and pushed her dildo into the cavity 'Hawk had just vacated.

Lori's eyes opened wide and her mouth fell open when she felt a second probe enter her from a lower angle than the first. Someone else was fucking her but she didn't know who.

When Tiên Le's slave finished cleaning 'Hawk's prick, 'Hawk patted the slave's head to say she approved before putting it away. She reached under Lori's breast, found the nipple and tugged it out where it could be seen. Taking advantage of Lori's open mouth she put the cue ball into it as a gag and freed the other nipple. The object ball under her breast shifted to a place where it could be seen but was no longer under the press of Lori's weight. 'Hawk liked the visual effect the ball created so she left it. She sat at the bar to watch.

Tiên Le was long in coming, too, but she finally did and stepped aside to have her cock serviced by the slave, who knelt next to the table. As she moved away, Tiên Le motioned to the next person in the pecking order, Shirl.

It wasn't until the third woman began to use her that Lori realized what was going on and she was terrified. She closed her eyes and fought back the tears. She hadn't meant to make 'Hawk angry. She was sorry. She'd do anything to keep this from happening if 'Hawk would just give her a chance, she wanted to beg. She'd heard of gang rape and knew everyone would have a stake in proving she was up to this activity. Ego and pride were the operative words, not passion and certainly not *com*passion. And it was beginning to hurt. Lori was sore inside and aching outside. No whipping could ever have been as bad as this promised to be.

Tiên Le joined 'Hawk at the bar to watch with her friend. She felt a chilling stare boring into the back of her head and turned around to see Maggie taking off her apron and rolling it up. She tapped 'Hawk's arm. 'Hawk turned in time to see the normally unflappable bartender throw the apron on the counter angrily. They both watched as the woman put her coat on and left.'Hawk motioned for Tiên Le to follow Maggie and got up to take over Maggie's abandoned station.

Tiên Le hung back for the first block of Maggie's brisk, aimless walk to give her time to cool off some before approaching her. If she'd known how mad Maggie was she might have followed for much longer before catching up to talk.

Maggie wasn't surprised when Tiên Le silently appeared at herside. It was a foolish move to take off into the night fueled by anger; she wouldn't be as cautious on the street when her mind was engaged by her hatred of what was happening in the Subway Club. She had her knife, but still. . . .

"Come on, Maggie. You've seen gang-rapes before —" Tiên Le began but was cut off abruptly.

Maggie whirled around to vent her emotions. "You make me sick!" she shot back violently. To anyone watching the two looked like lovers fighting. "What if that were your sister?" she suggested meanly.

Tiên Le stopped sharply. She was stung by Maggie's words. The hurt and surprise showed in her face and eyes. Maggie almost twisted her ankle she'd pulled up so hard when she saw it. Tiên Le's reaction hit her like a blow to the stomach. Her hands came to her cheeks and she said softly, "Oh, Tiên Le, I'm sorry. That wasn't fair. I had no right. . . ." A root canal would have been preferable to the pain of hurting Tiên Le. She took a step back and touched her friend's arm, begging forgiveness.

Tiên Le patted Maggie's hand. "It's all right. You were pissed." But it wasn't all right at all. Tiên Le knew in her heart that Maggie's suggestion *was* fair. *Too* fair. Painfully fair. What if that had been her sister? Or someone she cared about? She had never thought of it like that. But then neither had Maggie. So why now?

"What's wrong, Maggie?"

Maggie's shoulders deflated. She turned and began to walk again, slowly. "It's Lori," she sighed.

Puzzled, Tiên Le joined her friend asking, "Who's Lori?"

Maggie clucked, looked skyward then stopped again. Pointing behind her she answered, "That *girl* back there, that everybody's having such a good time with."

"Lori," Tiên Le swallowed the name like a bitter medicine she knew she had to take. Her stomach knotted up on the realization that that *girl* was a person. It had been so convenient to accept 'Hawk's attitude: that *girl* wasn't a person, just a thing. But Maggie didn't see it that way. Tiên Le didn't think she could see it that way any more either.

Maggie walked on urging her friend to join her. "I'm sorry, Tiên Le, I just couldn't stand it any longer. That poor girl has never hurt anyone, no one's getting revenge here. What point is 'Hawk making? Cloud isn't going to benefit from this little display of power, and God knows 'Hawk doesn't have to prove her sexual prowess."

"She's sharing, Maggie, it's part of the code," Tiên Le offered lamely. Maggie's argument was pretty solid.

"Why gang rape?" she questioned passionately. "Why not on an individual basis? Why did she build it up like this, keeping it from them, and keeping it from them? Then sicks the whole pack on her at once. It doesn't make sense. Do you know Lori thinks she's being punished for responding to Carla?" Maggie plopped herself down on a bench, disgusted.

"No. Why would she think that?" Tiên Le asked genuinely.

"That's how her mind works. She is scared to death that 'Hawk is going to get sick of her and toss her out like so much garbage."

"Did she say that? Doesn't she know 'Hawk would never do a thing like that?"

"She said nothing. She hardly ever says *any*thing. I have to work to get her to talk at all. But I can read between the lines. And after tonight I'm not so sure 'Hawk wouldn't dump her.

"I'm not going back until they're done, Tiên Le. And when I do I'll find a bloody mess of a girl with a broken spirit and probably no will to live. She's done nothing but try to please 'Hawk since the first day 'Hawk had her. And 'Hawk, well, she treats whores better than she does Lori," Maggie insisted helplessly. She'd tried so hard to help that girl and gain her trust. That sweet, loving spirit was being snuffed out and there was nothing she could do to stop it. Her belief that 'Hawk cared about Lori was being snuffed out too.

Tiên Le's heart ached. She'd never known that Maggie could care about anything or anyone, except 'Hawk. Maggie's heart had always seemed so frozen. She took Maggie's hand in hers and sat quietly with her friend until it was time to go back — and pick up the pieces.

Maggie's passionate plea for the girl's sake and against 'Hawk's cruelty would haunt Tiên Le for many nights to come. She, herself began to worry about the extent of 'Hawk's inhumanity.

* * *

Maggie dreaded going to work the night after the rape. Lori had looked just as she expected when she and Tiên Le returned to the bar. 'Hawk hadn't even let the girl free from the table; she'd just abandoned her as had everyone else. Maggie had been hard-pressed to get the key to Lori's wrists from 'Hawk before the leader went on her rounds. Maggie knew Lori had been subjected to assaults with pool cues and knife handles and fingers with sharp, dirty nails. The felt on the table had been wet from the tears even a survivor like Lori couldn't contain.

It was going to be hard enough to face Lori again without frightening her still further, but Maggie had to have the girl examined, didn't she? She wished Tattoo weren't the only person who could do it.

Maggie steeled herself before opening the door to 'Hawk's apartment. You've seen worse than this, she reminded herself. If only that flimsy bit of comfort had been adequate to ease the ache when she saw the look of stark terror shoot across Lori's face once Lori saw Tattoo follow her into the room.

Lori bolted from the couch-bed to the corner where she pressed her back against the wall and shook with fear. The lack of sun had already bleached her skin pale, now her face was chalk-like from panic. Her soft brown eyes were shot with blood and swollen from crying. Her head shook violently. Even in her silence she was saying "no" in a language that could be understood by anyone.

The whole affair sickened Maggie. She found it difficult to reach beyond her disgust to comfort the girl. "It's okay. She's not going to hurt you, I promise. She's here to check your . . . wound," Maggie said fishing about for a way to explain. She was normally heartless in situations like this and almost hated Lori for reawakening her dormant compassion. It had been so much easier not to care.

Approaching the girl cautiously, she touched Lori gingerly then took her by the arm to get her to sit on the couch-bed. Relieved that Lori had a shred of trust left, Maggie succeeded in coaxing the girl to open her legs for Tattoo.

"Be careful," she warned. Tattoo was mildly surprised by the admonition and took heed. She held the speculum under the hot water faucet to warm it, which she normally didn't do before an examination—unless cautioned by someone who had a right to.

Lori sucked in her breath when the instrument entered anyway. Her vagina was raw and tender. She bravely endured the probing and looking of the latex-gloved artist because Maggie seemed to think the procedure was necessary. The outcome of all this was of no importance to her. She withdrew into the darkest recesses of herself—back to that place she had been before Maggie had come in, that place where she intended to remain for as long as she lived, that place where no one could get to her to hurt her any more.

Maggie watched the blank stare take over Lori's expression and knew it for the same curtain that had fallen over her own face just before she'd become a heroin addict many years ago. It was a look that went beyond hopelessness and despair to lifelessness. She, at least, had had the drug to turn to. Lori had nothing. She was startled from her reflections by a dispassionate comment from Tattoo.

"No uterus in this one, Maggie."

("When I told her what Cloud did to me so I can't have periods, she got real angry and left.") Maggie remembered the girl's statement as though it had just been spoken to her. So Cloud Three Eagles had given 'Hawk a head start on breaking this girl's spirit, Maggie thought unhappily. The girl just looked out into space, completely unfazed by Tattoo's remark.

Tattoo finished her work and started to leave. She turned to Maggie and said, almost as an afterthought, "I've seen worse. I'll get my doctor friend to give you something to use to heal it.'Hawk should be able to use it again in a few days."

Maggie whirled around to freeze the artist with an angry glance but the woman had gone. She was boiling with rage and ready to score a hit but the target was too quick for her. She couldn't believe that Tattoo would think the reason for this examination could have been to benefit 'Hawk.

But what else would she think, Maggie, she wondered realistically. Deflated, she turned back to Lori who was now back at work, sweeping the floor. Her actions were listless and automatic — robot-like.

"Damn you, 'Hawk," Maggie swore under her breath. Lori didn't hear. Maggie finished the statement in her mind, You wanted a thing, now you have one.

* * *

Lori's response to the rape suited 'Hawk well. Not anticipating it made it no less convenient. Had 'Hawk examined her motives for the rape, she would have been aware of a pit of possessiveness smoldering just under the surface of her callous nature. 'Hawk had avoided sharing that private part of the girl because, unconsciously, she didn't want to stand by while others used what she wanted so badly but wouldn't allow herself to take. Getting-it-over-with was the end; rape was merely a means.

She had stood behind the bar, coldly watching two dozen women taking advantage of the singular opportunity to fuck the piece of white meat, and felt nothing. She had *that* much control over her emotions. Lori wasn't a tempting, alluring female anymore; she was an object, a fixture, part of the bar. That was what 'Hawk had said she was going to be and now that was what she was, barely distinguishable from the pool table she'd been attached to.

For several nights Maggie had been able to keep the girl out of the bar. The time had come when she could no longer succeed, even she knew that. Lori's behavior was so disturbing to her that she stopped coming to the bar earlier than was needed. She couldn't bear to be alone with the tragedy that was Lori.

When 'Hawk did override Maggie's insistence that she didn't need help and brought the girl out anyway, she was relieved to see that 'Hawk had replaced the lock on Lori's sex lips. Maggie was still trying to understand 'Hawk's behavior toward Lori. None of it made any sense. And she had been so sure that 'Hawk cared about the captive.

It was not surprising that Lori would silently wander about the bar, bussing tables and waiting patiently, but unresponsively as the women resumed the sexual abuses of her body. Maggie speculated that perhaps something good might come of all this if these women grew tired of the hollow, ghost-like shell they were left with and began to ignore Lori altogether.

Whatever happened Maggie was certain 'Hawk felt no remorse. In fact the leader seemed relaxed and relieved now that the barbed thorn had been pulled from her side. She was beginning to think that Lori had been little more than an inconvenience for 'Hawk. Wondering what good it was to care about people if all it brought was pain, Maggie proceeded to get very drunk for the first time in years.

Chapter Six

"Sophia, it's 'Hawk and Kramer," 'Hawk declared clearly to get the woman inside to open the door. She clenched her teeth together to keep her growing arousal from getting ahead of her. Just thinking about Sophia worked her up. Looking at the woman, standing in the doorway dressed in a thinning chenille robe, smiling broadly, made 'Hawk's fingers ache.

"'Hawk, Kramer! Good to see you. It's been a long time, Kramer. How's your mother?" Sophia asked, coyly ignoring 'Hawk's hungry gaze as she stepped aside to let them in. She hadn't known when to expect her friend to return. The anticipation hadn't been nearly as much fun as the real thing promised to be judging from the radiating lust glowing around 'Hawk's tall body.

The boy was there or Sophia wouldn't have worked to keep up the appearance that this was a social call. From the looks of

'Hawk's slender friend, Kramer, the boy was the only one who was being fooled. When Kramer replied that her mother was fine it was only after heavily swallowing her own desire for Sophia's plentiful and welcoming body. She knew that favors like the one she was going to do for 'Hawk were what got the leader to call an associate by a first name. Getting the name Reneé to pass over 'Hawk's lips was worth having to wait to get at her own woman for a few hours. Watching the tops of Sophia's breasts bubble out of the front of her robe made Kramer envious of 'Hawk. Sophia's sexuality oozed and dripped from every pore even though she was well into her fifties and her hair was sprinkled with white. A woman like Sophia just got better with each passing year.

The boy came to stand opposite 'Hawk. He looked from her scarred face to Kramer's square, hard-looking one and wondered where this 'Hawk person found these steely women to hang out with. "You bring me back my gun?" he asked exactingly, arms folded over his chest.

The humorously arrogant demand brought 'Hawk's attention away from Sophia to his small, blustering presence. She wondered if the boy had nearly as much brains as he did bravado. She was glad he had stayed with Sophia. The woman had a gift for getting past angry, hardened shells to the child inside and teaching a person how to get something from life besides hatred and resentment. "That *gun*, little man," she said seriously, "would have blown your arm off if you'd fired it."

The wavering look in the boy's eye gave him away. He couldn't have fired the gun, 'Hawk knew, and the boy knew she knew. Still he made a show of his right to have and use a gun. "I don't believe you," he huffed. "You're just trying to keep my gun." (If an adult had said the same thing, 'Hawk would have doubled up her heavily ringed fist and rearranged a face.) 'Hawk expected the response and knew what was behind it: a frightened little person who had been forced to grow up too fast.

"I didn't think you *would* believe me," she replied taking a black object from her jacket pocket. She handed the removed barrel of the boy's gun to him. He took it suspiciously. "That is the barrel from the gun you were totin', little man." She pulled a similar object from her other pocket for the boy to inspect. "Here's one from a *good* .22. Look inside them. Even you can see there's something wrong with the one you had," she instructed.

He looked both over carefully before he soberly handed them back to 'Hawk. The defect was obvious. His young mind was quick to see that 'Hawk wasn't jerking him around. Sophia's pacifying effect was already in evidence as he nodded his head gravely, acknowledging that this tall, rugged woman knew what she was about and had saved his life by disarming him.

'Hawk dissipated the heavy scene by taking the boy gently by the arm and leading him into the kitchen area to talk. Everything smelled so familiar and good and comfortable. She was soothed by the surroundings and it showed in the edge she took off her voice. "Listen, little man," she began calmly as she took the boy's coat from the chair and started to put it on him, "I thought you might like to go home with Kramer for a little while. Her people have heat and Kramer has a couple foxy sisters who'd like you real well. But I need your help on something," she said invitingly.

The boy looked at her receptively, amazed that someone like 'Hawk would need help. 'Hawk leaned down to talk closely, taking him into her confidence. "You see, Kramer's a little high tonight. . ." The boy looked out the corner of his eye. He knew high when he saw it. The woman was leaning against the door, sucking on a toothpick and eyeing Sophia indiscreetly. 'Hawk was right, she was on something. He nodded in agreement.

"Well," 'Hawk continued, "she likes to go home by way of the pool hall and frankly, I'd enjoy my visit with Sophia a lot more if I didn't have to worry about her getting into trouble. Catch my meaning?" she asked in the low tone of a conspirator.

The boy nodded his head enthusiastically. He was excited about being asked to escort an adult home and make sure she got there safely without taking any detours. 'Hawk didn't mind that the boy didn't see she wasn't at all worried about Kramer. Kramer could take care of herself, but chances were good that if the boy thought he was being escorted to Kramer's house so 'Hawk wouldn't have to worry about him, the boy would be trouble enough for two.

The door was closed and locked behind Kramer and the boy. 'Hawk's eyes fell on Sophia's body like a pouncing cat. She took her hat from her head and placed it on the kitchen table. Her breathing was hard and visible to this woman who had so much power to excite. 'Hawk unzipped her jacket, slowly took it off and hung it on the chair back all the while watching Sophia's eyes soften with yearning for her rigid brawn.

Sophia's mouth quivered as she reacquainted herself with 'Hawk's appearance. 'Hawk wore a close-cut natural hairstyle so she didn't have to bother with it. Sophia still couldn't get used to those eyes and, without the hat brim to diffuse their power, it was close to impossible to look at them at all. She looked instead at 'Hawk's firm breasts. They showed brazenly through the black net shirt: raven black nipples hard and tempting as they defiantly pushed the fabric into little tents. The breasts themselves were mounted like trophies on 'Hawk's well-developed pectoral muscles. The left breast nudged up against a black holster holding 'Hawk's trained-to-kill gun. Her long arms were wrapped with iron hard muscles that descended from her solid shoulders. The warrior, conditioned and ready to fight. 'Hawk unfastened the studded leather cuff that held her wrist knife and laid it next to her hat.

"You still got that thing I gave you?" Sophia asked provocatively.

'Hawk reached for the bulge in her pants and squeezed it suggestively. "You know it, mama, and it's *hard* for you," 'Hawk confirmed feverishly, openly displaying her ragged desire.

Sophia moaned deeply. Being desired by the Nighthawk was like nothing else in life. Having 'Hawk need her this way was the greatest excitement she'd ever known. She was thankful for her strong heart as it began to double its pace in response to this amazon walking toward her with a focused look of determination and will.

'Hawk stopped in front of Sophia and untied the sash of the robe. It fell away from her splendid nakedness. Her front side was dominated by the two most beautiful breasts 'Hawk had ever seen. The giant, round pillows of flesh hung from this thoroughly feminine woman like gifts from the gods bestowed upon an already wealthy body. While Sophia carried a lot of weight on her round upper arms, thighs and ass, she didn't let herself go. Her skin was smooth and tight all over her brown and gold burnished body. Her face showed cheer and beauty and her neck held her head majestically above soft womanly shoulders.

'Hawk's long fingers caressed the hard knobs of Sophia's dark nipples, gently, then less and less so until she was twisting them roughly making Sophia hiss with pleasure.

"I want to sit on your hard thing," Sophia told 'Hawk urgently. Her cunt was aching to be filled with cock.

"Huon," 'Hawk let out as agreement. She walked to the side of the bed and put her gun on the nightstand. (The piece was never out of her reach, even in the shower.) She stretched her long frame along the length of Sophia's old bed, ready for her partner to straddle her taut and needy body.

Sophia shed her robe and climbed aboard the bed as 'Hawk took her dildo from her pants. Holding it straight up, she groaned deeply when Sophia lowered herself onto the pole. Sophia's eyes closed blissfully and her mouth opened limply as she sighed. This was heaven and it would go on for as long as she wanted it to.

'Hawk dug her fingers into the lush thighs and lowered her own hips so the black rod would pull partially out of its cave, thus beginning the slow, rhythmic movement of her pelvis: up and down, pushing the thing in and dragging it out. Part of what 'Hawk saw as special about Sophia was how everything was so *visual* with her. Always a feast for the eyes no matter what went down between them. Nothing was hidden on this woman's body: her long fleshy sex lips, the little finger of a clitoris, the generous amounts of foamy white sex cream clinging to and dripping from every inch of her long, wide slit. How could anyone get enough of it?

'Hawk always let Sophia set the pace of this activity to guarantee the woman got all she could stand. Sophia had always said she never found a man who could keep it up long enough to suit her, and that she always had to use her own dildo after they were gone. But 'Hawk had been the perfect and willing student. As Sophia felt the smoothly paced fuck, she knew 'Hawk hadn't forgotten a thing.

"Oh, *mama*, I love fuckin' you," 'Hawk said breathily.

Sophia's legs began to flex making her hips rise and fall at an ever increasing rate. With natural grace and perfectly in tune with her partner, 'Hawk matched this incredible woman's pace. Faster and faster they worked until Sophia's breasts were bobbing and swaying to delight 'Hawk's transfixed eyes.

"Ride it, mama!" 'Hawk demanded fiercely. Soon her legs were slapping against Sophia's great buttocks and the woman was freely bouncing up and down on 'Hawk's glorious prick. The bed groaned and creaked underneath the couple. Frenetically they joined together and separated. Sophia's breasts were flopping around and clapping together as moans erupted from her to announce her readiness to climax.

'Hawk was fighting against her own impending orgasm. Her excitement was well past what she normally experienced with other women. She hadn't waited for a partner to come in a long time. This was a true test of her discipline and control. Sophia had always made her give her best, reach down inside for that something extra to go the distance. It was always worth it, though.

"Fuck me!" Sophia screamed pressingly. 'Hawk responded with breakneck speed, stabbing the woman mercilessly as Sophia cried, "Oh, yes, oh yes, yeeessss. Come with me," she begged mindlessly, somehow knowing 'Hawk could comply.

"Yeah, ohn, mama," 'Hawk responded, braking the furious fuck down to a final few vicious ruts as their minds exploded in tandem. Sophia's body shook with seizures of release then collapsed heavily and gloriously into 'Hawk's waiting arms. Except for the slowing down of her breathing, 'Hawk was motionless under the satisfied woman, giving her the peace and time she needed to recover from their intense copulation.

Drained and happy, Sophia raised her head to look into 'Hawk's eyes. This was the one time when they wouldn't be so unsettling. They were actually quite loving and filled with admiration, and yes, she wasn't imagining it, gratitude. She had thought there was something troubling her former charge, but now wasn't the time to ask.

"You're the best there is, Sophia," 'Hawk said warmly and sincerely. Sophia was the only person who had gotten past 'Hawk's thick coat of steel to the warm heart within. If it had not been for this generous, loving woman, 'Hawk would never have learned what intimacy was or what it felt like or how to return it. Tiên Le was perhaps the only other person to come close to touching the truly human side of the Nighthawk. Sophia used her needy and giving body to get to it. Tiên Le used her loyalty, devotion and courage to get to it.

'Hawk was refusing to see and steadfastly running from the one person in her life who encompassed all these qualities. The one person who just might have enough inner power and strength of love to conquer 'Hawk's heart. 'Hawk would never admit that she was on the path that would lead, ultimately, to the destruction of the best thing that ever came her way: Lori Smith.

'Hawk couldn't afford to have her heart conquered, only soothed and pacified and caressed from time to time. All other times her heart had to be hard or she couldn't shoulder the tremendous responsibilities she'd taken upon herself. To think it was possible to *share* her burden with others who were equally capable wasn't even an option she'd considered. She didn't know how.

Sophia kissed away the flicker of sadness that crossed 'Hawk's face to bring her back to the known and now. "Want me to dance for you?" she asked seductively.

'Hawk's heart skipped a beat and her belly tingled sweetly. "Have you ever asked me that and heard me say no?" she teased.

"Never. That's because you know I'm the best dancer in the world," Sophia bragged in fun then sucked in her breath as she dismounted 'Hawk's cock.

'Hawk watched the creamy thing fall out of Sophia to lay against her leather pantleg. She stayed on the bed enjoying her lethargy and the cigarette Sophia handed her.

Sophia put a record on her old record player and turned to face her contented audience. Just like the fuck they'd just had, the music started out easily enough. Sophia moved and swayed in rolling, wavelike progression. Her hands caressed and smoothed her flesh — slowly over her great ass, her long fingers pulling the buttocks apart then letting go to send the mounds of flesh swishing back together. Keeping her back to 'Hawk she pushed her hair up away from her neck and turned to one side so her breast would fall into view. Then she did the other side and grinned. It worked every time. 'Hawk stubbed out her cigarette, put her gun in its holster and got up to sit on the hard-backed chair next to the dancer. She wanted this woman dancing right in front of her, not across the room.

Sophia kept her back to 'Hawk, letting her hands roam over her breasts in broad circles, moving her hips from side to side. Her fingers trickled over her nipples until they were hard again. To aggravate 'Hawk she took each hard tip between her forefingers and thumbs to pull it up and to the side separating the masses of flesh and holding them painfully apart. She knew 'Hawk would grab for the nipples so *she* could pull them apart herself making each nipple support the weight of its own breast. But Sophia danced lightly away from the leader's long reach.

It was exciting and dangerous to keep something from 'Hawk that she wanted. Sophia wanted 'Hawk to act just a bit mean toward her—aggressive and domineering. They'd already "made love", now Sophia wanted to *play*. She didn't want to play safe either; she wanted to take risks with this unpredictable warlord. She glanced over her shoulder and was thrilled by the darkening look on 'Hawk's face.

"Get me my smokes, cunt," 'Hawk ordered tersely. While Sophia daringly took her sweet time getting 'Hawk's cigarettes and matches from her jacket, 'Hawk changed the record to one with a fast beat. Impishly, Sophia tossed the cigarettes to 'Hawk who caught them deftly but with mounting annoyance. Just short of true insolence, Sophia abruptly stuck the match sticks under 'Hawk's nose. 'Hawk took the matches with one hand and a nipple with the other. Caught in her tight grip, Sophia wasn't going to get away this time. The hand pulled down, forcing a wide-eyed Sophia to her knees.

"Now *dance*," Hawk snarled, baring her teeth in earnest. At that moment Sophia would have done anything the ruler commanded.

Confidently, 'Hawk released the nipple and sat back to enjoy Sophia's wonderful body.

Sophia stood, glowing with heated arousal. She pivoted three times to a halt facing 'Hawk. Bowing, her breasts dangled; she shook them side to side, back and forward, in circles. 'Hawk lit a cigarette, her inhale was audible. Sophia straightened and wrapped an arm under each massive breast separating them at the base. She carried them like two wobbling bundles and danced quickly to the music letting each breast bounce in front of her working 'Hawk up more and more.

When 'Hawk took her cigarette away from her mouth, Sophia moved directly up to her to let the great breasts loose so they would capture 'Hawk's head between them. 'Hawk's groan of pleasure was unbearably sweet to Sophia. The leader's hands came up to rest on Sophia's chest to hold the engulfing flesh around her. Buried in the womanhood, 'Hawk kissed it worshipfully.

One by one, Sophia removed the rings from 'Hawk's right hand and slipped them onto her own fingers. 'Hawk's passion made the ache between her legs even more insistent. She rescued the spent cigarette from the other hand and dropped it into an ashtray.

"'Hawk, do me, please," she begged needfully pulling away her front to turn and present her rear. She bent over and reached behind her to spread her gaping sex lips wider. Mindlessly, 'Hawk slid her fingers into the inviting sex cave. She took her time easing the penetrating movements to coax the opening to accept more and more until the muscles finally gripped her hand and swallowed it whole. Her large hand glided inside and curled into a fist and Sophia let her sex lips go so the entrance closed around 'Hawk's wrist.

"Fuuuck," 'Hawk exclaimed senselessly. Her mind was barely operative, so overcome was it by the thrill of invading this burning orifice. To ground herself in some way to the real world she lit a cigarette. The hand holding it rested on Sophia's buttock. She twisted her fist inside Sophia producing a gasp. The woman had placed her hands on her thighs to brace herself for the onslaught.

Some more twisting and turning inside the cunt, a couple more-drags on the cigarette and 'Hawk turned her full attention to this nympho pussy. She pummeled the greedy thing for several minutes, entranced by the sucking noises and Sophia's whimpers of fulfillment. The sight of Sophia's expansive jiggling ass, round thighs and soaking lips was surpassed only by her breasts in all their glory. The woman's whimpers turned to moans. 'Hawk responded by intensifying her attack. Sophia replied with an outburst of wails. 'Hawk's fingers dug into the shaking ass, gripping it tightly.

'Hawk fisted the cunt harder and faster, demanding, "Give it to me, slut!"

Sophia screamed 'Hawk's name as the orgasm kicked its way through her. She ripped herself from the fist and fell against the cold metal bars of her bed's footboard.

'Hawk acted quickly before Sophia would recover to the point where she might be unwilling to participate in the next act. She flung the end of the mattress up and folded it in the middle to lay bare the coil springs and the length of rope that was still there from the last time she'd been with this amazing woman. She hauled Sophia up so that her breasts fell over the metal bar across the top of the footboard. She tied the rope around the base of each breast and the bar securing them in a position that made the nipples point straight upwards. She knelt on the springs and thrust her cock between the tits fucking them viciously, groaning loudly.

'Hawk's fervent passion held Sophia's sexual excitement and willingness at a high, compliant level. She reached up and began to play with her own nipples, tugging on them and pinching them for 'Hawk's benefit. The black stick poking through her cleavage attracted her—closer and closer—until her face was just out of its reach. Her eyes were filled with longing as she waited for 'Hawk to approach her zenith. She knew 'Hawk wouldn't yank her head near to violate her mouth until the right time. When 'Hawk cued her with a sharp slap on her tit, Sophia took in a large gulp of air. A second later she felt the large hands grip her hair and yank her head into the soft pillows of her tits.

'Hawk jabbed the end of her cock into the waiting mouth. Her arms crushed the breasts closer together and her hands gripped the head she was now suffocating with cock and tits. Sophia continued to torture her own nipples knowing the incredible sight she was creating would push 'Hawk over the edge.

Perfectly timed, 'Hawk's orgasm was just a moment beyond the reach of Sophia's oxygen supply. Sophia's ears rang, she saw stars and went blank. The "little death" made her body go limp and she sagged against the bed, her hands dropping to her sides.

Almost immediately the sight of Sophia's unconsciousness toppled 'Hawk over her climax. She wailed and growled ferociously and let go of the head which fell backward, the mouth yawning open. Sophia's body resumed its breathing on its own. 'Hawk freed her and helped her into the restored bed.

'Hawk set her gun aside and joined the weak and happy woman on her bed. Spent for now, 'Hawk allowed herself to be gathered into Sophia's arms.

When 'Hawk seemed calm Sophia asked, "Something troubling you, 'Hawk?"

"Nothing, old lady, I'm fine," 'Hawk told her gently.

Sophia smoothed her hand over 'Hawk's head urging the big woman to rest it on her soft breast. 'Hawk very naturally complied. Sophia looked down and smiled thinking, She might be too old to bring her problems to me, but she's not too old to fall asleep on this old lady's bosom. 'Hawk's eyes were closed and her breathing was soft and low. Sophia's taming influence had worked its magic once more. The mighty warrior had innocently and trustingly fallen asleep.

During 'Hawk's brief nap Sophia put the rings back where they belonged. Drawn to the big hand and long fingers, Sophia moved the object of her fascination between her own legs and pushed one of the sleeping fingers inside her cunt and left it there. The unmoving thing tormented her: she wanted it to come to life inside her as she was coming to life around it. She *had* to have 'Hawk again. To that end she shifted her body to let 'Hawk's fine head rest on a pillow so she would work her nipple into the unsuspecting mouth.

'Hawk woke and moaned. She hadn't even opened her eyes and already her body was overtaken by long, sharp currents of need. To find a delicious nipple in her mouth and her finger inside a hot, wet snatch was heaven itself. She massaged the hard thing with her teeth and tongue to the strains of Sophia's pleading sighs. Her finger had barely gotten going before she heard her partner begging for something more.

"'Hawk, something else wants your mouth on it."

'Hawk pulled away from the wonderful nipple and smiled wickedly. "It wouldn't happen to be that hard little finger between your pussy lips?" she asked infuriatingly.

"Yes," Sophia admitted urgently. "Please, 'Hawk. It *wants* you."

"But does it *need* me?" 'Hawk pressed.

"Oh, yes," Sophia nearly wailed.

"How bad?" came the taunt.

"More than anything!" Sophia said frantically. 'Hawk's teasing was making her need it even more. "You're the only one who can satisfy it."

"I'm the only one who can satisfy anything you got, slut. Ain't that right?" 'Hawk insisted.

"Yes, yes, yes. You're the *best*. Oh, please, 'Hawk, please," Sophia begged desperately.

"Bring that pretty thing up here, slut."

Sophia was quick to obey, straddling the head as 'Hawk moved down the bed so she could bury her face in Sophia's goodness. Sophia spread her lips open to expose her oversized clitoris to 'Hawk's hungry eyes. She closed her thighs about the head and rested her ass on 'Hawk's strong chest.

'Hawk licked the finger-like protuberance; it was stiff and erect and fascinating. She had never encountered another woman with a clitoris this large. What a delight it was to roll her tongue around it, flick it, suck on it, nibble it, all of which she did continuously.

Occasionally she would let her eyes gaze upward to take in the sight of Sophia's breasts hovering just above her and would be inspired anew to please this woman.

Sophia could think of nothing; she just knelt there supporting the head that owned this gifted and tireless mouth and slowly went mad. Soon all of her thoughts focused on that one place on her body. "Suck me, please, oh suck me," she begged. 'Hawk sucked the clit so hard it would leave a mark. Sophia jerked and screamed as the ultimate satisfaction turned her inside out with its fierceness. Somehow she managed to lift up and part her legs to free 'Hawk, otherwise she was completely out of it.

Knowing Sophia was useless, 'Hawk coaxed the dazed woman to lie on her back on the bed and straddled her middle. She mashed the breasts together around her cock and brutally fucked the helpless tits until she achieved her own satisfaction.

Content, and proud of her sexual prowess, 'Hawk got off the bed, pulling the cover around Sophia's spent and happy body. She kissed Sophia's cheek then put her gun away. Before she put her knife, coat and hat on she took some papers from a pocket and laid them on the kitchen table. She had had someone take her money to pay off all Sophia's utility bills; the papers were the receipts. Sophia wouldn't take money from 'Hawk, even to help the boy, so 'Hawk found other ways to help this woman she owed so much to.

Picking up her cigarettes, she turned to look at Sophia and smiled.

"Going?" Sophia asked, still dazed by the involving bliss she was feeling.

"Yeah, mama. I'd like to stay and fuck you till dawn but I got work to do." 'Hawk pulled another slip of paper from a pocket and held it up for Sophia to see. "Tiên Le said for you to play these numbers on lotto this week."

Sophia smiled and nodded her head weakly; moving was difficult. They both knew that Tiên Le didn't give her numbers to just anyone. Her luck with the lottery was almost legendary. If Sophia played Tiên Le's numbers, she'd probably win a tidy little sum. 'Hawk was certain the money would go to help with the boy and Sophia wouldn't feel like she was taking a handout.

The paper was placed on the record player. Standing in the doorway 'Hawk parted with: "Get up before long and bolt this door," and a sly wink that said she'd be back some night.

* * *

Winter was a time of trade-off for 'Hawk. The long nights gave her more time to operate, but it always came when she least needed it. Summers were when tempers flared and young people had too little to occupy them and keep them out of trouble. If another summer passed like the last one had, 'Hawk might have to start coming out in the open while the sun was out to help keep her youths in line. The prospect didn't please her. As much as she hated rain, late day storms went a long way toward dousing hot-beds of temper and boredom.

Winter violence was usually of the domestic variety. As 'Hawk surveyed the young people assembled in this dirty smoke-filled tenement basement, evidence of family abuse could be detected easily by the trained eye. The ages of the kids who had proven themselves as worthy gang members were lower now than when 'Hawk had first established her "organization" some thirteen years ago. Life was harder for kids now than it had been when she had been a child. Or so she thought. Looking back at how she had survived, race riots and whole city blocks razed by fire a distant memory, she could at least say she had survived. The hardened, sometimes frightened looks in the eyes of some of these kids made her realize many of them *wouldn't* survive, now matter *how* hard she tried to help them.

Fatalistically she turned her attention to the "council meeting" grateful that they had found a meeting place that was warm. She doubted the old boiler hissing in the corner was safe, but at this hour of the night it was lucky there was heat at all. In her part of the city safe places to gather were rare; she relied upon the individual youth gang leaders to find these hideouts. Every month the location was a different one, and no one knew better than these kids where to go to be safe. Only the trusted core of each of the seven groups were allowed to attend with 'Hawk and her "command".

She could always tell who had the least to eat or might be in poor health. Those boys and sometimes girls, would stay close to the boiler. She stayed away, in the coldest corner of the room. Her body was hardened to the cold. In extreme weather she zipped her jacket zipper higher and wore gloves to keep her shooting hand warm. Several others took her lead and were glad of it. Tiên Le was the obvious exception. Her thin tropical blood had never adjusted to North American winters. Grudgingly she wore state-of-the-art skier's long underwear beneath her cotton outfit and a capelike wool coat over it. She was mostly just miserable and envious of the boys next to the boiler. For as much as she admired 'Hawk, Tiên Le wished her leader would stop believing feeling the cold to be a sign of weakness.

'Hawk's president, Shadow, was addressing the meeting. This young man had been hand-picked by 'Hawk several years before to learn the job of main leader for the seven gangs. He had risen through the ranks and been groomed by his predecessor and 'Hawk to command, train and guide these youths. Chosen for his cool head, intelligence and articulate speech, Shadow had earned the respect of each boy and girl there. In a world where the possession of firearms made everyone relatively equal, brains were what counted. His position carried power and responsibility which he bore with dignity.

He was a solid role model for those who looked up to him. He knew 'Hawk depended on him to keep the organization running during the day when her presence wasn't as strongly felt. Her faith in him made him proud. He was *somebody*, and her belief in him made him feel like he could accomplish anything he set his mind to. Being eighteen, his future was somewhat uncertain. He couldn't hang around youth gangs forever, but he had risen as high as he could go in 'Hawk's organization.

That 'Hawk was warlord was an unchallenged fact of life. She had been since he was five years old, and before some of these gang members had been thought of. He and the others had grown up with 'Hawk as their neighborhood's warlord. Her gender didn't seem to matter. Certainly many a schoolyard brawl had begun because of taunts from rival children about the warlord's womanhood. But all anyone had to do was look into her eyes to know there wasn't a man any tougher than the Nighthawk.

By rights, Shadow, or one of his predecessors should have been able to look forward to the possibility of becoming 'Hawk's general. 'Hawk hadn't had a general chosen from the ranks in several years. Not since the last one had been murdered by the police and had been replaced by Tiên Le. There had been a great deal of resentment among the individual leaders of the seven gangs (collectively known as the "Guard") and the president because 'Hawk had selected an outsider *and*, some complained, another woman.

'Hawk had heard them out and agreed the grievance about Tiên Le lacking a birthright as her successor was a valid one. (The objection over Tiên Le's gender had brought a dark cloud of resentment into 'Hawk's eyes and the objection had been immediately withdrawn.) She'd answered them by explaining that Tiên Le had greater battle experience and was more accustomed to accepting responsibility for large numbers of people. She'd granted them the opportunity to challenge Tiên Le to hand-to-hand combat saying, if anyone were to defeat their new general, she'd reconsider her choice. Three tried. Three failed. To help these vanquished fighters save face, Tiên Le offered to instruct them in the martial arts. Since that time Tiên Le had been accepted and it was considered an honor to train with the general.

Shadow could only hope to serve as president one more year and would have to move on. The young man he was training to replace him was coming along well. Standing to Shadow's right behind the makeshift table, the boy had a sure career as a boxer. Shadow wished it were easy to define his own strengths in terms of a career. But 'Hawk believed in him and had said recently that he was the best president she'd ever had, and she had her eye on a special job for him although she wouldn't say what.

Shadow kept the meeting flowing smoothly, covering various points of importance. Looking out over the group of hardened, but disciplined teenagers he spoke about the upcoming Golden Glove and karate tournaments they were scheduled to fight in. Enthusiastic shouts of encouragement for the entrants who were favored to win helped to warm and enliven the gathering. Also a sense of excitement was building — rumors of war lay electrically beneath the surface of the official proceedings.

Shadow could feel the stirrings within his own young body. It was at these times he was thankful for the training he and others had been given by 'Hawk in the use of firearms. The times he had gone to the Gun and Rifle Club with 'Hawk were special to

Shadow. 'Hawk treated him like an adult who could think and reason and make decisions on his own. Because she never talked down to him, he always listened closely to everything she said.

In turn he instructed others about the responsibility of carrying weapons and how having a gun didn't mean they had courage or brains. They learned how to disarm an enemy and take care of their weapons. She helped them to see that their anger could be vented without discharging bullets and senselessly killing other people for such insignificant reasons as stolen combs or insults. Their young, fiery, angry emotions were channeled through basketball courts, boxing rings, street dancing, art and rapping.

With extreme pride Shadow announced that the neighborhood's rap group, Knights of 'Hawk, had been awarded a recording contract with a major record company. Two of the group's members stood to accept their applause. More important than the applause to these young men was 'Hawk's surprised, pleased expression. Her smile and nod of congratulations would live with them long after the money and fame that awaited them. The dark sparkling eyes of the younger members showed their desire to one day please 'Hawk in a similar fashion.

Tiên Le ate up 'Hawk's happiness as greedily as the others. She liked to see tangible evidence of her leader's brilliance in administration and guidance. Although there were no members of established society present at these meetings to commend 'Hawk for her effectiveness with these tough, difficult children, Tiên Le knew how the clergy and social workers felt about the mysterious, sometimes deadly but always concerned warlord. The official stance was that there were fewer lost causes per capita on 'Hawk's turf than other places in the city. Unofficially, those who worked with the youths in these neighborhoods were impressed by 'Hawk, and secretly sanctioned her methods even when those methods exceeded the lawful boundaries they were restricted to.

'Hawk respected these young people. Tiên Le never tired of watching the steely-nerved woman work with them. Tonight the meeting was going smoothly but that was not always the case. It wasn't possible to put anywhere from twenty to forty angry, defensive, prideful youths in one room without friction developing. And it very often did. While these seven gangs were outwardly united, underneath all this discipline were twenty to forty time bombs waiting to unload.

Tiên Le marveled at 'Hawk's patience and inner calm when tempers snapped and fights broke out between one gang and another. It seemed 'Hawk was at her best when pandemonium surrounded her. She had a keen ear for listening to the real problems thinly masked by sharp insults and accusations that heated up about every other meeting.

Somehow these kids knew they were safe from one another and themselves when 'Hawk was around. She would let them rant at each other for awhile then step in. As much as anyone 'Hawk knew these fights, while valid blood feuds or claims of injustice, were cries for attention and attempts to test her. These young people had to make certain, over and over, that 'Hawk was there for them, rock solid, caring, adult and loving. No one here would admit they wanted to know 'Hawk loved them, but they all wanted her to. She could not be brought to admit she loved them either, but she did love them — intensely.

Once order was restored to one of these meetings 'Hawk would cut to the core of the argument and create a dialogue that showed the combatants how to listen to and validate each other's needs. If by no other means than by rote these children were learning the rudiments of communication which they applied, without realizing it, to their daily lives when 'Hawk wasn't around to help them.

'Hawk didn't lay raps on these kids. She didn't say, "stay in school". She hadn't stayed in school. These kids wouldn't stand for hypocrisy; they were too smart for that. Her advice was never heavy-handed or moralizing. She made them work through their problems using what they already knew about life, which was considerable. When she saw someone making a mistake she had made, she truthfully related her own experience and the result of her actions. Sometimes her youths found it hard to accept that their hero had made a mistake but in the end were willing to re-evaluate their actions based on 'Hawk's understanding. She was one of them and knew what they were about and didn't criticize them.

Tiên Le thought 'Hawk's directness and honesty refreshing in this tangled bureaucratic world. The meeting was winding down and the excitement was winding up. The word had gotten out that 'Hawk was going to speak before the meeting was over. The word "war" had been passed through this gathering like an infectious disease.

Shadow announced that 'Hawk had called for a general alert; a tense silence gripped the gathering. All but Tiên Le shifted their attention to the cool, dim corner where 'Hawk was sitting. Tiên Le had already been briefed; she withdrew into herself to listen and feel for any uneasiness or fear in the group. Everyone was waiting for 'Hawk to talk to them.

Casually perched on a sawhorse, back against the brick wall, one booted foot resting on the horizontal board the other braced on the concrete floor, she scanned the expectant faces for any signs of dishonor or treachery. Seeing only open faces she took the toothpick from her mouth and twisted it between her fingers as she spoke.

Her voice was low and her words came carefully. Some had to strain to hear but they all were breathless. To release some of the tension, she confirmed their fears/wishes from the start. "I feel a war comin' on," she revealed gravely. Whispers hissed and spit like burning sap. 'Hawk had been disturbed by what she had learned from her spies, Sid and Bad Man. A positive nod from Tiên Le told 'Hawk everyone in the room could be trusted. She relaxed and began again, bringing about quiet once more.

"The members of the old Imperials can't be trusted until they prove their loyalty," she said succinctly. If a war really were on the horizon, the cause would be revenge for the brutal killing of the former leader of that organization. The members who had crossed over to 'Hawk's fold were now suspect and were to be watched carefully.

"Everything has been too quiet since Candyman was wasted." Eyes darted around the room as if to reaffirm the pact never to speak of who had killed the warlord. They *all* knew 'Hawk had done it. Even the police "strongly suspected Candyman had been executed by a rival leader believed to be the woman known only as Nighthawk". The case had never been followed up due to lack of manpower and had been closed as an unsolved murder.

"The Twins," 'Hawk stated, referring to the warlords who really were twins and co-ruled the turf west of hers, "have their hands full right now. The school bus bombs and all the arson fires in their area lately are getting a lot of press. They're laying low and aren't likely to start a war for a bloodfight that isn't really theirs. Keep your eyes and ears open down there anyway."

A flurry of agreement rustled through the group. It was always exciting to hear 'Hawk talk, but it was even more thrilling to be included in her war plans. 'Hawk needed their help and they knew it.

"Any trouble will probably come from the south and Dapper Toni. He's unpredictable and will accept any excuse for a fight," 'Hawk cautioned. D. Antonio Petrazzia, or Dapper Toni as he liked to call himself, had been a thorn in 'Hawk's side for many years. With Candyman out of the way, 'Hawk had just traded the frying pan for the fire. He was as close to insane as anyone could be, 'Hawk thought, without being bagged off to the state hospital. Now with the powerful title of warlord to bolster his ego, he was likely to do anything.

"I think this bombing and these fires are diversionary tactics of D. Antonio's. I think he's planning something but no one's talking. If you hear of anyone talking big about having explosives," she warned seriously, "or think any fire looks suspicious, report it to me."

The youths reflected her demeanor. She was worried, they all could tell because she didn't normally require direct reports to her alone. The weightiness of this matter settled onto their hearts. This was war. People died in wars. Suddenly it wasn't quite as exhilarating.

"Remember—staying cool and not over-reacting to rumors and talk is what got us through the last war with few lives lost. Shadow, stay on top of training. Your jobs are to keep people safe and your own heads right. Let's get out of here," she closed sharply. She didn't like belaboring points.

As the youths filed out she acknowledged each one in some way. A boy of twelve shook her hand bravely. 'Hawk knew him for one of the street artists whose work she'd seen on the sides of several buildings. A shiver ran up her spine when she looked into his eyes. Tiên Le had felt it too. This boy was going to die soon, she could sense death hanging around nearby. "I like your work, son," she told him, thinking she'd make sure his art was never defaced in his memory. He smiled but the look in his eyes said he also knew something was going to happen.

Chapter Seven

The small apartment smelled of fish and curries, incense and sex. The glow of tall votive candles adorning the small altar provided the only light, and large flickering shadows danced on the walls of faded, peeling paint.

Tiên Le's slave gripped the thick quilt under her, quivering with anticipation. Moments before she had been roughly stripped and thrown, face down, onto the foam pad that served as the mattress of her Master's bed. She drowned in the rising tide of her Master's passion, overcome by the intensity of her Master's need. She moaned when she felt the head of the loved dildo brushing against her open and ready asshole. She had not grown numb to use over the years as some might have, but craved for and needed it more than ever. To give herself completely to her Master was all that she lived for.

Tiên Le had been surprised when she realized she'd missed her little tôi (servant) while in Vietnam. She had taken the girl for granted over the years but had recently come to an awareness of how special this servile creature was. How fortunate she was to have found a *female* who was willing to have her personhood obliterated, to be without ego, to need only one thing in life—a chance to serve. This sort could easily be found among the male population. To find a female, not just any female, but one who aroused her sexually, was the best of fortune. Tiên Le had renewed her commitment to care for this girl, had come to a fuller sense of her responsibility to protect her slave since returning. And she resolved never to leave it alone for an extended period of time again.

The slave knew nothing of her Master's deepened pledge; she saw only that her Master paid more attention to her, touched her more, held her more and, most importantly, used her more. She sighed happily when her ass became filled with her Master's cock.

Tiên Le shifted her weight so she could reach under her naked slave, one hand seeking the elastic nipple hidden under the mashed breast, the other hand sliding downward to the pulsing sex. When she found what she was looking for she became heavy on top of the helpless body. She stretched the breast to the side so the well-used (tortured) nipple could be seen to the slave's side. Tiên Le twisted and stretched it while her other hand massaged her slave's black clitoris. Completing this multi-focused picture, Tiên Le began to fuck her slave's needy asshole as she viciously gripped a black trapezius between her teeth.

Her slave thus pinned, she let go her internal restraints and went for a wild ride. Tiên Le felt her excitement building as her dildo tugged in and out of its tight sleeve of flesh, as her hips and pelvis pumped and ground into the firm ass beneath her. Again and again she hammered into it as her slave's quaking tension grew.

Her slave's ecstatic cries struggled to become intelligible words, but come they must. Aided by her years of training, the slave began to beg through her shuddering moans. "Master, may I come . . . please, may I come . . . please, please, pleeease?" she cried. Her Master was so incredibly skilled at making her body peak, it was extremely difficult to hold off her orgasm. Hold off she must or be beaten severely for having an orgasm without permission. "Master, *please*, I beg you. May I come? Oh, oh, please . . . ?"

It was only after her slave looked like she was really going to sob that Tiên Le let go of her mouth grip to whisper the throaty command. "Come," she breathed passionately accelerating her motion over the clit and pinching the nipple so hard a bead of blood congealed on her thumbnail. The slave twitched and twisted like a small landed fish, crying like an amorous cat as spasm upon spasm passed through her. The only thing between her and being called to heaven by her god was the knowledge that her Master had not had enough to satisfy her own needs and required more.

Letting her slave rest and recover from her orgasms was something Tiên Le rarely did. Her panting, hoarse breathing would not subside until later. *After* she had used and abused her servant still more. Dildo pulled free from the ass, Tiên Le dragged the small woman from the bed to the wall next to the altar and its collection of candles. She lifted the weakened body so the back lay against the cool wall.

The slave knew its role perfectly. Up-side-down, she braced her weight with her arms while Tiên Le fastened her ankles into the metal restraints bolted to the wall. Spread-eagled, dangling from her ankles, her arms were pulled apart to fit into the wrist clamps (also bolted to the wall). In this reversed position her mouth was at the exact height to accept her Master's cock as her Master knelt in front of her.

Tiên Le pushed the dildo into her slave's mouth and took a lighted candle from the altar. Carefully she lowered the base into her slave's gaping cunt. The flame danced three inches above the lips of the "candle holder". The angle of the thick rod of wax allowed a steady drip of hot liquid to fall down the slave's front, tormenting her. If she flexed her internal muscles, the angle would shift making the wax flow directly down the side of the candle and onto her clitoris. Tiên Le watched the wax strike three times, and listened to the hisses of pain/pleasure coming from the mouth around her cock.

Her hips moved into a rhythmic fuck that shook her slave's body and the candle. The wax began to jump and fall landing on the outstretched breasts below. Tiên Le held the pointed pendulous ornaments away from the body they were attached to. The undersides were coated with the white liquid which showed so prominently against the dark skin. Even more in contrast were the splatters that Tiên Le managed to catch on the coal-colored nipples. Her own fingers and thumbs caught the hot rain as well, and it dotted her outfit of black gauze. She paid no attention, focusing instead on the throb of need built up in her abdomen, fighting to let go.

Her hips moved faster, pounding her weapon into the roof of her slave's mouth. Her pace quickened to furious, the wax splashed about and the nipples were stretched to their painful limit. Tiên Le joined with the gods of excess and snapped. Her cries of fulfillment swelled her slave's heart. The eyes of the slave were closed contentedly as the Master's squinted shut in ecstasy.

The luxurious, silent moment that passed between them was ended abruptly by a knock at Tiên Le's door. The knock startled the slave and her jump rewarded her with a new, unexpected dose of wax which made her hiss. Tiên Le wasn't startled by the knock; she had known for some time that someone was outside her door. Waiting, she presumed, for the obvious sexual encounter to sound over.

Tiên Le's hand sliced the air next to the candle, extinguishing the flame. She pulled the candle from her slave's cunt and poured the reservoir of liquid wax directly into the sex cave. A muffled scream of agony bubbled around her cock. Her slave's blood-filled face puffed out like a balloon. Tiên Le could tell the girl's teeth were digging into the dildo for all they were worth. The knock came again. Tiên Le had to concentrate to answer.

"Yeah, what?" she said somewhat crossly. It was hard not to get lost in the writhing, straining struggle her slave was displaying in her bondage.

"Tiên Le?" came the beautiful voice that was instantly recognized (not without a flair of excitement). "It's Maggie. I need to talk. Please. . . ." The voice was hopeful but reluctant.

"Oh! Maggie! Sure, just a minute," Tiên Le answered, pulling her cock out of the mouth to disappear into her pants.

The body before her was sagging and heaving, the front line of pain searing through it like a military assault. Tiên Le released the catches on the wall fetters and the legs slumped over her shoulder. Her soft-soled foot kicked the wrist latch free with brisk ease as she leaned over to open the remaining bond. Nearly forgotten, the slave was poured into its little sleeping nest and Tiên Le answered the door.

Maggie was not unaffected by what she'd just overheard through Tiên Le's door. She'd walked up the stairs and down the hall with her heart in her throat anyway. To hear what was going on inside her friend's apartment was nothing short of daunting. Or compelling, which was why she had stayed. Completely without her consent her belly tugged at her with ripples of delight such as she'd never felt before. Sex went on around her all the time and left her unmoved. Why, then, had this aural voyeurism gotten to her so? Seeing the vibrant left over arousal clinging to Tiên Le's welcoming face told Maggie everything she didn't want to know. That it hadn't been the passion per se, but that that passion was produced by and coming from Tiên Le.

Maggie swallowed and tried to remember why she'd come. Seeing the shine of expectation and twinkle of hunger in Tiên Le's black eyes didn't help matters much. Suddenly, the look passed and became serious and concerned. Tiên Le knew that in all these years Maggie had known where she lived and had not come to see her. This was no social call. The magic moment between them passed and Tiên Le stepped aside, motioning for her friend to come in.

Maggie entered the small room sensing her own wonder. There was a small cove that served as a kitchen and a door that could only lead to a private bath, a luxury in this section of the neighborhood. Maggie was surprised that the kitchen clearly saw regular use; she couldn't imagine Tiên Le cooking anything. She looked curiously at the altar with its picture and flowers and candles, the wall restraints and, almost startling her, between the antique wardrobe and the corner, lying in a heap, the little slave Tiên Le kept. She realized then that it was the slave who did the cooking.

She'd grown accustomed to Lori's nakedness but she was oddly embarrassed by the slave's unclothed body. It was strange to her that the girl should look so much a part of the mass of blankets she was curled into with no apparent shame.

Tiên Le felt humbled by this visit. Her native yet dormant desire to please fidgeted restlessly under her reserve and calm. In her culture, having a guest in one's home was a supreme honor, and she wanted to share all she had and was with this special guest. She bowed slightly and gestured toward the only place in her small home that was suitable to sit on: her bed.

"Please, sit," she invited almost nervously. She was worried Mag-

gie might misinterpret the gesture as a come on. "You are cold.
Allow me to share some hot tea," she offered quickly.

Maggie understood and was charmed by Tiên Le's generosity and
warmth. She sat and said hot tea would be nice.

Tiên Le snapped her fingers and sharply called, "Toi." The slave
scrambled into the kitchen to prepare the tea without further instructions. A trail of crumbled wax lined the floor where she had
walked. Maggie noticed it and the one candle on the altar not
burning. She saw the splashed wax chipping off Tiên Le's garment
too.

"I'm sorry to disturb you, Tiên Le," she apologized. "I haven't
been able to sleep much all day and thought since I was awake
anyway I might as well get up. I didn't want to go to the bar
early. . ." Her voice trailed off sadly. They both knew life at the
Subway Club had gotten pretty grim. 'Hawk hadn't improved her
attitude toward Lori at all. "I hope you don't mind. I just wanted to
come see you . . . to talk," she added to cover for any feeling she
might have had to say, "Just to see you."

"I don't mind at all, Maggie. You're always welcome here." A
silence sat stilly between them until the slave served the tea. Maggie
took in the sight of the solid wax cracked and broken on the slave's
small cunt and the undersides of her breasts and nipples. Tiên Le
had been absently peeling it off her gauze and silk and dropping it
carelessly next to the bed.

"It's 'Hawk," Maggie sighed after thanking Tiên Le for the tea.
"She's been acting . . . strange for the last couple nights. Irritable
and mean." Her eyes were pleading for an answer. A glance sideways showed her a guarded look of jealousy in the slave's eyes
which was doused the minute it was noticed. The slave buried its
head in the nest to keep from betraying itself. Maggie ignored the
look but would wonder later what the slave could possibly have to
be jealous of.

Tiên Le had missed the exchange because she was gazing
thoughtfully into her teacup. Maggie sipped the strong brew finding it pleasant and relaxing. She suddenly wanted to know more
about this complex woman sitting next to her.

"Maggie," Tiên Le looked up and fought against her desire to
kiss Maggie's well-shaped lips, "how long has it been since 'Hawk

has had her . . . ?" Tiên Le found it difficult to think of 'Hawk and menstruation as occurring together.

So did Maggie. But it happened a couple times a year anyway and woe unto anyone in her path when it did. She calculated the months and nodded. "You're right. That has to be it." Then something else occurred to her. "Oh, Tiên Le, what do I do with Lori?" she asked urgently.

"You have to keep her out of 'Hawk's way, that's for sure. Can you put her in the bar?"

The two decided how to handle the volatile situation before Maggie had to leave. At the door, Tiên Le bolstered her courage to ask, "Maggie, may I take you out to dinner some evening before work?" Tiên Le had never gone on a date before; the idea intrigued her.

Neither had Maggie and the idea made her blush. "I'd like that, Tiên Le," she answered softly then left briskly to cover her shattered reserve.

Tiên Le closed her door and stood staring at it, savoring the moment. With her eyes closed she could still see the glowing image of Maggie's hard-edged, soft-cored brown eyes smiling at her. It dawned on her that if 'Hawk did come down with her bloods, then the bar would be closed for a couple nights. Maggie wouldn't go to work at all and might want company.

She walked over to her slave's nest and petted her charge kindly. The girl's eyes peeked out from under the covers, timid and loving. She adored Tiên Le and thrived on every scrap of attention paid to her.

"Do you want to go to the Youth Center with me?" Tiên Le asked gently. She was feeling right with herself and life, centered. She liked having tôi with her when she felt this way. Her slave nodded yes, eyes wide with eagerness. She loved to watch her Master teach the martial arts to the fearsome young men and boys at the Youth Center. It was thrilling to watch this smallish woman, a compact powerhouse of strength, train and discipline men who were easily twice her weight and a foot or more taller. The youths obeyed her instructions with pride and marvelled, as tôi did, at Tiên Le's skill. To watch her fly silently through the air to execute some of her kicks was joy itself.

It was the slave's job to bathe her Master's back and wash her silky hair; she knew that she alone had seen the steel-edged muscles under all that black cloth, the hidden strength inside this mysterious woman. As she finished dressing and helped her Master put on her cape the thought of the hidden weapons that looked like stars made her shiver. She'd seen her Master produce one from inside the folds of her clothes once. The object had flown across the room and lodged into the wall next to a boy who had been misbehaving at one of her lessons. Everyone in the room had been stunned into silence, knowing she'd deliberately missed. Tiên Le didn't have to remind these youths of her deadliness very often. Silent reminders were usually the most effective.

If tôi had been allowed to talk to these boys, *she* could have reminded them. This dangerous female came with a temper, too, and she had the healed broken bones to prove it. Yet she would follow her Master into the fiery furnace if asked. For now she felt blessed to be allowed to follow her down the snow-covered sidewalk to the Youth Center.

* * *

Maggie had gone by her own apartment, which she shared with a sister and her two children, to pick up a couple things she needed. Her timing was perfect. She hadn't been in the Subway Club more than ten minutes before she heard a loud crash and 'Hawk's violent "FUCK" coming from the leader's apartment.

She used her key to open the door. As expected, Lori was blanched with fear. Maggie took a few things from the refrigerator and ordered, "Get your blanket, you're coming out in the bar."

Lori was more than happy to follow Maggie — anywhere — as long as it meant getting away from 'Hawk. Behind the bar Maggie placed the food on a shelf and tried to explain.

'Hawk just started her period, kid." To Lori's amazed expression she said, "Yeah, I know. It's hard to imagine. But she *is* a woman, no matter what *she* thinks. She only gets one once every six months and it only lasts a couple nights. But she's *impossible* to be around when it happens. That noise you heard was probably her throwing a bar bell or something. She gets *real* pissed and *real* dangerous right now, so you have to stay out of her sight. The bar will be closed so nobody will be here but 'Hawk and you. She doesn't go out at all. And nobody comes in. Not even me." Maggie showed

Lori the stack of *True Romance* magazines she'd brought and put a long sweater around the girl's shoulders.

"It isn't as warm out here as it is in the apartment so I brought this to help you keep warm. If 'Hawk sees you in this, she'll beat the shit out of you. So be careful. Hide back here and read. There's some food. Sleep on one of the benches and use the toilet out here. I'm sure you don't know there is an upstairs to this place, but that's where she goes at night. You'll probably hear her walking around up there. When she is, you're safe but listen sharp because it's when she's down here is when there's danger. Good luck, kid."

Maggie left quietly, hoping Lori had all the common sense and survival skills Maggie thought she had.

* * *

Maggie's sister had answered the door and invited Tiên Le inside. Tiên Le tried not to appear uncomfortable while she waited for Maggie. A niece and nephew stared at the tattoos on Tiên Le's hands until their mother noticed and scolded them, then yelled down the hallway to get Maggie to hurry up. The nervous atmosphere was at once dispelled and heightened by Maggie's appearance in the front room.

Tiên Le stood sharply and nearly forgot to say hello because she was so overcome by Maggie's beauty. She had never seen Maggie in a dress or make-up and was almost without words to express her pleasure.

"Hello, Maggie," she said awkwardly but with a smile.

Maggie smiled warmly, somewhat pleased with herself for managing to rattle her cool friend. It felt nice to wear a dress for something besides church. She'd bought a new one just for this occasion and her sister had fussed over her like a mother. Earlier Maggie had felt silly: she was forty and going on her first date. Thoughts of Tiên Le revived her confidence; there was no one she'd rather share this American custom with than her long-time friend from Vietnam. *Who* the date was with was more important than when it was. She knew that in her heart, and resolved to make it special for both of them.

Her dress of combed wool was a deep blue with sequins along the slightly daring neckline. Her black shoulder length hair had soft waves and was caught in a rhinestone comb above her right ear. She wore black pumps and no jewelry. Simple and mature.

To Tiên Le she was the most beautiful woman she'd ever seen. She'd asked one of the social workers at the Youth Center about the fine points of American dating. From him she learned about flowers and such but the man hadn't prepared her for being this moved by the object of her attention.

"I suppose you two *could* just stare at each other all night, "Maggie's sister interjected, "or you could go to dinner."

Maggie fought a blush and Tiên Le cleared her throat.

"You look wonderful, Maggie!" Tiên Le announced breathily, finally finding her voice. "I brought this for you," she said, producing a clear plastic box from inside her cape and opening it.

Tiên Le was dressed as she always was. Maggie didn't mind; she liked the way her friend looked. What she hadn't seen before was the look on her narrow face. She'd never seen that expression on anyone, ever, and she was having trouble believing it was for her. The look said: I'm interested in you, I like you, I want to be with you, you appeal to me. It was all done with such intensity and honesty. She wanted to say, For me?! Me alone? Instead she said, "*Thank* you, Tiên Le. That was very thoughtful of you." She pried her eyes from Tiên Le's and gazed at the corsage of red sweetheart roses and white baby's breath. It was intoxicating to be the object of such involving attention.

The act of having the corsage pinned above her breast was electrifying. Being touched so tenderly by this pantherlike woman excited her. This was a moment worth the years of waiting. She didn't feel slighted for having gone so many years without knowing it was possible to have a special someone, for her, just for her. She knew now that no one but Tiên Le could have made her feel this way. Had she not been so happy, she would have cried.

Maggie floated through the process of having her coat put on, doors opened, the taxi ride to another part of town. It wasn't until they were greeted at the door of the dark restaurant that she became aware of reality. It had been the foreign language that had brought her out of her daze. It was Tiên Le . . . speaking Vietnamese.

The hostess was taking their coats and smiling genuinely, motioning the couple to be seated in an intimate, candle-lit booth. She seemed to know Tiên Le and was happy to see her. Maggie looked around seeing the fierce beauty of the place and noticed the tangy smells.

"What a beautiful restaurant. Where are we?"

"Little Asia," Tiên Le said proudly. She enjoyed coming to the part of the city where much of the Asian population was beginning to settle. Were it not for her deep involvement in 'Hawk's neighborhood she would move here herself. And persuade the family who looked after her sister to move too. Sometimes fitting in was easier. For now she contented herself with visiting and relaxing in the company of her countrymen. She hoped Maggie would find it enjoyable. "They serve dishes from Southeast Asia here. Do you trust me to order dinner for you?"

Maggie didn't even pick up the menu. She always trusted Tiên Le. "Please."

After a few minutes of adjusting to the atmosphere and the pleasing musical language, Maggie relaxed. She began to draw out Tiên Le's background. Her own life as a hooker could wait. Even though Tiên Le knew she had been a prostitute, she wasn't proud of it and was worried Tiên Le might change her feelings toward her.

"How did you learn the martial arts?" she probed.

Tiên Le paused before answering. She didn't usually talk about her art. Only 'Hawk and her Master knew the whole story. It would feel good to tell Maggie, she decided.

"My father began to teach me when I was three. Teaching girls self-defense wasn't a popular idea then. With the threat from the North and Viet Cong always present, my father felt I should learn anyway. He wanted me to be able to protect myself." A sparkle showed in Tiên Le's eye; she was proud of her ability. "Before long I was better than my older brothers and my father said I was gifted, a natural athlete. And then *they* came." Tiên Le snarled and her eyes went dark with hatred and pain.

"Who?" Maggie asked, suddenly concerned.

"The enemy," Tiên Le spoke venomously. "They slaughtered our entire village and burned everything. Only me and my baby sister escaped."

"Americans?" Maggie asked fearfully.

"The North Vietnamese," Tiên Le answered with such hatred her date winced.

"How old was your sister?" Maggie's breathing was short; she wanted to get away from the mental image of the disaster.

"Just a few days old. I was only able to save her because I could run so fast. My mother thrust her into my arms and told me to run for it. I did. Once I knew there was nothing to go back to, I took out on my own."

"How old were you?"

"Eight."

Maggie was stunned by the answer. "How did you survive?"

"Luck mostly. I went south finding women to help with em gái until I was well away from the fighting. I came across a support unit of American military men and found a woman in a nearby village to take care of the baby while I tried to find a way to survive. That's when I learned to play poker," Tiên Le said, her smile returning. They were being served a curious flattened bird, rice and vegetables. Maggie bravely took the piece Tiên Le offered to her and bit into it. Her eyes lit up with surprise and Tiên Le laughed.

"This is barbequed chicken!" she commented with surprise.

"Did you think Americans invented it? That's Laotian fast food."

"It's delicious. You learned to play poker?" Maggie probed, knowing her friend made her living at the game and wanting to know how she'd gotten so good at it.

"From the Americans. They thought I was *cute*." Tiên Le wrinkled her nose in mock disgust. Maggie giggled. "Except that I kept winning. They decided I was good luck and kept me around as their mascot. I didn't mind. They taught me English and I made enough money to support myself and my sister."

Maggie swallowed a bite of her food. She hadn't even attempted to use chopsticks. The porcelain spoon proved sufficient. "Are they the ones who taught you more self-defense?"

"No. One day they found me practicing what I had learned and, as a joke, thought to get me in to study with the Master in town. They cut my hair and dressed me as a boy to go before him to ask to be admitted as his student. They laughed for days when he accepted me."

"Did he think you were a boy?"

"Not for a minute. He let the Americans have their laugh. He accepted me because I was talented, sincere and not prideful." Tiên

Le calmly took another bite of chicken. She was enjoying her "date".

"You *were* lucky. How did you come to America?"

"When the Americans were pulling out of Vietnam, a friend helped me disguise myself as military personnel and I stowed away on a transport to West Germany. I was fifteen then and needed to keep making money to support em gái. Europeans couldn't tell how old I was so I could get into casinos and learned more about gambling. I was *very* good at it, too. I studied my art with different Masters as I traveled around the world for a few years until I finally decided to visit a friend in Los Angeles. It was there that I heard about 'Hawk and I've been here ever since."

"What an exciting life you've had," Maggie said almost sadly.She couldn't imagine how she could possibly interest someone like Tiên Le.

"I suppose so," Tiên Le agreed unenthusiastically. "But it's been spent mostly in the company of men. I'd never been with a woman until I went to France," Tiên Le revealed.

"Really?" Maggie was amazed.

"If she hadn't seduced me I might never have learned about women. She taught me a lot. I made up for lost time after that. But only when I could *find* the time. Between studying and gambling I didn't have much."

"That's hard to conceive of. You're always so confident around women."

Tiên Le pushed away her dishes and leaned toward her guest. She peered meaningfully into Maggie's rounded eyes. "It's just sex, Maggie. I never cared about anyone until I met you. But I couldn't get through to you until recently. You've always kept yourself hidden away where no one could get to you. Except when you talk to 'Hawk. Then a light comes on in your eyes and shows what a gentle, good soul you're hiding in there. I've always longed for you to look at *me* that way.

"I know we promised not to talk about 'Hawk tonight. I hate what is happening down there but if helping Lori has made you less afraid to be yourself, then I'm glad she's there."

Maggie had never had such a candid conversation with anyone before. She was uncomfortable yet relieved to be seen in her true form for once, if only just for a second or two. 'Hawk never recognized it in the way Tiên Le just had. She was sure crying wasn't the way to behave on a date but she cried anyway. Tiên Le held her close, unashamed by the public display of emotion.

"I'm sorry, Tiên Le," Maggie said softly, "I'm a raw nerve I guess. I feel childish . . . it's just that. . . ." Maggie's emotional fluency broke down before it could get started. She didn't know how to proceed. How to share that special part of herself that had been locked away for so many years. Being kind to Lori wasn't as difficult because the girl didn't expect anything. Maggie didn't have to worry about falling short of expectations that weren't there. But with Tiên Le . . . that was different . . . Tiên Le *mattered*. Maggie couldn't bear it if she were "less than". Less than what, she couldn't say.

Tiên Le sensed the struggle her date was engaged in but couldn't identify it. However she had her foot in the door with Maggie, finally, and wasn't going to back off now. 'Hawk could confide in her; surely Maggie could too.

After Maggie dried her eyes and blew her nose, Tiên Le took Maggie's hand between hers. The weathered extremity amplified her next words. "We've all led hard lives, Maggie. We've done what we had to to get by," she stated reassuringly to invite this special woman to open up.

"But you didn't prostitute yourself to get by," was Maggie's bitter rejoinder.

So *that* was it, Tiên Le thought. The revelation was like a slap in the face. She tightened her grip on the hand as it tried to withdraw from her. She wasn't about to let Maggie pull away from her now. She had worked too hard to get this far and wasn't going to let misplaced Christian guilt stand between her and what was rapidly taking on every appearance of love.

"I would have failed miserably at it if I had, Maggie."

Maggie's mouth fell open. Tiên Le had just burst her balloon of self-pity with the same quick ease she would have used to block a punch. And without blinking an eye. She tried to imagine Tiên Le standing on a street corner dressed in trashy, revealing clothes and too-high heels. The mental picture made her laugh. A joyful, self-deprecating laugh. "You're right, Tiên Le, you would have."

"And rightly so. I'm not beautiful, Maggie. *You are*," Tiên Le remarked forcefully. "And whoever got you started hooking knew it. And knew how to capitalize on it."

Maggie stopped laughing then. Her eyes blinked rapidly and she quit breathing for a second. It was only at that moment that she remembered how it first happened. Suddenly she felt suffocated by the onslaught of memories and feelings. "Can we go?" she asked hurriedly. "I need some air." She picked up her purse and moved out of the booth leaving her meal unfinished.

Tiên Le scrambled after her, paying for dinner and giving her thanks/apologies to the hostess and grabbing their coats. Warily,she caught up with Maggie, mindful of the last time, when the Puerto Rican temper had flared so brightly. But Maggie was introspective and calm. Her walk slowed to an amble when she felt Tiên Le tenderly placing her coat over her shoulders. She put the coat on, careful to cover the corsage so it wouldn't freeze in the winter night.

"That's exactly the way he put it, too," Maggie recalled sadly. "He said I was beautiful and could go far and make lots of money. It's funny, I didn't even care about money. I wanted attention and he was so charming and kind and nothing like my father. Or so I thought. It turned out he was just exactly like my father—an alcoholic, womanizing, vicious . . . *bastard*," Maggie pronounced meanly. "I really fell for all his smooth-talking. He got me in bed, told me how good I was. Before long he had me sleeping with this friend or that friend. Then my father found out. He beat me terribly and threw me out of the house; it was weeks before I was healed."

"So you moved in with this guy, right?" Tiên Le asked, knowing the answer in advance.

"I had to. No one in my family would take me in because they were afraid of my father. They may have thought he would change his mind, but I didn't care any more. I wanted to be away from him."

"How long was it before this guy started beating you, too?"

"A couple months—when I tried to keep from going out to make money 'to earn my keep'," Maggie sighed painfully. She knew Tiên Le was aware of how pimps operated. That her experience was common by anyone's standards. Another pretty, abused girl-turned-whore. Then came meeting the other girls in the "stable" and then surcease: heroin. Maggie rubbed her arm, unconsciously trying to cover up the track marks.

A biting breeze blew by them and Tiên Le drew closer. Hesitantly she took Maggie's arm and locked it into hers, but she wasn't rebuffed. They walked on, joined like lovers on a date. Which was what they had just become. Maggie accepted the gesture with a quick glance that embraced Tiên Le with warmth and trust.

"I was thirteen and had no where else to go."

"And nothing else you could do—except survive. I'm glad you survived, Maggie."

"I had help," Maggie added to cover her feeling of shyness. She hadn't learned yet how to accept such genuine affection, "from 'Hawk. We sort of took care of each other—off and on—for about twelve or thirteen years. When she took over as warlord she helped me get off junk and gave me the job in the bar. I haven't done much in my life in the twenty-five or six years I've known 'Hawk . . ." Maggie felt Tiên Le stiffen. She looked to see what was the matter but her date was smiling. She had no way of knowing she'd touched a sore spot with her friend.

Maggie had known 'Hawk almost as many years as Tiên Le had been alive and the revelation underscored Tiên Le's sensitivity about the difference in their ages.

Maggie couldn't clearly define the subtle shift in Tiên Le's attitude so she continued. "But I like to think I helped make 'Hawk a better person." There, Tiên Le's okay again, Maggie thought, deciding she'd imagined the problem. "Between me and Sophia, 'Hawk kept from turning so hateful she would have destroyed herself."

"Did you ever want to do anything else?" Tiên Le deftly changed the subject as they came to the other side of the street they'd been walking on.

"What do you mean?" Maggie was puzzled.

"I mean when you were young did you ever dream about what you wanted to do when you grew up?"

"No," Maggie replied sharply.

But Tiên Le could almost hear the teeth grinding against the dream of a young girl. A dream beaten and fucked and drugged out of her. Tiên Le stopped and turned toward this survivor. Her eyes forced open the wall, pried back the barbed wire fences and stole into the vault of Maggie's soul.

"Tell me," she begged. "I want to know."

Maggie shook her head and tried to walk away. Tiên Le held on to her arm surprising Maggie with her show of strength. Stubbornly, Tiên Le held her fast to that spot on the sidewalk in the middle of "Little Asia" and pleaded with her eyes to know.

"It's silly, Tiên Le. Just a childhood dream," Maggie offered, trying to minimize it. Tiên Le didn't budge. Determination settled into her dark eyes.

"Oh, all right," Maggie consented. "I wanted to be an artist. I used to draw all the time . . . what?"

Tiên Le's eyes had become big and her mouth parted, breathing foggy surprise into the crisp night. "No fooling?!" she asked sounding endearingly American. "Me too. My father used painting as a meditation and was teaching me to help discipline my mind. When he died I swore I'd never paint again because I was so angry." A drop of tear had accumulated in the corner of Tiên Le's eye. It fell along her cheek when she blinked — the first tear to pass that way in almost twenty years.

The couple stood in silence, unable to vocalize the millions of things they wanted to say to each other now that they had found in one another a kindred spirit, an understanding and something neither of them had ever had: possibilities — something bigger than just existing — purpose. Purpose, to be shared and encouraged. Something to live for.

Awkwardly, and because she didn't know any other way to express herself, Maggie said, "My sister saved my drawings from when I was a girl. Would you like to see them?"

"I'd like nothing more in life, Magdalene," Tiên Le answered respectfully.

Their date ended up with the two women sprawled across the rug of Maggie's bedroom admiring the youthful, innocent and yellowing drawings of women, flowers and cityscapes. The two didn't even kiss goodnight but stood, gazing into each other's eyes, silently acknowledging the fact that they had fallen in love.

Chapter Eight

Lori emptied the ashtray and wiped the table clean. Methodically she went about her chores scarcely noticing that Carla and Big Mary were the only two bar patrons who still abused her sexually. The others either lost interest in her or had surrendered to the visual hostilities coming from Maggie and Tiên Le.

Lori was unaware that the bartender and general had banded together to try to put a stop to the flagrant use of Lori's defenseless body. Or that the couple were acting as her protectors behind 'Hawk's back. That they consistently failed to intimidate Carla or Big Mary who patently ignored the dirty looks and stern disapproval.

If asked, Lori might have been able to recall that she'd already been assaulted by both women that night. The assaults weren't anything Lori ever thought about. She just did what was required, then went about her work without acknowledging anything had happened. She had truly become a bar fixture — with no feelings or identity. 'Hawk ignored her. Maggie avoided her. She barely existed.

The act of overestimating Lori's non-existence was Carla's biggest mistake. Carla didn't even stop to think Lori might be listening to her conversation on the pay phone next to the lower entrance to the Subway Club. Indeed she didn't even notice the figure in the shadows cleaning a table. Her over-confident but covert statement was picked up cleanly by the girl. "They're all down here, Toni, like a bunch of sittin' ducks."

Lori didn't know who Toni was but she knew who the sittin' ducks were: 'Hawk, Tiên Le and Shirl. Lori wasn't surprised by the statement. She'd always known Carla didn't fit in with this crowd. Betrayal wasn't something Lori was overly familiar with but if she would have suspected anyone of being capable of it, the cool, haughty Carla would have been her first choice.

She hadn't thought through anything in so long she barely knew how. Her heart took over where her mind left off. She could not stand by and watch these people get hurt. That she might also be hurt wasn't a consideration. As soon as Carla's back was turned to her, Lori stole out of the shadows, crept past the woman and ducked behind the bar.

Maggie felt the tug of her jean pantleg and looked down to where it came from. Seeing Lori's anxious expression shocked her. It was the first sign of life on the girl's face in some time. She leaned down and asked what was wrong. Shakily, Lori relayed what she'd overheard. Maggie's face turned to stone; she told Lori to stay put.

Calmly, Maggie leaned over the counter to quietly warn 'Hawk, careful not to look concerned. There was no hesitation on 'Hawk's part to tell Maggie to issue the alarm. War had been sitting on the horizon like a resting cat ready to spring at the slightest provocation. Questioning Maggie's information might prove fatal and she couldn't take that risk.

The sound system was turned off and the lights in the bar came on, flashed three times, then stayed on. Instantly everyone in the bar who had an assignment moved into action.

'Hawk, Tiên Le and Shirl spread out. Big Mary threw the heavy iron bolt across the steel door and locked it into place. 'Hawk activated the spring-loaded latches that opened to reveal three doors that had been wall a moment before. Inside the exit 'Hawk stood next to was a small arsenal of weapons.

As the second rifle was being handed out, Carla realized what was happening. Desperate to stop this escape (she had tried to find out if there were any other way out of the bar but every time she asked no one seemed to know) Carla grabbed Maggie and pulled a gun on her.

"Everybody freeze!" she yelled as she viciously surrounded Maggie's neck with her arm and pulled the bartender to the steel door. Maggie's body shielded hers and the barrel of her revolver was poised at Maggie's temple.

Everybody froze.

Maggie tried not to look frightened. She knew now that Lori's information had been correct. The bar was going to be attacked or Carla wouldn't be trying so hard to keep everybody down there where they could all be slaughtered. Maggie didn't want anyone to risk their lives to save her. And would have said so had Carla's grip not kept her from talking.

Tense milli-seconds ticked by seemingly drawn out by indecision. This stalemate could go on for as long as Carla wanted. No one would risk shooting at her, missing and hitting Maggie instead.

A flash of steel zinged across the room and struck Carla in the head. No one had counted on Tiên Le's deadly accurate reflexes. What had seemed like a small eternity had actually been a couple seconds. The shuriken Tiên Le threw hit its target full force and knocked Carla's head against the steel door. The gun hadn't been cocked; it dropped to the floor without firing. Carla's grip gave way, freeing her hostage as she slumped, unconscious, to the floor, the shuriken still lodged in her bloody forehead.

Big Mary picked up the gun and took the baseball bat Shirl handed to her. 'Hawk quickly armed everyone she could trust while barking out commands. "Shirl, find Shadow and take over the top. Tiên Le, get the Guard and take over the streets. Reneé, get your brother and take over the subways. Go!"

While the final command echoed in the air the bar emptied through the three hidden doors, each group of women attaching by strength and rank to their assigned leaders. Reneé Kramer took her group through the lowest maze that terminated in a women's restroom on the first level of the subway that honeycombed the city. She didn't have time to savor hearing 'Hawk address her by her first name thereby admitting her into the closest circle of 'Hawk's friends.

Shirl's maze through the "vacant" building above the Subway Club opened onto the rooftops she knew so well. Tiên Le's maze fed into the dark empty alley.

Left behind, under Big Mary's ruthless protection, were Maggie and Lori. Maggie because it was her job to put all the money in a safe and double-check the bar for fire hazards; Lori because she'd never been factored into 'Hawk's complex emergency get-away plans. Even the door guard had locked the outside entrance and disappeared through a vent above her chair. Except for Carla's fallen body and Big Mary's concerned presence the Subway Club looked as it would at closing time.

Lori crouched behind the bar afraid. From the sounds going on around her she could tell everyone had gotten out.

Maggie seemed so calm to Lori; it was reassuring. A movement caught Lori's eye and she turned toward it. Carla wasn't dead! She had come to and was pulling a small gun carefully from her boot. A thousand thoughts flashed through Lori's mind until she saw Carla aim the gun at Maggie's torso. Driven by blind instinct Lori jumped up and shoved Maggie out of the way in the same instant the gun was fired. She felt a strange sharp pain in her thigh, and her body flipped sideways to land on its back on the floor next to Maggie's feet. Her hand came to her thigh; she screamed sharply. A warm, wet sensation covered her hand as she doubled over trying to crawl away from the pain.

The gun fired only once. Big Mary bashed Carla's skull in with the bat immediately after the attempted murder. Satisfied Carla was dead, Big Mary walked behind the bar to make sure Maggie was all right.

"Mag, Mag! Hey!" Big Mary shouted trying to wake the bartender by shaking her.

Maggie came around and groaned. She had bumped her head when Lori pushed her. "Ohn. I must have hit my head. What happened?"

By way of an answer Lori stifled a groan with her fist. She'd been biting her hand and crying, totally overtaken by pain and completely unaware of her surroundings.

Maggie turned abruptly toward the sound. "Lori! My God, what happened?" She pulled Lori's hand away from the wound and swore. "Shit!" She knew a bullet wound when she saw one. "How did she get shot?" Maggie demanded fiercely.

"Mag, I thought Carla was *dead*. I didn't see her till she pulled the trigger. . . ."

Maggie looked around the big woman then away from the gruesome sight. The small gun was still in Carla's hand.

"She was aiming at you, Mag," Mary revealed.

"Me! But Lori pushed me . . . ," Maggie put it all together in her head and realized that Lori had probably saved her life.

"Jesus, kid. You're really something, you know that?" Maggie didn't think Lori was listening to what she said, though. "Mary, help me get her into 'Hawk's apartment. She doesn't need to see that," Maggie instructed, pointing to Carla's gory body.

Once inside the apartment Maggie had Mary apply pressure to the wound to slow the bleeding while she made some phone calls to find out what was happening outside and how long it would be before it was safe to have Tattoo come to remove the bullet. She swore all the while knowing that, without drugs for Lori's pain, they were in for a long night.

* * *

Jesus looked over the corner of the wall he had just finished painting and was proud of the results. His mother would lay into him for staying out late again. Still, he liked to work alone and this alley was virtually deserted after dark. Tiny flakes of snow appeared from the sky and blew in this direction and that, unable to decide where the wind wanted them to go. The temperature had taken a sharp drop making Jesus shiver. His twelve-year-old body wanted to go home and find some hot food, if any was left. He stashed his spray paint inside a hole in the brick wall and headed out to the street. Walking briskly along the sidewalk weaving around toppled trash cans, Jesus turned down an invitation to join the boys on the block who were walking the opposite direction. They had some bottles and were going to get high. It was Saturday night, man, and come on with us. But Jesus smiled charmingly and walked on.

There was something funny yet familiar about the slow driving, black Caddy cruising down the street. Something about the sleek red pin-striping on the car caught Jesus' attention and he slowed his walk to watch the car creep along. Six dangerous-looking men were crowded into the vehicle. One of the men was staring at Jesus. The light from a street lamp made the paint on the car sparkle, reminding Jesus of something. Candy! The car looked like shiny candy. That was how everyone knew the car belonged to Candyman. But Candyman was dead and Dapper Toni was warlord in the south now. So if that's Dapper Toni's car, then . . . Jesus' thoughts screamed shrilly in his mind, Dapper Toni is on 'Hawk's turf — and he's soldierin', declaring war, and driving toward the Subway Club!

Jesus could think of but one thing to do: call Shadow. He broke into a run toward the pay phone booth on the corner. He pulled a quarter from his pocket, put it in the phone and pushed the buttons hard and fast.

"Answer, answer, damn it. Shadow! Jesus. Yeah, man, I just saw Dapper Toni. . . ." The long car began to speed toward the phone-booth. A man was leaning out the window with a machine gun in his hand. "He's headed for the Subway Clu . . . ahh." Bullets riddled the booth and Jesus' young body. The car sped away, turning the corner in the opposite direction of the Subway Club. The phone receiver dangled and swayed. A voice screamed through it saying the name Jesus over and over, then quit. Sirens could be heard in the distance and people began to crowd around the bloody heap of a boy, women crying, men shouting angrily. Boys tried to run after the fleeing car but soon realized their chase was futile and started to walk sadly back to their murdered friend. They did not yet realize that Jesus' death was the *second* death of the night and that the war had already begun.

* * *

'Hawk waited for her door guard to escape from the vulnerable ground level entrance of the club and catch up. They left through the same exit Tiên Le and her group had just gone out of. The two women ran down the alley, checked the street for danger and ran across it to the next alley then repeated the process until they reached the pool hall on Haverson.

'Hawk was exhilarated but cool. She was at her best when in the midst of crisis; her thinking was always crisp and rational. She was a natural, charismatic leader who felt at ease giving orders and seeing that things got done. When called upon, 'Hawk was completely selfless, courageous and tireless. She took care of her people, her neighborhood and was completely without ego when doing it. She didn't have to struggle for power or prove herself. She already had power – real power – and had proven herself many times.

Still the pool hall on Haverson was pivotal. How well she did there determined how well the whole war would go. For as much as she needed her youth gangs, she needed these loosely organized adult men more. All the leadership ability in the world wasn't going to help her if she couldn't get past their macho belief that *they* were running the neighborhood.

Inwardly 'Hawk found these men laughable. There wasn't a true leader among them. At times there were ex-military men around – the pool hall was well known as a place to recruit mercenaries for foreign wars – and some very vicious men hung out there. But they were all followers.

This pool hall was where 'Hawk had set the record straight about her womanhood some seventeen years ago. She'd been wearing all her rings even then and had hit a man in the face, blinding him in one eye for trying to advance on her sexually.

Holding up in the shadow of the building to catch her breath, she wished she had another level head with her instead of one of her door guards – a woman who was chosen for her ruthless ways. Especially not the bear of a woman with her now. This one had a chip on her shoulder and was trigger happy, too. But this wasn't the time to go in the hall alone.

The duo covered each other and slipped into the long building. The usual Saturday night assortment of hustlers, dealers and hardcore survivors were present. On the surface these men were having fun but an underlying thread of mistrust and tension cinched them together. Undercover police intermingled here and drug busts were a common occurrence. Black men made for easier targets than black women. 'Hawk didn't always look like a woman, though, especially during war.

Her very presence alone was cause for uneasiness in this all male environment. She only enjoyed a guarded welcome here. Her arrival with another woman was immediate cause for alarm. 'Hawk never showed up with one of her women unless something was seriously wrong. Even more so that she was heavily armed. Someone was always watching this place. Seeing two armed people enter the hall was going to draw the wrong kind of attention. And soon.

'Hawk didn't waste time being congenial. She took in who was there and who wasn't and started talking.

"There's a war going down. We got a tip Dapper Toni was gonna come down on my club, and took off. We've already taken one of his people out," 'Hawk informed the men briskly and loudly. The men stopped their games and drew near—eyes jumping and fingers flexing. 'Hawk had said the magic word: war. Drugs, nine-ball and tall stories could wait. They began picking up their coats and putting them on—the hall would empty out soon and the cops would catch wind of things.

"We all know D. Antonio isn't playing with a full deck," 'Hawk warned. Grumbling assent filled the restless air. "If he was after my club, then he's going for big, vulnerable targets where he can take out a lot of people with little effort. There's a prayer meetin' goin' on at the Riverfront Church and a dance at the Youth Center. Who's havin' parties tonight?" 'Hawk asked.

"Anduhar's nightclub is," volunteered one man.

"Fuck," 'Hawk swore. That club had some wild parties and would be close to impossible to control. "We'll have to double the guard at Anduhar's. . . ."

"Who says we got to listen to you anyway?" came an angry voice from the left of the crowd.

"I don't have time for this," 'Hawk replied.

"Well make time for it," the man demanded as he stepped forward trying to take control away from 'Hawk.

"Man, shut up," came another voice. "'Hawk is *war*lord around here, fool," another man asserted.

"Yeah. Well maybe I want to be warlord," the tall interloper insisted.

'Hawk was silent and alert. She'd faced these challenges from over-brave loudmouths before. She sized him up and shifted her stance placing a hand out to caution her partner from acting rashly. This one could be put down easy; he was taller and probably stronger but not smarter or more experienced. 'Hawk wasn't the only one who had arrived at that conclusion either.

During the staredown that ensued 'Hawk spoke smoothly. "These are your wives and children and mothers we're talking about protecting, gentlemen. D. Antonio is partial to firebombs," she said confidently showing she had knowledge of the situation and how to handle it. "You can bet D. Antonio is on *his* way right now." 'Hawk skillfully played on their sensibilities and natural desire to protect.

A big man with a deep voice said, "I'll take Anduhar's, 'Hawk." Another said he'd cover the prayer meeting and a third the dance.

"Let's do it, men," 'Hawk ordered.

The big man responded by grabbing the tall challenger by the arm. "Come on, son, one warlord is enough for us." A moment later only the owner was left in the pool hall on Haverson.

* * *

'Hawk scanned the street for anything that looked suspicious. It would be dawn soon and 'Hawk couldn't go home. The snow had turned to sleet which pelted her leather, bouncing off its hard surface and sounding like tiny drum beats. A garbage truck lumbered noisily along in front of the row of caged shops that lined the street.

The night had gone badly. As far as 'Hawk knew the only casualty D. Antonio had suffered was Carla. She'd learned about the boy Jesus who had kept the enemy away from her club. Beyond that sad news she had little to go on. She'd been right about the nightclub party; it had gotten out of control. A blessing in disguise because the police had arrived to break it up, making the gathering an unlikely target. In fact, police were everywhere.

'Hawk hoped the war didn't intensify because the city leaders had a tendency to overreact to neighborhood violence. The last thing 'Hawk needed was the National Guard and curfews. She checked the rooftops above her and waited for the musical whistle that would signal the approach of her general. It was a reassuring sound.

Tiên Le and her slave moved into the shadow of the wall across the alley from 'Hawk. She was cold and wet and miserable and short-tempered. Twice she had just missed being spotted by police. Meeting 'Hawk right on her southern border made her feel unsafe. But Shadow had relayed the message, so here she was. Something was wrong about this place and Tiên Le was irritated with her leader for choosing it.

"What's *she* doing here?" 'Hawk hissed by way of greeting. She wasn't even-tempered either. This sleet was worse than rain for throwing her out of sorts. None of the three had eaten in hours. The slave was tired, cold and frightened. They were all at their worst.

"I couldn't take her home," Tiên Le answered bitterly. Didn't 'Hawk think she would have left tôi somewhere if she could have? "Cops are swarming around the building I live in. Bad Man got picked off on the roof by a sniper," Tiên Le explained. "It's not safe here," she added, glancing down the street seeing part of a slow-moving car sticking out beyond the trash hauler laboring past them. She tensed and put her arm out to push her slave back against the wall.

'Hawk spotted her movement and turned to look in the same direction, her rifle poised.

The car stopped. The trash truck moved on. Exposed, Tiên Le and 'Hawk saw the gun aimed at 'Hawk. Both rifles fired lighting up the area with red streams of fire and splitting the quiet early morning with loud blasts.

The vehicle's tires spun on the wet pavement before digging in and squealing out.

Tiên Le never looked to see if the shooter had been hit. Her next action was to stand over 'Hawk's body to protect it from further attack, crouched and ready.

Lying in the cold water accumulated in the lowest part of the alley 'Hawk struggled with the fiery pain below her left clavicle. The bullet's trajectory and force had spun her around and dropped her face down on the pavement.

She knew that if the shooter had just been a little more accurate, she'd be dead. This wasn't her first bullet wound, but it didn't hurt any less. What she wanted more than anything was to maintain her dignity. And to that end she was concentrating on keeping her bladder from letting go. She could take anything but having her bladder give way again.

"Master, she's alive!" tôi said, alarm in her voice.

Tiên Le broke her stance to look out the alley to assess the situation. Lights in windows came on, people peered out to see what the sounds were, knowing they were gunshots but wishing otherwise.

"Fuck!" Tiên Le cursed. A police car was headed toward them, lights flashing and siren shrilling.

Tiên Le picked up the shell casing and 'Hawk's rifle and slung its strap over her shoulder. "'Hawk! Come on, the cops are coming." She bent to help her friend up. "Hurry."

The word 'cops' forced 'Hawk into action. She pulled herself up and scrambled down the filth-strewn alley with her comrades and disappeared into the darkness.

The police car screeched to a halt at the alley entrance and the officers jumped out of it. They pulled up and looked around. They were all alone. One officer looked up but the people who had seen the shooting had disappeared, too, lest they might become falsely accused. The other officer looked down, scouring the alley with his flashlight. They were too late. The crime was committed, the perpetrators were gone and all they were left with was a small splattering of blood that was quickly washing away in the gathering sleet.

* * *

The sky was beginning to lighten and the city was waking up. The three women had traveled five perilous blocks, avoiding police and enemies. 'Hawk was slowing down. Her adrenalin had played out and her strength was fading. Her shirt and coat lining were saturated with blood. Tiên Le was worried.

"Half a block more, 'Hawk, and two flights of stairs," she advised with concern. She hoped her friend could make it. She had to.

'Hawk pulled her hand off the wound and looked at it. Why wasn't the bleeding stopped? she wondered. "Yeah, go," she said bravely. She was worried, too. She made it up to the first landing and stumbled against the wall. Tôi tried to assist her to no avail.

"What's wrong?" Tiên Le asked gravely.

'Hawk grabbed Tiên Le's shoulder, gripping desperately. "Tiên Le, I don't know how much longer I can hold this."

Tiên Le's eyes enlarged with wonder. "You mean you . . .?" implying that she realized 'Hawk had held her bladder all this time. "No," 'Hawk breathed impatiently.

Tiên Le sprang up the last flight of stairs stopping at the door on the left. She pounded on it and yelled, "Bac si, Bac si," and went on to identify herself and the emergency in Vietnamese.

The door was opened cautiously. Once the residents of the small apartment were confident their caller was who she said she was, the door was opened the rest of the way. These people were used to being awakened with medical emergencies. Tiên Le had never been one of them. Her visits were usually pleasant and welcomed.

Tiên Le flew down the stairs and together with tôi managed to get 'Hawk the rest of the way up and into the apartment. Ignoring the excited activity around them, Tiên Le escorted 'Hawk to the bathroom and closed the door. While 'Hawk was helping herself in the private room, Tiên Le began giving instructions in her native tongue.

She placed her slave in a corner and asked the woman of the house to find some food for herself and the slave. A man in his fifties came out of the sleeping area to prepare the couch for his patient whom he had not yet seen. He was expressionless and calm. His sideways glance toward the corner revealed nothing about what he thought of the small black girl cowering in the corner. The smell of wet leather, wool and denim mixed with the odors of fish, herbs and fried food. He next noticed the rifle propped by the bathroom door. The toilet was flushed and a giant black woman was opening the door.

Tiên Le hastened to lead 'Hawk to the couch and coaxed her to lie down. She spun on her heels to speak to the Bac si (doctor).

'Hawk thought it seemed strange that Tiên Le sounded like she was begging this man for something. Then everything went dark.

Tiên Le *was* begging this man. He was an herbal doctor, skilled in surgery but not licensed to practice medicine in the United States. And he knew it was illegal to attend to a gunshot victim without reporting it to the authorities. Tiên Le was speaking quickly but respectfully. She turned to motion toward her friend and cried out when she saw the big woman's head had rolled back and her mouth had gone slack. "Hawk!" She rushed to her and began to take her coat off, after taking the Colt .45 from the holster and placing it on the table next to the couch.

"Who is this person?" the doctor demanded coldly. He resented this intrusion, even if it was Tiên Le. Who were these strangers?

Abandoning her patient, respectful tone, Tiên Le turned and hissed, "Nighthawk."

The name reverberated around the room. The doctor, his wife, a young woman and three children were standing there watching. One of the few words the doctor knew in English was Nighthawk. He'd never seen the woman but he knew about who and what she was. She was respected and feared by the people of this neighborhood. Accounts of her work made her sound nearly legendary. It was almost hard to think of her as being constructed of real flesh and blood. Yet she obviously was for here she was, on his couch, bleeding too much.

He immediately became a focused whirlwind of activity. Orders were given and obeyed. The coat and holster were removed and shirt cut away, the wound cleaned and prepared. A strong smelling brew of tea was placed on the table next to the gun.

'Hawk came around. Tiên Le held her head up and offered the tea. "'Hawk, drink this. It will help the pain and slow the bleeding," she told in part. "The doctor is going to remove the bullet."

'Hawk groggily drank the rank stuff and drifted off again. What Tiên Le didn't tell her friend was the tea would also induce a deep sleep for several hours. She knew 'Hawk would not agree to be put out of commission and would try to go out to fight the minute the bullet was out and the bleeding stopped. But the warrior had already lost too much blood. Her life hung in dangerous balance as it was. Temporarily, at least, Tiên Le was warlord, and she had to act in everyone's best interest. Keeping 'Hawk alive was in everyone's best interest.

After the surgery was performed and 'Hawk was resting easily,Tiên Le found she had some explaining to do. About what had happened to 'Hawk, why the warlord trusted her, who tôi was. The family and young woman listened quietly, growing to hold Tiên Le in great awe. Especially the young woman who expressed her concern for Tiên Le's safety.

Tôi watched her Master comfort this woman with renewed interest. She had watched this woman's looks of fondness toward Tiên Le and felt jealous. It disturbed her that the woman seemed so familiar to her. All the Vietnamese being spoken had made her feel quite left out until she heard a phrase she recognized: em gái. Of course, this woman is my Master's little sister, tôi thought with relief. She relaxed after that and finished eating the food she'd been given, feeling safe and content in her corner.

Tiên Le rose to leave, informing tôi, "If 'Hawk wakes up, tell her I went back out on patrol and will check in soon. She won't feel like going anywhere until tonight . . . I hope," she speculated on her way out the door.

Chapter Nine

Tiên Le's spirit brightened when Maggie opened the door of the apartment she shared with her sister. Maggie's sleep had been fitful and she welcomed this daytime intrusion. Her sister was at Mass with the children and wouldn't be back for an hour or so. Maggie had gotten home too late to even think about going to evening Mass later. A late novena appealed to her more. There were people she wanted to *pray* for. Seeing her weary lover in the doorway meant she had one less candle to light, one less rosary to say.

"Oh, Tiên Le, thank God you're all right." She didn't have to ask for Tiên Le to hold her. The warrior closed the front door and closed in on a powerful, heartfelt embrace of relief and love.

The last sixteen hours had been hell. Just a couple hours after she'd left 'Hawk in the doctor's care, D. Antonio had fire-bombed Beniña's restaurant killing Beniña and two of her employees who were getting ready to open for business. The death toll from the "outbreak of neighborhood violence", as the press was calling it, now stood at six that Tiên Le knew of. The press and the mayor were discounting the idea of a "neighborhood war".

Officially turf boundaries and warlords weren't recognized by established society. To ignore the existence of neighborhood hierarchies was to take away their power. Doing so also left the establishment without realistic explanations for the bloodshed. After all, no white people had been killed. But reports of shots fired, innocent children gunned down in the streets and firebombs spelled trouble in any city. Five reported deaths in less than twenty-four hours, armed and agitated youth gangs patrolling the area, rumors flying and tempers flaring couldn't be ignored. Without an identifiable enemy the authorities didn't know precisely how to react. So they did what they always did in situations like this one: they arrested people.

Tiên Le had just come from the bail bondsman where she had arranged bail for Shadow. Enough people had pointed the finger at the man whose name the authorities were "not prepared to release" that they surely would have stopped the wholesale arrests of 'Hawk's people. Tiên Le knew the police couldn't *find* D. Antonio Petrazzia, or they would have stopped picking up every suspicious individual they encountered.

Holding Maggie was good medicine for Tiên Le's heavy soul. She wished she could have left the strain she felt outside Maggie's apartment but it was right there with her — vibrating her nerves like a plucked tension wire.

Maggie was feeling the energy, too. Some of it was her own from worrying about Tiên Le, 'Hawk and Lori, among other things.

The couple had been holding each other, giving silent comfort, when their cheeks brushed electrically. Tiên Le capitalized on the shiver the contact produced by bringing her slightly parted lips within a hair's breath of Maggie's soft mouth. She lingered there letting her stuttering breath and desire-filled eyes speak of the possibilities.

Without shoes on Maggie stood an inch or so taller than her lover. She was drawn to the lips that reached for hers, ready for at least *some* of what was being offered to her. The kiss began sensually enough, as Tiên Le had meant it to. How quickly the tender touch fanned the coals of her craving for Maggie into sparkling flames surprised Tiên Le. Her breathing came in long tugs; her hand moved up to Maggie's head where it grasped the soft, thick hair. The deepening kiss moved through her like a storm front flooding her with the years of wanting. She hadn't wanted to push Maggie into this but her need welled up over her sensibleness. She pulled away from the beautifully answered kiss to let her passion plead its case.

"Magdalene, let me make love to you . . . please." Her request was doubly underscored by the longing in her eyes.

Maggie had never been *asked* for the favor of her body. Not once in her life. Everyone had always taken. She was so honored by Tiên Le's respect, she was left speechless. To consent, she unfastened the catch of Tiên Le's damp wool cape and let it drop to the floor. She nodded her head slowly, transfixed by her lover's black lightning eyes.

Tiên Le was overcome with excitement. Her lips moved to Maggie's ear. "Mag . . . dalene," she breathed, "I've wanted you," a small kiss on the neck, "for so long." Maggie's soft robe parted easily to lay open for Tiên Le the graceful, feminine body she had fantasized about having in her grasp all these years. The creamy brown skin was tight and smooth and looked several years younger than the face and hands. The gentle curve of breast, waist and hips captivated Tiên Le.

Maggie's breathing was deep and rapid and demanding in spite of, Tiên Le suspected, her carefully cultivated immunity to sexuality. She was pleased with herself for succeeding where others had failed with this desirable woman. Her hands were warm now and throbbing to explore the architecture of womanhood before her. As were her lips. She knew her timing had been right when she heard Maggie's gasping moan pull from her, created by the feel of knowledgeable lips surrounding a hard, brown nipple. Tongue flicking over its sensitivity. Awakening it from its forced hibernation along with it every other cell in the body it belonged to. Belly and sex filled with blood, engorged with need.

The couple found themselves on the couch — every part of Maggie's body demanding its due and receiving it. Tiên Le expertly read, fondled, caressed, nibbled and kissed every spot she could reach, working them both into a sharpened, panting state of craving. Tiên Le couldn't hold back any more. Eyes huge with lust she let the final request free so it would stop hammering against her teeth to get out. "Magdalene, I want to fuck you." Tiên Le thought, Please don't say no, I'll go mad.

Maggie had sworn for years that she would never let anyone fuck her again. Anyone. But Tiên Le wasn't just anyone. Tiên Le was her lover. And she *did* love her. *No* one had ever wanted her this badly either. She knew that if she said no, Tiên Le would respect her—and would find *some* way to deal with it. She also knew withholding that part of herself from Tiên Le would put up a wall between them that might eventually seal them off from each other. She couldn't bear that.

"Yes," she said softly, thinking it was a small price to pay for Tiên Le's genuine love and kindness.

"Ohnn, yeah," Tiên Le moaned. She reached into the folds of gauze and pulled out the prong strapped to her lower belly. With great care she spread the moist lips of Maggie's vagina apart and gently introduced her cock to the opening. It came as no surprise to Tiên Le that this woman was more ready than she knew to accept this insertion. She would bet a month's winnings that no one had ever taken the time to arouse Maggie enough to get the opening to lubricate and stretch and relax to take a full penetration. She bet as well that sex had always hurt Maggie and had never left her ful-filled. She was prepared to change all that.

Once the head of her cock slowly passed through the gates, Tiên Le laid her body evenly over Maggie's. She moved her hips into her partner to allow the pole to glide completely in.

Maggie had been braced for the pain but it never came. Instead she felt full and vibrant and expectant. As Tiên Le moved the shaft in and out, gradually building the tempo and moaning softly, Mag-gie pulled her knees up near her shoulders to open more and deeper. Her hands grabbed Tiên Le's buttocks and pulled them in closer. Neck arched, mouth open to sighs and wails, Maggie learned what sex could be and had never been: exciting, animalistic and satisfy-ing. She also found she had the endurance needed to keep up with her lover.

Which was just as well because Tiên Le was beyond rational thought and compassionate patience. With Maggie responding as she was, Tiên Le felt free to let loose the years of wanting this woman and all the stress of this war. This excitement had given her a second wind to fuel her hard-driving intercourse. As long as Maggie kept taking it, she fucked harder and faster, pushing closer and closer to that place where it would all squeeze through the tunnel of ecstasy and burst through to the other side. Where it would all explode away from her and leave her clean and free of its oppressive constriction.

Just when she thought she'd have to go through the tunnel alone, Maggie snagged the comet's tail and shot through with her, screaming and gasping and heaving, too. They held each other with the little strength left them — sighing, smiling, calling endearments and each other's name and kissing their way back to earth.

"I never knew it could be like that, Tiên Le," Maggie told her lover with awe.

"Me either. That was the most incredible orgasm I've ever had," Tiên Le agreed.

"It's the *only* orgasm I've ever had," Maggie confessed, both embarrassed and pleased. She couldn't even get angry for never knowing before now. There were a lot of things she hadn't known before Tiên Le came into her heart.

Tiên Le was amazed and proud. "Thank you for waiting to share it with me," Tiên Le said reverently.

Maggie smiled wickedly. "Any time," she said invitingly. "An-ny-time."

"God, you're sexy when you're satisfied." Tiên Le pulled out of her lover's sex and let the cream-covered thing lie between them as she shifted her weight to lie on the outside of the couch, facing her contented, beautiful woman.

The two were so involved in their loving, appreciative gaze they didn't hear Maggie's sister open the door. It had been done quietly because Maggie should have been asleep. "Oh," the sister exclaimed when she saw the bodies on the couch, acting quickly to keep the children turned so they wouldn't see, but not above watching herself. It intrigued her to watch Tiên Le shift and look like she was tucking something away. She'd seen her sister's body a thousand times so wasn't interested in how quickly Maggie pulled her robe back together and stood. "Couldn't sleep?" she asked teasingly. "Hello, Tiên Le." Tiên Le made a quick movement that brought her gracefully to her feet. She bowed slightly and returned the greeting, completely unruffled at being "caught".

Maggie's sister ushered her children down the hallway saying, "It smells like a wet sheep in here. Bring your cape in the kitchen, Tiên Le, and let it dry over the register."

Maggie picked the cloak up. "I'll do it, if you can stay for a little while?"

"A small while, I want to talk."

Maggie started to walk into the kitchen then turned soberly. "Rumor has it 'Hawk is dead but I know in my heart she's alive." Her eyes pleaded for confirmation.

"Wounded. Lost a lot of blood. She'll be okay. She's with a friend of mine who knows medicine and is taking good care of her." Tiên Le's eyes looked sad. The burden of reality brought her back from her brief vacation. Still, she was calm now and better able to cope.

"Hungry?"

"Yeah."

"I'll bring you some hot soup and fresh rolls." Maggie caressed the damp cloak, loving it because it was part of Tiên Le, and walked quietly toward the kitchen to leave Tiên Le alone with her heavy thoughts for a short time.

Maggie curled into the chair next to the couch and watched Tiên Le restore herself with the robust food she'd served her. As a small gesture of celebration for consummating their love, Maggie had opened the good wine.

Tiên Le sat back in the couch and savored the drink. She rarely had alcohol and was enjoying the warmth it added to the meal. "I feel much better. Thank you."

"Good," Maggie replied. "Tell me what happened to 'Hawk."

Tiên Le sighed. "She was going to go after D. Antonio," she said, careful to keep her voice low. "We were at the border when we were spotted by one of D. Antonio's patrols. 'Hawk got a round off before she got hit. I don't know if she got the man who shot her. She took it right here." Tiên Le pointed to the place on her body that would illustrate where the bullet had gone in. She reassured Maggie that 'Hawk was forced to rest and would probably be up and around soon. She told her to keep quiet about 'Hawk's condition one way or the other.

"So you're warlord for now," Maggie stated flatly.

"Doesn't make it any easier to kill people," Tiên Le responded unhappily.

"If you mean Carla, you didn't kill her. Big Mary did," Maggie informed the warrior bitterly. She wished Tiên Le had killed the traitor.

"What are you talking about?" the leader demanded darkly.

"I'm talking about Carla didn't die right away and had another gun and tried to shoot me after everyone left. Lori pushed me out of the way and took the bullet in the thigh. Big Mary bashed Carla's head in with a baseball bat. She killed her, not you."

Tiên Le was stunned and it showed. Not only by what had happened but by the acrid way Maggie told it. It took awhile for Tiên Le to take it all in. She had no idea she'd left Maggie in peril. "I'm sorry, Magdalene. Everything happened so fast. There wasn't time to check to see if she was dead."

"I know that, Tiên Le. Any one of us could have checked. You did what had to be done so everyone else could get away. Big Mary is just sick about it because it's her job to protect me. And Lori, too, I suppose. No one ever said." She rubbed her forehead. It was all too sad. "Anyway, I finally got Tattoo to come down to remove the bullet and sew Lori up. She'll be fine. Found some drugs and knocked her out with them. I've got to go check on her soon.

"What happened to Carla's body?" It was a cold question but warlords had to consider these things.

Maggie shivered and shook her head. "I don't even want to know what Big Mary did with it. Something appropriately ghoulish I'm sure."

Tiên Le nodded her agreement; Big Mary was a bit off.

"God I hate war," Maggie sighed, her body deflating in the chair. She saw the flint-hard look in Tiên Le's eyes and realized what a stupid thing she had just said. Six deaths and at least two serious injuries and it wasn't over yet, but what was any of it compared to what Tiên Le had endured in her homeland? "I'm sorry. That was an inexcusable comment." Maggie wanted to be forgiven for it.

Tiên Le changed the subject. "I've got more rounds to do and I have to check on 'Hawk. She needs a new shirt; where can I get one?"

"The army surplus sells them. Here I'll write it down for you."

Maggie gave the information to her now withdrawn lover who kissed her quickly and left.

* * *

'Hawk opened her eyes and looked around. The pain in her shoulder reminded her of how she had come to be in these strange surroundings. She recalled being told a doctor was going to remove the bullet from her and feeling relieved that *some*body was.

She looked at Tiên Le sitting on the floor by her, cross-legged and eyes closed. Next to the general was her slave, stretched along the colorful room divider that separated the three women from the rest of the small apartment. It was nighttime. 'Hawk remembered coming here in the morning, which told her she had been out for several hours. She was annoyed that her injury was severe enough to put her down for so long. Knowing her body as she did, she realized her wound must have been more life-threatening than she'd thought. She could easily have bled to death were it not for Tiên Le's actions and this doctor's skill. She owed these people her life. She stood in awe of that debt and hoped she could find some way to honor it.

For now she had work to do. She pulled the blankets back and sat up. The new net shirt lying on the table with her gear told her Maggie was okay. Half through struggling to put the shirt on she noticed Tiên Le staring at her reproachfully. 'Hawk halted a second to consider the general's attempt to keep her in bed, then pulled the shirt the rest of the way on. She reached for the studded knife sheath and began snapping it around her left wrist. She may be injured but she was still warlord. She was prepared to sacrifice her health to stop D. Antonio Petrazzia.

'Hawk called for a report. "Where do we stand?"

Tiên Le sighed. 'Hawk had had that same focused look of determination before she'd killed Candyman. There was no arguing with her when she was acting like this. "Beniña's was firebombed this morning, killing her and two others," Tiên Le reported matter-of-factly. She knew the leader wouldn't allow herself to be affected by the news. True warriors never did. Until the fighting was done. Then the personal hell would rise to the surface and demand attention. No one ever knew how 'Hawk took these things. Even Maggie had no knowledge of the nightmares, inability to sleep and severe spells of cold sweats 'Hawk endured to purge her demons after she killed someone, or when someone who mattered died senselessly.

"It's been quiet since then. Mostly because every available police officer is on duty."

"The National Guard?" 'Hawk queried.

"Not yet, but it's being considered."

Tiên Le roused her sleeping slave and stood herself. 'Hawk continued to dress while Tiên Le saw to their dinner. Checking her boot for the silencer she'd shoved into it at the bar, she clucked at the bullet hole in her blood-stained holster strap. She winced when she strapped the holster over her dressing.

The slave knelt before 'Hawk placing a tray with a hot stew and coffee on it before her leader. Tiên Le shook her head with disgust when she saw 'Hawk stubbornly ignore the pain.

'Hawk checked the magazine of her pistol and snapped it back into place. "I need some paper and a pen."

"At least *eat*, 'Hawk," Tiên Le said sternly.

"Huh? Yeah, in a minute," 'Hawk replied absently.

Tiên Le handed her the requested items. 'Hawk wrote a quick note that read:

> Paulo,
>   Hit, not down. ~~DAP~~ Time to promote our
> presidents. Meet at 2.
>   Nighthawk

She was certain that her friend and warlord to the north, Paulo, would understand from that note that she intended to eliminate their common enemy and that she intended to replace the wayward southern leadership with people she could trust. Paulo would know the meeting place: the site of the torn down soda shop where the two of them had hung out as teenagers. She handed the note and the emblem ring she slipped from her finger to Tiên Le's slave.

The girl took the note and ring cautiously, looking to her Master for permission. Tiên Le nodded. Tôi was wide-eyed; her heart beat quickly with fear; 'Hawk had never noticed her in a non-sexual way. She admired and feared this great woman intensely and could scarcely cope with the contact.

"Do you know who Paulo is?" 'Hawk asked gently. She would have preferred to use someone besides this skittish girl as a messenger. The slave nodded, looking at her lap, hypnotizing herself with the heavy silver ring carved with 'Hawk's device. No way could she go through with anything 'Hawk needed her to do in a fully conscious state. The mention of the northern warlord made her even less likely to succeed without this self-induced trance she was creating. Tiên Le was watchful. The slave had been taught this technique as a part of sexual discipline, and as something to use as a pacifier during stressfully long absences from her Master. She was confident the girl could perform for 'Hawk.

"Do you know what he looks like?"

Tôi did not.

"He's a big, handsome Puerto Rican with a Maltese cross tattooed on his left palm. Go to the barber shop on Cole and tell whoever confronts you that you have a message for Paulo from me. You'll be taken to him. Give him the note and ring. When you've done that go to Sophia and tell her I asked her to look after you until it's safe. Do you understand?"

Tôi understood. Her face was a mask of peace; she was empty of herself. Dismissed, she left quietly on her errand.

'Hawk knew that if she'd been asking too much of the girl, Tiên Le would've spoken up. She felt sure the mission would be completed. At Tiên Le's renewed urging 'Hawk ate, thoughtfully working her plans through her head. Between sips of coffee she asked for the address of the building they were in.

Not understanding her general's hesitancy to reveal their location, she said, "Tiên Le, I *have* to know where we are." Tiên Le mentally scolded herself for being paranoid and gave the information. If she couldn't trust 'Hawk, who *could* she trust? 'Hawk nodded and returned to her absorption in her plans.

Greatly restored by her long rest and nutritious meal, she reached for her rifle and dismantled it. Tiên Le could see her leader was nearly ready to leave so proffered some advice. "If you plan to express gratitude to these people, keep it low key. They embarrass easily and understand very little English."

'Hawk handed the butt of her rifle to her general to hide in her cape. "Starting with you, my friend. You saved my life by bringing me here."

Tiên Le stuck the rifle part in her sash and put on her cloak. "You would have done the same for me," Tiên Le replied softly, trying to minimize the gesture. She helped 'Hawk put on her heavy leather jacket and handed the motorcycle hat to her leader. 'Hawk checked her pockets for ammunition, stood tall and stretched the stiffness from her body. Fully armed and dressed she felt herself again. She looked her general in the eye and said, "Always." The bond between these warriors was strengthened by this ordeal, and on some level they could understand but not express those feelings.

Before going Tiên Le introduced 'Hawk to the family that had cared for her that day. 'Hawk offered her hand to the doctor. He took it and they shook hands. 'Hawk simply told him, thank you, but it was the deep sincerity in her voice that broke the language barrier. 'Hawk knew the man wouldn't accept a bold offer of payment for his skilled services. She'd left a few one hundred dollar bills on the table when Tiên Le wasn't looking. To 'Hawk no amount of money would repay this man, nor did she think her gratitude ended with the money. To Tiên Le she said, "He knows that if he ever needs help, he can count on me, doesn't he?"

"I believe he feels you are genuine and can be counted on."

The doctor's wife and three children stood slightly behind him, shyly interested and smiling.

"I thought I knew all the children on my turf. I've never seen these bright ones."

"They don't go out much and receive their education at home," Tiên Le explained. Actually there were several children in this building 'Hawk didn't know about. Neither did the government.

'Hawk touched the brim of her cap and gave the woman a short nod of thanks.

Tiên Le pulled the young woman forward to meet the warlord.

"'Hawk, this is my little sister, Tuy Kim," Tiên Le said proudly.

'Hawk smiled broadly at the girl. It did her heart good to know Tiên Le trusted her enough to let her meet the almost mythical em gái. She put her large hand around the base of Tiên Le's neck and leaned down to talk directly into her ear while keeping her eye on the girl. "Are you sure, good buddy? She's awfully pretty," 'Hawk teased.

Tiên Le smiled and told her sister that the warrior found her attractive. The girl blushed and giggled.

"Is she the one who washed the blood out of my coat lining?" 'Hawk thought the gesture was something a very impressed young woman might do.

"Yes . . ." Tiên Le confirmed, amazed that 'Hawk figured it out.

'Hawk straightened and pointed to the lining to show she'd noticed. "Thank you, Tuy Kim."

The girl lowered her head bashfully and coyly looked at the warlord through her eyelashes.

'Hawk thought Tuy Kim was very charming but business was business, war was war. "We're going to need gloves where we're going, Tiên Le," 'Hawk warned.

Tiên Le pulled a pair of black kidskin gloves from her cape pocket to show 'Hawk.

"Let's do it."

* * *

In the basement of the building they were in, 'Hawk pulled up sharply when she discovered a family using the boiler room as living quarters. "Jesus, what are *they* doing here?"

The family began to pull together in a tight huddle. They were afraid. Tiên Le ventured forward speaking Vietnamese to the oldest male. The man acknowledged they were countrymen.

"He understands you?" 'Hawk asked.

"Yes."

"Good. Tell them we mean them no harm and we will disturb nothing. If they leave for an hour, we'll be gone and everything will be cool."

Tiên Le was at her charming best as she persuaded the people to leave even though she herself didn't know what was going to happen.

'Hawk walked into the room and sat on the floor, leaning her back against the back wall. She lighted a cigarette and sighed, relaxing her head against the wall.

"Now what?" Tiên Le asked curiously.

"We wait," 'Hawk responded mysteriously. Tiên Le was skilled at waiting. She sat quietly with her friend.

'Hawk came alive when she detected a rumble coming toward them. It got louder and louder until it shook them for a minute or so then moved along and away. A subway train had passed by close to the foundation of the building.

"God, I don't know how they live down here with all that racket," 'Hawk wondered. She stood and reached up to find a latch well above her head. She got the old thing to work and it let loose a part of the cinderblock wall.

Tiên Le looked on, fascinated by what she saw.

'Hawk braced her foot into the opening and wedged her body into the space.

"Aren't you worried that family might find this?"

"No offense, Tiên Le, but none of them are tall enough and probably not strong enough to worry about," 'Hawk explained. Tiên Le squeezed through behind 'Hawk and helped her close the secret door after them. The darkness was eerie. Rats were everywhere. 'Hawk's eyes adjusted to the faint light coming from the underground traffic signal and she headed out. Tiên Le followed but not happily.

"How do you know we're safe down here?" the general asked, not at all confidently.

'Hawk was almost flip about how comfortable she was traversing this underground network of tracks. "That was an uptown train and it only runs once an hour on Sundays."

"'Hawk, don't you think it's about time you started teaching me about these things?" Tiên Le asked somewhat crossly. For the first time in years she was seeing, first hand, how her leader got around so stealthily. It had never occurred to her before, but 'Hawk really did come and go almost like a ghost. She was mad at herself for just accepting it as 'Hawk's way of going and never questioning the leader about how she did it. Or realizing that 'Hawk had probably made that door and others like it throughout her neighborhood. It was so convenient to just accept the mystery as part of the legend without thinking about 'Hawk spending her whole life working out practical things like moving through places where other people wouldn't dare go.

It wasn't until the general asked, that 'Hawk realized Tiên Le didn't know about her network of entrances and exits and paths through the underworld. Her recent brush with death brought home to her that she was getting older and that she wasn't immortal. That someday Tiên Le might have to take her place. Tiên Le was right — the general needed to know these things.

"Tiên Le, if we live through this, I'll teach you everything I know."

The light of the station platform was a welcome sight to Tiên Le. The few people on the platform who saw them climb the ladder from the tracks acted like nothing was out of the ordinary and went about their own business. 'Hawk had instructed her general to board the train at the opposite end of the platform and to disembark at the next stop. 'Hawk was not fond of riding subway trains unless they were empty. People always looked at her like she was one of those people they'd heard about; why they shouldn't ride the subway at night. Looking non-threatening was something 'Hawk never managed to do.

The next station was situated in D. Antonio's turf. So was the Gun and Rifle Club where 'Hawk often went to practice marksmanship. Residents of the area were accustomed to the sight of their neighboring warlord on her way to the firing range. If she didn't come alone, she had a youth with her but the youth never wore colors and 'Hawk never looked like she was spoiling for a fight. She paid for carefully watched passage through this part of town. She emerged from the subway casually as though she had nothing more on her mind than innocent target practice. Tiên Le reached the street five minutes later and walked the opposite direction.

'Hawk's plan worked. She created an illusion: no one would believe a warlord would walk through enemy territory, alone, during a war. So she went unchallenged, playing on people's lack of belief. Disappearing in a blind spot, she doubled back to the building where she'd sent Tiên Le.

She joined her general at the bottom of the fire escape. "Put your gloves on," 'Hawk instructed, "there's a lookout on top of this building. Tiên Le," 'Hawk's voice became grave and commanding, "I don't want any witnesses."

Tiên Le smudged her face with dirt, put her gloves on and nodded. She understood and was prepared to do what was necessary. They encountered the lookout almost immediately after reaching the rooftop. Silently, cold-bloodedly, Tiên Le broke the man's neck using a technique that would end his life without suffering or

150

screaming. They left the dead man and stole quietly to the other side of the building.

Crouched behind the ledge, 'Hawk reassembled her rifle, added the silencer and loaded it. She braced the gun on the ledge, snorting contemptuously. D. Antonio was right where she thought he would be. In his apartment, probably plotting his next senseless act of revenge. She could see one other man with her enemy in the lighted room. Their arrogance amazed her. How this man could leave himself so completely open to attack with practically no protection was beyond her.

She set her sights, aimed carefully and squeezed the trigger. Then instantly repeated the process three more times to strike each man with two bullets to eliminate their chances of survival. The bullets shattered the window and found their marks. The bloody bodies slumped over the table. 'Hawk grunted. Disgusting but necessary business. She broke the hot, smoking rifle apart quickly, gave part of it to her general, picked up the shell casings and they fled the same way they had come.

Chapter Ten

'Hawk and Tiên Le could have easily returned to the Subway Club through the front door. Maggie had opened the place up because the bar served as a protected meeting place for war councils, the only circumstances under which the youth gang hierarchy was allowed into the establishment, and the only time the Subway Club became a juice bar. The last thing 'Hawk needed was to get busted for serving alcohol to minors.

'Hawk chose instead to begin her general's lessons of the complex physical operations she had perfected over the years. The two women entered through the rooftop of the three story building above the Club.

Tiên Le was filled with wonder and intrigued by the internal structure of the place. It was a virtual fortress. Its most predominant feature was that it was fireproof, reconstructed almost completely of cinder blocks and asbestos. It was well-stocked with supplies, too.

"You did all this?" Tiên Le asked, astounded.

"Most of it. I had an ex-Marine help me. He had a habit. . . .'" 'Hawk explained. Tiên Le could fill in the blanks to surmise the man had worked for drugs as payment.

"You own this whole building?"

'Hawk stopped to inspect a metal cabinet of supplies. "Yeah, I bought it when I was fifteen with money I made from selling drugs to rich white kids."

"Now you had to have had help with that," Tiên Le put forth.

"No shit," 'Hawk agreed. "Rich white girl runs away from home; I find her; daddy is grateful; to repay me he negotiated the purchase for me." 'Hawk shrugged her shoulders as if everybody did things that way. It was simple to her.

Tiên Le leaned against a pillar, suddenly perplexed. *"Fifteen."* She was fascinated by 'Hawk's thoroughness. Did 'Hawk prepare for *everything*? "How old *are* you?" Tiên Le inquired.

'Hawk looked into the distance briefly puzzling over the question. It had been awhile since she'd last figured her age. "Best guess . . . thirty-three. No one seems to really know. All anybody would say was something like 'when my Randy was five, you were around then,' and then they'd figure from there by trying to remember how old I looked at the time."

"So you've spent over half your life preparing and maintaining this place. Incredible. Why?" Tiên Le asked boldly.

'Hawk placed rat poison around and changed a light bulb before answering. "Security, I suppose. I knew no one but me was ever really going to take care of me. But taking care of me is easy, Tiên Le. I needed *more* than that. I think I always knew I wasn't like other people. And it's more than my eyes. I like protecting people. It makes me feel good. I'm better at it than other people. Even Paulo. He's good, but I'm better."

Tiên Le read between the lines (something she did well). 'Hawk was telling her that she had to protect *herself*, too, and she was better at that than other people. This fortress over her club was a manifestation of the fortress around her heart. And very few people ever got inside either place.

Tiên Le blinked when she discovered 'Hawk staring at her.

"Where were you?" 'Hawk said cautiously, unsure how to ask something so personal.

"Thinking about Maggie," Tiên Le revealed. Interacting with 'Hawk with such honesty felt warm and safe.

"Oh?" 'Hawk wondered guardedly.

"Do you think she takes me seriously? I mean with me being so much younger? Hell, I've only been alive two years longer than you've known her." Tiên Le couldn't see that she placed an unreasonable value on chronological age.

"Of course she takes you seriously. Everybody does. She's what? Forty? And you're . . . ?"

"Twenty-eight."

"So?"

"So, I couldn't bear it if she thought I was too young for her," Tiên Le insisted, wanting some kind of reassurance that this thing between her and Maggie would withstand pressures from outside the relationship.

'Hawk appraised her friend closely. "You're in love with her, aren't you?"

Tiên Le was surprised 'Hawk even knew what being in love was. She admitted she was in love with Maggie.

Studying the general, 'Hawk asked, "Have you slept with her?"

"Yes, I have."

'Hawk laughed out loud, giving a congratulatory slap on her friend's arm. "Way to go, Tiên Le! That woman hasn't slept with anyone for *years*. Was she good?"

Tiên Le smiled, remembering the event. "Very."

"And you're worried about age differences? Do you know how many women have been trying to nail her? Christ. You lucky shit. She more than takes you serious, good buddy. You cracked the big one, my friend. Just see to it you take good care of her. Maggie is special people," 'Hawk cautioned.

Tiên Le's smile widened. "You can count on it, 'Hawk. Thanks."

'Hawk patted her general's arm and motioned toward the staircase to the club below.

A heated discussion going on among the members of 'Hawk's army (comprised of women and youths) covered 'Hawk and Tiên Le's surreptitious entrance through one of the secret panels in the wall. They stood quietly in a dark corner listening to the argument.

'Hawk's president, Shadow, was maintaining his cool while maintaining that 'Hawk was still alive. It was clear that the rumor of her death had begun to foster doubt among her followers.

"You should be warlord now, Shadow!" one young man asserted. Another picked up the tone of insurgency. "Yeah, now, while you have the chance." There was always someone whose nature it was to instigate violent actions no matter how loyal they professed to be.

"No," Shadow insisted crossly. "'Hawk is *not* dead. Anyway, Tiên Le is general, and next in line is Shirl. *Then* me. That's the way 'Hawk wants it and that's the way it's gonna be."

'Hawk was pleased that she had not misjudged or over-estimated Shadow. She felt honored by his loyalty.

"Well if 'Hawk ain't dead, where is she?" someone else demanded.

"I'm right here," 'Hawk spoke up striding confidently out of the darkness into the fracas. Tiên Le followed, slightly tickled by her leader's ability to manipulate people and situations. Both women stopped amid the surprised murmurs and exclamations of relief to hug Maggie. 'Hawk whispered to Maggie that she was fine in response to the bartender's worried expression. Tiên Le didn't entirely let go of her lover but turned to watch 'Hawk take control of the situation. To one of her women she questioned, "Where are Shirl and Reneé?"

"Out on patrol. We were worried about *you*, 'Hawk . . . ," the woman ventured.

'Hawk ignored the concern. She shook hands with Shadow, nodding favorably to him before she turned her steely gaze on the young men who were agitating against the outline of her leadership. "If I ever see another breach of discipline like that again, you two gentlemen will be looking for a new place to live." The young men looked at the floor uneasily shifting their weight from one foot to another. They could take anything but hearing 'Hawk scold them in clear, precise English. When she talked street-talk to them they knew she was never seriously angry with them for their infractions of the rules. But a trial by fire would have been easier to face than having 'Hawk single them out to upbraid them with the same language a teacher or youth worker would use. She meant what she said and they understood it. Others looked at them with a mixture of fear and sympathy. The stricken, apologetic looks on the boys' faces convinced her she need say nothing more and lost her anger instantly.

"I have it on good authority that D. Antonio Petrazzia is no longer with us." 'Hawk let the gathering express their relief and happiness for a minute before continuing. "We are still in a state of war. There is no way to know if he initiated any attack plans before he was wasted." She let the seriousness of her statement take affect. It didn't trouble her that this group was probably speculating about who had eliminated the enemy leader. They could be trusted not to speculate too loudly or around anyone who couldn't be trusted. "Shadow, you're coming with me. Tiên Le is in charge while I take care of some other business," 'Hawk ordered before leaving.

Tiên Le knew her leader could not risk spending any more time with her, especially where 'Hawk was going. She turned her attention to getting everyone through the balance of the night in one piece.

* * *

On the way to the place where they were now waiting, 'Hawk had told Shadow about her plans for him. That special job she had in mind for him was warlord of the neighborhood to the south of hers. He was pleased, excited and apprehensive. "I know you're ready for this, Shadow," she had said. "Me and Paulo are going to make certain everyone else understands it, too."

Shadow wasn't overly thrilled about having someone else fighting his battle for him. Under normal circumstances he would have commanded his own hostile take-over of a neighborhood. But it would have been of his own neighborhood. Not someone else's neighborhood. And these weren't normal circumstances. Something extreme had to be done, and now. "I'm tired of fighting wars against nut cases. I should have done this months ago," 'Hawk had lamented. She blamed herself for the recent deaths of her people, and had no forgiveness for herself for her lack of foresight. With Shadow as warlord and one of Paulo's people as general, she could expect peace between her and the southern neighborhood. Right now, peace appealed to her.

The police helicopter that had been hovering over them, shining its searchlight all around them, moved on. The streetlamps seemed dim by comparison. Everyone not wanting to be in the spotlight breathed easier and began to move about. The black step-van 'Hawk had been waiting for came into view, cruising slowly. The vehicle's headlights blinked twice and the sliding door on the passenger side came open. 'Hawk and Shadow broke from their cover, running up to the moving van and leaping into it smoothly. The van continued to move down the dimly lit street at its same lazy pace.

'Hawk smiled at the tall, cool man leaning against the panel behind the driver. His smile was equally warm with welcome. These two warlords respected each other. There was a deep admiration for the others' strengths and abilities. They held a common belief in the power and responsibility of leadership being put to use to benefit people. The depth of their kinship and friendship had withstood the test of time, transcending gender and race and ego. It was an extraordinary relationship.

The presidents accompanying the warlords watched the greeting carefully and suspiciously, each knowing his leader well and looking for signs of conflict.

But the warlords fell into an easy rhythm of comradeship. They had been excited about seeing one another again, although they were careful not to show it.

"Thanks for coming, Paulo," 'Hawk said gratefully. They shared a solid handshake.

"I'll always be there for *you*, 'Hawk," Paulo stated with something akin to love in his voice. He pulled the ring from his pocket and handed it back to its owner. The gesture spoke of guarded tenderness. 'Hawk slipped the ring back on the empty finger. Paulo had had the ring made for her nearly twenty years ago. It felt just as special now as it had then.

"And D. Antonio?" Paulo asked darkly. Their emotional communion could only go so far before it grew uncomfortable. 'Hawk took the cue and was all business once more. She leaned against the opposite wall of the vehicle and lit a cigarette. "Wasted."

Paulo grunted his approval. There were two things Paulo saw as constant about 'Hawk: her courage and her aim. "This is Isaiah." Paulo motioned for the muscular, bearded black youth to greet 'Hawk. "Hey," he said, leaning forward to shake 'Hawk's hand. He was surprised by the strength in her hand. What he'd heard about her eyes was true. They were spooky. She appraised him quickly and nodded. The same applied to Shadow. Isaiah was surprised this tailored looking person had such a firm grip. Paulo was pleased to see the sharp youth return his gaze gracefully without giving an inch. 'Hawk had herself a well-groomed and no doubt expertly trained leader on her hands. The choice for warlord was obvious, but he had to make a show of promoting Isaiah anyway.

Before the van crossed over into hostile territory, Paulo had his driver hold up. "We need to talk about who's going to be warlord."

'Hawk let her cigarette dangle from her lips. She raised her cap and hooked her thumbs in her studded belt. "Yes, we do," she agreed, sternly locking Paulo's eyes with her own. "Shadow is highly motivated to straighten these people out."

"He's how old?" Paulo demanded.

"Eighteen."

"Isaiah is nineteen and has fought in two wars; one to the west and one to the north," Paulo maintained. He wasn't at all surprised when 'Hawk told of Shadow's four wars, all with the south.

The two young men in question waited anxiously, almost resentfully while their betters decided their future without consulting them. When Paulo made his concession, it was with the reassurance that if Shadow couldn't cut it as warlord, Isaiah would be close by, able to take over. For now the older youth was given the title general. Paulo was sure Shadow would win Isaiah's confidence and loyalty in short order.

Now came the difficult task: getting the southern people to accept these hand-picked leaders. Paulo told his driver to move along and the warriors tensed for the struggle ahead of them.

The van crept down the quiet street; its occupants were alert, scanning the area through the front windows and mirrors. Knowing where D. Antonio's apartment was was one thing. Knowing where his band of people hung out was another. The location changed regularly. The van turned the corner, the invaders were still looking.

"There," Shadow said quietly, pointing to the right rear view mirror. He had seen two youths with painted faces and bright clothing scamper across the street behind the passing vehicle.

The driver spotted three more youths in his mirror who were running toward the same place. He turned down the next alleyway and through to the next street. The sidewalk along the front of an abandoned building was littered with sleeping bodies. The van halted, those inside waited for another clue.

Isaiah perked up. "Listen." He heard music coming from their left.

"I've seen that car before," Shadow added. He'd seen it at an inner city basketball tournament. "That's the Jag Maulers' car," he said identifying the neighborhood's meanest youth gang. As if on cue one of the colorful individuals appeared in front of the building then slipped inside the front entrance.

The foursome jumped out of the van and split up; 'Hawk and Isaiah went to the back, Paulo and Shadow to the front.

Covering the back door, waiting for the signal for the ambush, 'Hawk drew her weapon. She rolled her eyes skyward when Isaiah pulled an Uzi machine gun from his coat. She sometimes forgot about delicate male egos requiring the support of that much fire-power. To have become Paulo's president, Isaiah had to have learned some discipline. 'Hawk had to go on trust that this young man wouldn't over-react. 'Hawk checked the door and found it locked. She hated admitting that her shoulder was stiffening up on her, but now was not the time to let her own pride and ego get in her way. "Son, I have a fresh bullet hole in my shoulder and I'd rather not break this door in," she confided. Besides, he was massive — this door would be nothing for him.

Isaiah puffed himself up with chivalry. "I'll do it, 'Hawk."

"Good man." 'Hawk favored him with a smile and grip on the shoulder.

They heard Paulo's shrill whistle and moved into action. Isaiah was good as his word, smashing the door in and rushing into the meeting place. There were men scrambling and women screaming everywhere. Two men charged 'Hawk and Isaiah; one dispatched by the butt of Isaiah's gun, the other by 'Hawk's back-handed fist. The heavily-ringed blow tore open the man's cheek; he screamed as he fell and rolled away in agony. Paulo and Shadow had countered similar attacks leaving five men either unconscious or doubled in pain between the four of them. The fighting stopped suddenly once the main line of defense collapsed.

The invaders began barking orders to move people into the center of the room and disarm themselves. They dragged the injured men into the circle and made everyone be quiet. 'Hawk was not impressed by this motley group. Evidence of three organized youth gangs and the fragments of an adult unit was detectable. She began unloading the small arsenal they'd collected, while Isaiah covered the front door and Paulo and Shadow guarded their captives.

A tall, pock-marked man stepped forward as the group's spokesperson. "Man, what you want with us? This is Dapper Toni's opera-tion . . ."

"Not any more," Shadow cut in. "It's *mine* now."

"Someone's coming," Isaiah announced.

The group seemed confident, thinking Dapper Toni was coming to rescue them. The invaders remained calm but alert.

A young man burst through the door and was taken from behind by Isaiah. The newcomer became compliant with a gun at his head. "Dapper Toni is dead," he said shakily. He had hoped his news would start a fierce battle for leadership. But he was too late.

Whispers flashed through the huddled gathering.

"That's right, D. Antonio is dead. And since you people don't seem to know how to do things down here, we're gonna do it for you." Shadow's speech was fluid and commanding.

"Who are you, and *says* who?" the spokesman demanded.

"I'm Shadow. I've been Nighthawk's president for three years. I'm your warlord now. This here is Isaiah. He was Paulo's president; he's my general now," Shadow advised smoothly. His confidence was disarming and reassuring.

More whispering and acknowledging. Some of them had recognized Nighthawk and deduced the third man was Paulo. Even the men who had been unconscious were getting clear on their situation. Their warlord was dead, and the two powerful warlords from the north were taking over with new leadership. They were left with no choice but to accept the mandate.

After a lengthy meeting, Paulo and 'Hawk left, taking the arsenal with them as a guarantee against an uprising. A truce had been declared in their wake and they both felt good about the chances of the newly promoted ex-presidents. Paulo dropped 'Hawk off at her club. The war was over. It was time to get some rest.

Chapter Eleven

Rest was about all 'Hawk could call what she'd gotten during the day that had just passed. Lack of activity was a better description. She had come home and fallen into bed, completely exhausted. She would drift off to sleep only to be terrorized by nightmares. Her sleep would end abruptly leaving her struggling for breath and shaking. Then the sweat would break out, cold and clammy as the touch of death on her skin. She would shiver and huddle into her blankets until she got warm and slept. Then it would begin all over again.

If she believed in God she would have prayed to him to free her of this living hell. She didn't know what else she could do to make good the lost lives; surely something could be arranged. But 'Hawk didn't believe in God or the devil. She believed in survival. Which meant all she could do was survive her ordeal — silently and alone in her dark bedroom. The thought that a young woman lay in the next room who could be called upon for comfort was as far removed from 'Hawk as a divine being to bargain with.

When night time came her internal clock let her know she could get up and take a break from the process . . . a process that might last as long as a week. She stood under the hot shower until it ran cold, then stayed there some more to shock her body into activity.

Dressed, she ignored Lori and the offer of food. She walked into the bar, unconsciously needing Maggie's company to soothe her nerves.

Maggie had extra gauze and tape that Tattoo had left for Lori's wound. She'd already helped the passive, distant captive change the dressing on her thigh. She was back to being emotionally available for Lori, hoping she could bring the girl out of her silent world. Mindful of how she had spent so many years of her own life, Maggie controlled the amount of pain drugs Lori received. She wasn't going to repay the girl's life-saving efforts by giving her a drug habit to support. In fact Maggie was seriously considering finding a way to free the girl to some situation where the girl's spirit could be rehabilitated. She'd even discussed the possibility with Tiên Le, who agreed with the idea and offered to help support Lori financially.

But any anger she'd been building for 'Hawk's callous treatment was set aside when she saw the drawn look on her friend's face. She set the gauze, tape and scissors on the counter in front of 'Hawk and walked around to her. She coaxed the coat off the leader, and less easily, the holster and shirt. Pulling the old, wet dressing off the wound, she tried to keep 'Hawk's mind off what she was doing. The big woman had little patience for being fussed over.

"On the news they said D. Antonio had been executed by a professional assassin. They think he was wasted over a bad drug deal. There were all kinds of drugs in his apartment when they found him. Now they're saying all the violence was drug related and now that D. Antonio is dead their troubles are over," Maggie related.

'Hawk reached into her jacket for a cigarette and lit it. "Assholes. Don't think a *woman* can pull off a clean hit," 'Hawk growled bitterly. Her pride smarted but her reason reigned. "Fine with me. They won't look very far for anybody who picks off a major drug dealer. Let the Mayor have a feather in his cap. Just so long as they stay out of *my* face. Thanks, Maggie." 'Hawk dressed again, looking around her. "This place is a wreck. Get white meat out here to help you clean up," she ordered imperiously.

Jarred by the heartless command, Maggie was frozen for a second of disbelief followed by the reactivation of the mad she had brewing against 'Hawk.

"That *does* it," Maggie breathed hatefully. In all her years as 'Hawk's friend she had never talked back to her. "I've had it with you, *war* lord." The words were like poisoned arrows shot from a powerful crossbow. "You can just get yourself another bartender, mister, because I'm not going to work here another minute." Maggie pulled off her apron and threw it meanly on the floor.

Before she could turn and stomp off 'Hawk grabbed her by the upper arm and yanked her close. Maggie's temper crackled and flashed even in the face of 'Hawk's deadly eyes.

"What the fuck are you talking about?" 'Hawk asked fiercely.

"I'm talking about *Lori*, and the shitty way you treat her. Especially after what she's done," Maggie answered with equal intensity.

"Who the fuck is Lori? What's gotten into you, woman?"

Maggie was about to hurl the term white meat back at 'Hawk when it dawned on her that 'Hawk really *didn't* know what had gotten into her. Mouth slightly parted she replied with a look of puzzlement. "You don't know, do you?"

"Know what?" 'Hawk said impatiently.

"That Carla wasn't dead when you left. She had another gun and Lori," Maggie pointed toward the apartment, "that girl you've been keeping all this time, spotted the gun, shoved me out of the way and took the bullet in her thigh. Carla was aiming at *me*, 'Hawk, and Lori saved my life. She saved all our lives."

'Hawk let go of Maggie's arm and staggered backwards to a stool. She let the stool help hold her up. Maggie was surprised by 'Hawk's reaction. The leader was completely stunned by the information.

"Lori heard Carla talking to D. Antonio on the phone. She told me what she heard and I told you. If she hadn't, we would have all been gunned down where we stood." Maggie was beginning to feel concerned about the leader. She'd never seen 'Hawk have trouble taking something in. 'Hawk had always dealt with everything that came her way, and immediately, without hesitation. Maggie felt like the big woman had just taken a dagger, square in her heart. "Are you all right?" she asked gravely.

'Hawk *had* taken a dagger, clean through her heart. An emotional stabbing. Maggie's revelation had paid no heed whatsoever to the impenetrable fortress around her heart. How could the information that Lori had sacrificed herself so completely for 'Hawk and others stop outside the blockade when it was what 'Hawk had wanted all her life? She had never consciously set it up that way but she had always been looking for a woman of courage and loyalty with the generosity to use them, even at the expense of her own life. Sure, Tiên Le fit that description, but the general was more of a reflection of 'Hawk herself. 'Hawk needed someone who would exist solely for her, not having any desire beyond pleasing her. Someone who was strong in a different way. A woman whose love went beyond the conventional to the exceptional.

The very idea that Lori might *be* that woman frightened and confused 'Hawk. Not only that she might be that woman but may have given the ultimate proof that she *was* that woman was barely acceptable to 'Hawk. And she hadn't even noticed the girl was injured! That was how effectively she'd ignored her. 'Hawk didn't answer Maggie's question. Instead she said, "Please don't quit, Maggie. I need you," and retreated to the far end of the club and sat down.

Maggie watched her friend carefully all night long. The big woman never moved. She just sat there, quiet and withdrawn, not speaking to anyone, smoking cigarettes and picking at the food she'd been given. She was still sitting there after the last patron had gone and Maggie closed up.

Maggie put her coat on and walked over to 'Hawk. She touched her gently saying, "See you tomorrow, 'Hawk," and left.

* * *

'Hawk warred with herself all night and her demons all day. When she rose from the battleground of her bed she had the feeling she'd lost in both the arenas of heart and spirit. She went through as much of her weight workout as she could without aggravating her injury.

She had tried for so many years to keep everyone out of that vulnerable place in her heart. Even Sophia, as dear as she was to 'Hawk, had never breached the chasm to get completely inside. But Lori had. Damn her. An innocent, docile, sexy white girl had done what 'Hawk was sure no one would *ever* do. Having stopped to think about it, 'Hawk discovered that she'd known from the first night Lori had the potential to win her way past the defenses 'Hawk built.

'Hawk had ignored the victory celebration going on around her the night before. She had been replaying all her interactions with Lori during the past months, remembering with precise clarity how the girl had endured the cruelty, the neglect, the destruction of her personhood without a single complaint.

'Hawk asked herself why, if she'd known from the beginning that she was attracted to and excited by the girl, had she not let her pass, unchallenged? Even more illogical was the proclamation of seizure, those tattoos, the banding. Why had she worked so hard to make sure that girl didn't get away from her? Why was she so relieved when she found out Three Eagles was in jail? Or so angry at the Indian for having hurt Lori? Or callous about the gang rape?

Could it have been because she wanted Lori for herself? When'Hawk dared herself to answer yes, just for the sake of argument, all she had done made sense. She'd spotted the girl, wanted her, taken her and found the perfect excuse to keep her. That was all well and good but there were a couple of flies in the ointment. Like the girl's race. There would be those who would argue that the girl was trying to save her own skin by alerting Maggie about Carla's conversation. But taking a bullet meant for someone else? That leveled the scales in anybody's book. 'Hawk didn't care what other people thought anyway. Lori had proven herself to be as worthy as anyone she knew. 'Hawk let go of her reluctance to be close to a white woman pretty easily. Not so easy to let go of was her concern that this girl might still be in love with Three Eagles.

She remembered the first and last drunk she'd tied on because she realized that, while she held captive the girl's body, Three Eagles possessed the girl's heart. You couldn't put a tattoo on a heart; you couldn't put a heart in shackles. A heart had to be given, freely. And 'Hawk had done very little to try to get the girl to change her mind about whom she chose to love.

'Hawk didn't like not being able to make Lori love her. But she could at least find out if the girl found her attractive, if she were even willing to have some kind of relationship with her. She wondered how Tiên Le had gotten through to Maggie. Maybe she would ask her friend one day.

For now, 'Hawk only knew of one way to relate to a woman with anything resembling intimacy, and that was with sex. She put her barbell down. Her shower could wait; she was going to take her chances with the girl in the next room. She took the two small-linked chains she'd used on Lori the night of the gang rape from her pants pocket, her cigarettes and matches from her coat pocket, and opened her bedroom door.

Lori was jolted from her work by the sound of the door opening. She always timed her work to coincide with the weightlifting sessions and then the shower so that she could have 'Hawk's breakfast ready when she came out of her room fully dressed.

She was just preparing to heat the pan for bacon when she heard the door open unexpectedly. She turned sharply toward the door, her hands coming to her mouth to cover her gasp.

There was 'Hawk, standing there with practically nothing on. No hat, jacket, pants, boots or knife sheath; all she wore was her net shirt, holster, gun and black leather strap that held her dildo. Lori was mesmerized and tantalized. The sight of 'Hawk's powerfully muscled legs and arms shocked Lori out of her tiny world. The midnight skin glistened with the shine of sweat 'Hawk had worked up with her weights.

Lori noticed the big woman set something on the kitchen table then lean back confidently against the door jamb. Lori's visual tour took in the hardened nipples and taut stomach showing through the fine netting of the shirt. The Colt .45 both frightened her and appealed to her. She had not heard the rumors about 'Hawk being dead and hadn't been told the warlord had been shot. The dressing under the holster worried her, but not for long. Her growing desire tugged her eyes downward to the long black pole dangling between 'Hawk's partly spread legs. Why was 'Hawk doing this? Why was she allowing herself to be so vulnerable (or as vulnerable as anyone who has a loaded cannon can be?) Why so deliberately provocative?

'Hawk was pleased with the girl's reaction. Those brown eyes had gotten so big, and that wonderful chest was heaving so *hard*. In a sexual context, Sophia was the only woman who had ever seen her full-grown body with her coat and hat off. *No* woman had seen her with her pants and boots off, too. She was really taking a gamble by letting this girl see her this completely.

"Like what you see?" 'Hawk asked with a low voice that betrayed her own response to this scene. The girl kept her hands over her mouth but her head moved up and down appreciatively, almost eagerly.

Their eyes met. This time Lori's didn't lower fearfully as they had in the past. This time they were foggy with unashamed desire. 'Hawk didn't think she could stay standing in the face of that great a need. She turned the kitchen chair so she could sit on it and still keep the contact. The thrill of it flashed through her. "Come here, bitch," she invited demandingly.

Lori's heart jumped a hurdle inside her chest. Her hands came away from her mouth to land over her heart as though she could just get it to beat normally again. 'Hawk had finally said the word she was literally dying to hear. And she'd said it to her. Not white meat. Bitch. Bitch; that meant 'Hawk acknowledged her. More than that! It meant 'Hawk was conferring a special status upon her. Could it be true? Was she really "'Hawk's woman"? Better yet: "The *Nighthawk's* woman?" Lori didn't think for a minute that this meant 'Hawk loved her. She didn't care. She was somebody again. 'Hawk's bitch!

She dazedly drew closer. A movement caught her attention. Looking downward she saw 'Hawk working her cock with her hand.

Gracefully she went down on her knees between 'Hawk's spread thighs. Totally focused she let her hand circle the black thing so she could guide it into her mouth. She gently caressed the base when 'Hawk's hand withdrew and worked more and more of the end into her mouth, remembering what she'd been taught.

'Hawk knew the more aroused her partner was the easier it would be for her to accept the rod into her throat. She smoothed her hands up Lori's arms to the bands of silver. She grasped the chains that extended from the armbands to the nipples and began to tug on them; rhythmically and with increasing intensity, yanking the nipple rings without actually touching them.

Her sex toy was beginning to glow and croon and moan and

flow. The beautifully skilled head was taking longer and longer glides down her pole getting closer and closer to her pelvis. Her fingers pulled harder and harder on the chains as the weight of the breasts resisted and strained. 'Hawk was pulling the breasts apart then letting them slap together then pulling them apart again. Her excitement was building, swelling, growing.

"Suck it, bitch. Take it *all* in. You can do it. Come on, bitch," she encouraged passionately. "Do it. Work it. Deeper," she commanded. "Faster!"

Lori's head bobbed up and down, her pace quickening. She knew she was working 'Hawk into a fever and she was loving it. Her own excitement was barely containable. What 'Hawk was doing to her nipples was incredible.

'Hawk couldn't stand it any more. The girl's soft hair had grown half way down her back and it had been so long since she had touched it. She dropped the chains and grabbed the head letting her fingers revel in the silky feeling stuff. She mashed Lori's face into her pelvis and fucked the mouth and throat furiously, her hips lifting from the chair. No more restraining her responses to this girl. She let it all free, and it came out in long, gurgling yells and "Fuck, yeahs". She came *over* and *over* and *over*.

She thought it a good thing that she was sitting in a chair because she doubted she'd be able to move for a week. This was the most fantastic release she'd ever experienced.

Lori was *filled* with pride. Seeing this mighty body heave and sigh with glorious relief made her feel special. 'Hawk made a feeble attempt to pull out of Lori's mouth but was too wasted. Lori emptied her mouth and turned to reach for a towel from the stove handle to clean away the spit and mucus and tears such a ravaging produced.

Sitting back on her heels, she waited quietly for 'Hawk to recover and either require more of her sexually or leave to take her shower.

When 'Hawk could move what she wanted was a cigarette. What a luxury it was to sit stretched out, smoking a cigarette and admiring this sexy girl. No more running from her need, *and*, she decided, no more thinking she didn't have time for a hot tumble with this desirable wench. The girl was hers, wasn't she? It was why she'd had all this sex jewelry made in the first place. To play with and enjoy. And the girl seemed willing to do *that* much anyway.

Hadn't the girl lighted up like a neon sign when she called her "bitch"? And, god, could she give head. Better than Shirl's bitch, if that was possible.

For the first time, 'Hawk actually really *looked* at Lori. And that was when she noticed the bandage on the girl's thigh.

"Does it hurt much?" 'Hawk asked.

Lori's head came up sharply, eyes filled with questions.

"Your thigh?" clarified 'Hawk.

"Some," Lori answered meekly. "Maggie gives me pills."

"Stand up."

Lori stood and looked on with fascination as 'Hawk peeled back the dressing to see. The girl would have a hole in her thigh and a none-too-pretty scar to show for her courage. "Tattoo dig it out?"

"Yes."

'Hawk put the dressing back. "She's dug a couple out of me, too. We're lucky to have her around." 'Hawk sat up straight. "You're a brave girl."

Lori couldn't respond to 'Hawk's comment. She didn't feel brave. She contended to herself that any one of 'Hawk's people would have done the same. She just happened to have been there. That was all. She reached out and touched 'Hawk's wounded shoulder with tender, inquiring fingers.

"I'm fine," Hawk said shortly. That her injury concerned the girl was more than the leader could cope with. She took the hand carefully away and changed the subject.

"God damn, you turn me on," she admitted letting her fingers fiddle with the chain dangling between Lori's nipples.

The breasts raised and lowered in response to the insinuating touch and exciting confession. She *wanted* to turn 'Hawk on, and please her and make her proud.

'Hawk picked up the chains from the table and attached them to Lori's cunt rings. She turned the girl around so she could fasten the other ends of the chains to the ring embedded in the back of Lori's waistband. Turning the girl back around, 'Hawk whistled her appreciation of the effect the chains created. The cunt lips were separated to completely expose the clitoris to view, touch and torment. It was a thoroughly exciting sight.

"Unbelievable!" 'Hawk breathed. She let her fingertips trickle over the organ, watching it get harder and stand out more prominently. She listened to the girl sigh and whimper her approval as she played with the red point. The vulnerable sex was wet and fragrant. 'Hawk's other hand began to tug on the chain between the nipples while she set about thumping the throbbing clitoris with her finger. Faster and faster she tugged and thumped until the girl was mad with pleasure. Suddenly the girl reached down and deftly pushed 'Hawk's finger inside her soaked cunt. 'Hawk took over from there, fucking the girl and grinding her thumb into the clitoris.

"Come to me, bitch!" 'Hawk ordered gruffly. "Come!"

Lori shook and screamed and bounced on 'Hawk's hand as the tension snapped and devastated her. 'Hawk pulled her so she would land against her, keeping her finger inside to delight in the pulsing contractions of Lori's cunt.

She waited until the girl was completely recovered before she left to take a shower and begin her night.

* * *

'Hawk didn't know which was worse: staying home with her nightmares and cold sweats or being out during the day to attend this funeral. She recognized one of the police officers guarding the entrance to the century-old Catholic church. One of them had been a member of her organization almost a decade ago and was a cousin to the slain boy. 'Hawk stopped at the top of the stairs, cautiously keeping her back to the same door as the officer. She greeted the officer prudently. "Roberto."

Roberto waved off his partner's suspicious glance toward 'Hawk. All eyes jumped uneasily down the street and up to the rooftops. 'Hawk's lookouts were in place as additional precautions against unwarranted violence. No threats had been issued by anyone — yet. Funerals were targeted regularly for retaliation between warring factions. Although the war was officially over, it was never wise to be too confident. The police officer was pleased to see 'Hawk attending this service; her presence reassured him that she still cared.

A youth worker stopped to stare at 'Hawk before going inside the church. He looked weary and sad. Briefly he looked accusatory, but the look faded. Like so many others, the youth worker wanted to find a scapegoat for the senseless killings. 'Hawk was an obvious choice. But then he arrived at the same conclusion everyone else arrived at: 'Hawk wasn't a god. 'Hawk couldn't protect everyone, all the time. When the officer Roberto greeted him, the youth worker had to admit to himself that 'Hawk had always done more good than harm. Roberto wouldn't even be alive today, much less a member of the force, had it not been for 'Hawk's guidance. 'Hawk had almost always succeeded where the system failed. Roberto was living proof of that. "Roberto, 'Hawk," the worker volunteered. Saying nothing more he went inside.

'Hawk relaxed a little. If the youth worker wasn't worried about an attack, the chances improved that the funeral would remain the solemn affair it was meant to be.

Roberto held 'Hawk up. "A man was found in an alley with a bullet in his head. He'd bled to death. The bullet matched the ones that killed D. Antonio."

"Really," 'Hawk noted blandly. "Whoever pulled the trigger has probably already destroyed the weapon," she speculated.

"Probably," Roberto agreed. "We haven't got any leads, and no witnesses are coming forward. The captain is still sticking with the professional assassin theory. It's believed the man who gunned down Jesus is the man who died with D. Antonio," Roberto added almost smugly. It wasn't necessarily American justice, but it was good enough for him.

"One less fool to look out for," 'Hawk concluded. The sun broke free of the clouds to announce the arrival of spring. Even with dark glasses on, it was too bright for 'Hawk's light-sensitive eyes. She went inside the crowded church for relief from the painful glare. So, she had hit the man who'd wounded her. Good, she thought, when all else failed her, her aim was still sharp. Knowing she'd also evened the score for Jesus made it no easier to face his family.

Members of the San Juan Social Club, the longest-organized youth gang in the city, stood at attention around the closed coffin of their fallen member, Jesus. Each young man wore a black jacket with their skull and crossbone emblem sewn on the back, white shirt, red bandana around the neck and blue jeans. It was a time-honored, traditional uniform that instilled pride in all of them. Jesus' jacket rested on the coffin next to a wreath. The San Juan Auxiliary, the girlfriends of the gang members, flanked the immediate family in the front pews. That Jesus had been a member of a gang appeared to be an accepted part of life for the couple who were obviously the boy's parents. That the younger brothers would probably follow in Jesus' footsteps seemed to weigh upon them. But the gang and their girls had been very supportive and sympathetic, offering to help the family in any way they could. And the funeral expenses, which were well beyond their meager means, had already been paid for. Anonymously, they'd been told.

In unison the members brought their fists to their chests to salute their warlord when she walked in the back door and stood behind the last pew. The action drew attention to her entrance, which she had hoped to avoid. Silently she removed her sunglasses and nodded her acknowledgement. The crowed rustled and whispered among themselves. They were surprised to see the Nighthawk attending the service. It had been years since she'd last been seen during the day. The leader was doing right by them all by making this special effort. As a show of solidarity, Aqueem, 'Hawk's new president, came to stand beside her. The long Mass got under way.

'Hawk had stood motionless and expressionless for the entire ceremony. The whole thing was easily as great an ordeal as her demon-ridden sleep would have been. She stopped the boy's parents before they left the church. "Your son died a hero. He will not be forgotten and his art will be saved," she told them reverently.

The mother looked away, unable to speak through her sobs and frightened by 'Hawk's frozen face. The father searched the stony, scarred face for solace but found none. He had heard the Nighthawk was a true warrior and now he could see he'd heard right. If she said his son was a hero, then that was what he was. And heroes never died in vain. The father nodded gravely and followed his family out of the church.

'Hawk closed her eyes, searching for the strength to go to the Riverside Church and go through this all over again at Bad Man's funeral. Her eyes came open when she felt a soft touch on her jacket sleeve. She looked down into Maggie's moist eyes. "Thanks for coming, 'Hawk. It meant a lot to everyone to have you here."

'Hawk had forgotten Maggie was close to the boy's family. She was glad to see her friend but she couldn't say so. Her large hand gently covered Maggie's knowingly. If anyone could guess how heavy was the burden on her heart, Maggie could. Together they walked into the noonday sun.

Three weeks had passed since the war ended. 'Hawk's nerves were calm for the most part. Shadow had made steady progress in the south. The prospect of peace between the two neighborhoods looked more realistic. Maggie and Tiên Le spent all their free time together. 'Hawk was charmed by the warmth and tenderness the couple engendered. The lover's uninhibited displays of affection inspired her to bring Lori into the bar to keep her company during the nine ball tournament she was hosting.

The Subway Club was crowded for the tournament; some of the women were from out of town and not familiar with the social structure of the hosting bar. Strangest and most fascinating to them was the naked white girl and the tension that surrounded her presence among them.

Most of the regular patrons had learned of Lori's role in sounding the alert that heralded the war, and being wounded trying to protect Maggie. Reactions to Lori's bravery ranged from completely impressed to resentful. There were still those who were unwilling to accept Lori no matter what she did. Most notably, Shirl's lover. For some time she had been 'Hawk's favorite sex partner and there was very little she wouldn't do to keep it that way. She was sulking anyway because Shirl was winning game after game. That meant she wasn't being paid any attention by Shirl, or 'Hawk. Because 'Hawk had that white pussy in her arms and wasn't even looking at her.

Since Shirl wasn't paying any attention, she began to drink more than she was allowed. Encouraged by her success with defying Shirl's rules, she began to flirt with one of the women from out of town (knowing local women wouldn't respond to her advances for fear of angering Shirl). She purposely chose a tough-looking woman who could be goaded into doing something dangerous. She told her unsuspecting victim about the white girl and how the girl was communal property and couldn't refuse the attentions of anyone who desired her. By the time 'Hawk got up to help Maggie bring some beer from the back cooler, Shirl's lover had fired the new woman up enough to risk taking advantage of Lori.

'Hawk surprised herself with the intensity of her possessiveness. New though the feeling was, she was quick to respond. From across the bar she shouted, "Hey, motherfucker, get your hands off my bitch!"

The whole of the bar clientele was stunned by the command. The interloper backed away instantly. Lori took in the sight of the stranger's hands letting go of her nipples; she turned sharply toward 'Hawk to see what it looked like to be fiercely defending the woman she owned. Lori was thrilled by the fire in 'Hawk's eyes. There must have been dozens of women who would have done anything to inspire that reaction from the leader. Lori was quick to cover her broad grin with her hands to avoid seeming *too* pleased with herself for winning her way into the warlord's heart and having it proclaimed loudly and clearly to everyone. She couldn't hide the sparkle in her eyes however. The happiness in them brought a smile to 'Hawk. There was hope in those wide, innocent eyes.

The guilty woman held up her hands and apologized. "Hey, man, I'm sorry." It was just plain stupidity to pick a fight over a woman in a strange bar with a full complement of locals in it.

"Forget it," 'Hawk replied good-naturedly. "You didn't know," she said, waving the incident off. She was having a good time and didn't really want to make an issue out of it. She'd finally admitted in public that the white girl was special to her. Who the hell was going to challenge her right to do so? Certainly no one she cared about. There had been a raised eyebrow or two followed by shrugs; even a congratulatory "It's about fuckin' time you took a woman." Tiên Le and Maggie blessed the announcement with favorable nods, and Shirl was far more interested in resuming her nine ball game.

Shirl's *lover* was fuming. She downed her drink and to avoid the woman she'd steered wrongly into 'Hawk's path, she went to order another, stiffer drink.

'Hawk took up her perch again pulling Lori to stand between her thighs. Completely relaxed she leaned into her woman's softness. Confident that she wasn't going to have to deal with any shit for her choice, 'Hawk allowed herself to enjoy the silky hair brushing her cheeks, Lori's quivering and sighs in response to large hands roaming over her blushing skin, her own belly shuddering with need.

Shirl had eliminated all but one of her opponents and was preparing for a best three out of five final match. She had been so focused that she had not noticed the increasingly louder, steadily viler insults spewing from the mouth of her drunken lover. Nor had anyone else particularly. Until the diatribe recklessly spilled over into a quiet break in the action around the pool table.

"Motherfucker's afraid of her own reflection," Shirl's lover jeered meanly. Filled with false courage, she had meant for the comment to be heard. She was pissed and wanted everybody to know it. She wasn't going to let 'Hawk's choice go unchallenged. Foolishly, she had expected Shirl to back her up. The glare coming back at her from Shirl was equally as deadly as 'Hawk's.

No fight was going to come from this situation. Shirl's lover had insulted Shirl's warlord. Shirl's loyalty was squarely with 'Hawk. She could *find* another lover, but if she lost 'Hawk's friendship, she'd *never* get it back.

'Hawk didn't look to see how Shirl was reacting. She knew how her friend felt about insubordination from mouthy bitches: they deserved what they got. She moved smoothly off her stool, pushing Lori away, and walked over to the defiant troublemaker. She grabbed the woman by the hair, pulled the head back and forced her to her knees.

It was only when she was on her knees, looking into 'Hawk's boiling eyes that Shirl's lover realized she was in big trouble. Her challenging angry expression was quickly traded for one of fear.

"I ain't afraid of *nothin'*," 'Hawk spat. "Least of all a cock-suckin', pussy-waggin' piece of trash like you."

"I'm sorry, 'Hawk. Please, I'm sorry," the woman appealed.

"You *are* sorry. Sorry-assed. But I'm going to give you a chance to do somethin' useful with that nasty mouth of yours," 'Hawk related mysteriously.

"Anything," the woman pleaded. "I'll do anything you say." She screamed when 'Hawk pulled her from her knees and dragged her across the floor to her stool and dropped her there.

'Hawk turned to the confused Lori who had no idea what had happened but could tell the woman on the floor was in serious trouble. Had 'Hawk not been so mad, she would have laughed at Lori's naivete. She hoisted the girl onto her stool and spread her legs. To Shirl's lover she instructed, "Let's see how much you disapprove of my bitch after you've licked her off."

The laughter that broke the tension was a cold, vicious laughter and was coming from everyone except Lori and Shirl's disfavored lover.

"No," the woman said defiantly. "No, I won't do it," she insisted. Nothing could be more repulsive to her than to orally pleasure the white girl she hated so much. Her head snapped back from the force of the slap Shirl delivered across her face.

"Do it, whore," Shirl demanded.

Wiping the tears from her eyes, the woman knew she had nowhere to turn. Her intractable lover and ruthless warlord had united in their desire to discipline her. She was being soundly put in her place and offered only one way to redeem herself. She knelt before the spread pussy and began to lick it; hesitantly at first, then enthusiastically as she realized it tasted good and was responding to her expert mouth.

Lori stopped questioning what was going on and began to accept the delicious attention to her clitoris and lips. The tongue swept over her flesh, the teeth pulled on the cunt rings, the pointed organ dipped into her cream-filled opening then lapped up the juices covering her clit again.

When she could, she opened her eyes to watch 'Hawk and Shirl playing with her breasts and tugging on her nipple rings. Coarse breathing and vibrant moans accompanied her sighs of delight and gasps of madness. The tempo increased and everyone forgot this was supposed to be punishment.

Shirl's lover was snagged by Lori's intangible lure and reeled in by the girl's potent attraction. She could see now why 'Hawk had been sucked in by this girl's involving sexuality. Like everyone else before her, she wanted to see this wench come. She wouldn't hate the girl any less for displacing her but she did feel compelled to prove she could answer Lori's consuming need. When she succeeded, she felt as deeply satisfied and aware of her own prowess as 'Hawk had that first night the girl had shown up. Watching the girl go limp in 'Hawk's arms was victory itself. She was calmed and willing to behave while Shirl finished her match. Contrite, sweet and coy, she rose to her feet and handed Shirl's stick to her and wished her good luck. Shirl chalked her stick and broke the rack as though nothing had gone on.

Chapter Twelve

Maggie couldn't believe her eyes. Cloud Three Eagles had just come through the lower entrance of the Subway Club. Things had been going so well between 'Hawk and Lori, she'd forgotten about the Indian. Cloud had to have come to the bar without stopping anywhere first, Maggie reasoned, or the Indian would have heard 'Hawk had it in for her and known better than to show up at all.

Her eyes never left the woman who was easily as tall as 'Hawk and, from the looks of her, still as strong as the warlord. The broad face with its high set, widely spaced cheekbones, narrow dark eyes, perfectly arched eyebrows, flat nose and full lips, was just as angry and mean-looking as ever. A rust-colored suede headband matched Cloud's earthy skin and set off her jet black hair which she wore in a thick braid down her back.

Knowing Cloud had fallen from grace didn't prevent Maggie

from falling under the spell of the Indian's charisma. She opened a dark beer for her and set it on the bar.

Cloud had received lukewarm greetings from the women she knew and was beginning to wonder if something was wrong. She paid for the beer and said, "Hey, Maggie, what's up?"

"Hi, Cloud. Not much. Little warm down here for that coat, isn't it?" Maggie was glad Tiên Le wasn't close enough to hear the question. She couldn't help herself; she wanted to see Cloud without her fringed buckskin coat. Cloud's native clothing interested her.

Cloud smiled and winked at the bartender. "Will you look after it for me?" she asked handing it to Maggie. Cloud wore a bone choker around her long neck, a buffalo skull necklace rested on her chest, and an earring with three silver eagle feathers in her left ear. Around each thick arm was an armband decorated with grouse feathers. A tan chamois vest and pants hugged her rigid body. The vest exposed more than it covered; like 'Hawk, Cloud had no modesty about her breasts which sat high and proud. A woven strap hung over one shoulder and fastened to the opposite hip. From behind Cloud, one could see a knife sheath and knife fastened to the strap level with her shoulder blade, a 9 mm pistol tucked into her pants, an ax on her hip and eagle feathers crowded around the beginning of her braid. Cloud always looked like she was ready for a fight.

Maggie noticed Lori bussing a table nearby. The girl's back was to the Indian but Maggie wasn't going to miss a minute of this reunion. She lowered the volume of the music, drawing attention to that end of the club.

Cloud turned around to see what Maggie was looking at and spotted the naked white girl. "Lori?" Cloud asked incredulously.

Lori nearly dropped the bottle in her hand when she heard her name being spoken by the voice she knew so well. She turned to answer the query. "Cloud!" she said nervously. Having utterly despaired of ever seeing her former partner again, Lori had done nothing to prepare herself for this now unwelcome encounter.

"What the fuck are you doing here?" Cloud demanded. Part of her question was answered by the "Property of the Nighthawk" tattoo on Lori's right breast. The tattoo riled her but it was a simple affair to tattoo over. The "Fuck Hole" tattoo and the elaborate sex jewelry turned her on. She'd leave that in place. But how did Lori end up here, and where were her clothes? Now she knew why Lori had never answered her letters.

Accustomed to arguing with the Indian, Lori said, "Funny you should ask, Cloud. After all these months. Been having fun with your *family*?" Lori asked bitterly. Cloud's excuse for leaving for long periods had always been that being with her tribeswomen was a family affair.

"No, baby," Cloud said smoothly. "I've been in jail. You never answered my letters, lover." She knew how to manipulate Lori into forgiving her. Her hungry look was genuine. She'd spent many a long night in jail thinking about her busty girlfriend and was itching to get her hands on the voluptuous, responsive body.

Everyone in the bar had stopped what she was doing to watch and listen. 'Hawk was standing out of view to keep from influencing the outcome; she was listening very carefully.

Momentarily, Lori was overcome by Cloud's charm and her own natural desire to forgive. That Cloud was looking at her like she could eat her alive didn't help matters. Lori felt the little fires ignite between her legs just like they had always done when Cloud looked at her that way. Of course, if Cloud had been in jail that would explain why she hadn't come to rescue her. But if it hadn't been for Cloud, she wouldn't have been here in the first place. Now she was glad she was, because she loved 'Hawk and had hope 'Hawk might one day love her. But all the months of hell she endured to get to this point were essentially of Cloud's doing. It had been Cloud's selfish neglect that had put her here, what would prevent the same thing from happening again?

When Lori's forgiveness wasn't immediately forthcoming Cloud decided to take things into her own hands. "Where are your clothes?"

"I don't have any," Lori revealed, almost proudly.

"I'm taking you home, Lori. I'll go up to my bike and get my rain poncho from my pack."

"No!" Lori proclaimed clearly and loudly. "I'm not going with you!"

Cloud stared at Lori, desire transforming to ire. Cloud took a step closer, leaned down and said, "Winyonwet 'kowin," using the cruelest tone she could muster.

Lori's mouth fell open. She was shocked. She remembered hearing Cloud say the big word when referring to streetwalkers; she remembered the hatred in her voice even then.

"I am not!" Lori insisted firmly, slamming the bottle she'd been holding on the table for emphasis. She was mad now. No one, not even Cloud, had ever seen her that way.

"Where do you get off calling me a prostitute? *You're* the one who invited me down here. Then when I got here *you* were gone. Tell me, Cloud. Who was it this time? Donna Standing Elk? Or maybe Ginny Mousseau; she likes to party. What the hell did you think was going to happen to me when I got here and you had left?" Lori left an appropriate pause for Cloud to answer. The big woman was too stunned, both by Lori's anger and the knowledge of having forgotten about Lori on that night.

"You didn't think, did you? And now you want me to go with you *again*? What happens if you *forget* about me again, Cloud? Who'd end up with me then?

"I belong to the Nighthawk, and I'm staying right here," Lori declared forcefully.

Murmurs moved through the on-looking crowd. No one would have believed Lori knew how to stand up for herself to anyone, much less this dangerous Indian.

"This is bullshit, Lori. You're talkin' crazy, woman. Have you been brainwashed or something? How often does 'Hawk beat on you anyway?"

"'Hawk has never hit me," Lori stated confidently.

"I've never had to. You've always acted right and done as you're told," 'Hawk interjected firmly, walking out from behind the pillar she'd been listening from. She was pleased by Lori's pluck. Talking back to Three Eagles was no mean feat. Openly declaring her loyalty to and preference for 'Hawk bridged the final moat surrounding 'Hawk's heart. Now she knew the girl's heart belonged to her along with her body.

The space between 'Hawk and Cloud cleared of people. Lori tried to move away but Cloud grabbed her arm and pulled her close.

"Let her go, Three Eagles. You betrayed me. If you'd played by the rules and shared her like you were supposed to this wouldn't have happened. She's mine now, and you're not welcome here." She didn't think words would suffice. A fight was inevitable. Out of the corner of her eye, 'Hawk could see her general poised for action.

"Fuck your rules," Cloud replied. With one fluid motion she let go of Lori's arm, reached over her shoulder, drew the knife and threw it. The blade lodged in the floor between 'Hawk's feet and vibrated from the force. The modern day equivalent of a gauntlet.

The knife was answered by 'Hawk's digging its point into the floor between Cloud's split-skin cowboy boots.

"Bare hands," 'Hawk instructed. Since the advantage in the bar was hers, she disarmed first. She handed her coat to Tiên Le who laid it down. Watching Cloud carefully, 'Hawk gingerly removed her gun from her holster. Tiên Le took the weapon, keeping a cautious eye on 'Hawk's opponent.

Cloud pulled her silver 9 mm from her pants and laid it on the bar.

With the guns out of the way, Tiên Le felt safe to dislodge the knives and place them next to the guns.

"The rings," Cloud said soberly. She wasn't going to get her face rearranged by 'Hawk's heavy jewelry.

'Hawk pulled the rings from her fingers and handed them over to Tiên Le. "The ax," 'Hawk added. She'd seen the Indian throw the ancient weapon; she was *very* good with it. The ax was placed on the bar counter also. Tiên Le motioned for two other women to join her as a barrier between the combatants and their weapons. Tables and chairs were cleared away to give these fighters plenty of room.

'Hawk took two sideways steps to take advantage of the larger field. Her bullet wound was healed now and she was well rested. Sizing the Indian up, she speculated Cloud may have suffered a loss of strength from lack of activity in jail. Still her opponent was one for fighting and may have been in a few. The accuracy of Cloud's knife throw indicated reflexes that were sharp and quick. Cloud had a reputation for fighting dirty. Hands out, fingers flexing, 'Hawk knew the one real edge in her favor was motivation. If Cloud won this fight, 'Hawk would probably never see Lori again. And she wasn't going to let that happen. Not now that she had finally found what she wanted in a woman.

Measuring time was over. Cloud lunged at 'Hawk who blocked

the fist upward to expose the ribs. 'Hawk punched the open target forcefully.

Anyone else would have gone down from such a blow. Cloud Three Eagles didn't. She let the force of it push her away and spin her. She took advantage of the twisting action to come full circle, fists interlocked and aiming upward. Powered by centrifugal force and surprise, her blow scored 'Hawk's left eye.

The crowd gasped as 'Hawk reeled backwards a few steps. Several people had to be held back from coming to their leader's assistance. The implications of the outcome of this fight went beyond possession of the little white girl. More than just pride was at stake here. If Cloud could defeat the Nighthawk, then she could conceivably try to claim the title of warlord. The idea was not an appealing one: Cloud was a free spirit and wouldn't like staying in this neighborhood for any length of time. What would happen to *them* if Cloud forgot about them the way she'd forgotten about the white girl?

'Hawk didn't share their concern. If Cloud won this fight and wasn't content with taking the girl, Tiên Le would break the Indian's neck. Her organization wasn't going to go down with one fist fight like it would in some neighborhoods. She'd spent too many years making certain of that.

Cloud followed her punch with a move that resulted in a stranglehold. 'Hawk was quick to respond with her elbow. This time she made sure the Indian doubled over. Cloud let go, grabbing her ribs. For as big as she was, she was light on her feet. She got away from 'Hawk's follow-up swing.

Cloud rushed 'Hawk, grabbing accurately for the throat. Her own throat was protected by her bone choker. 'Hawk felt the large-hands surrounding her neck with startling pressure. If someone had told her Three Eagles had choked a person to death before, she would have believed it. A sickening, sinking feeling engulfed her. The boiling gaze in Cloud's eyes spoke of more than victory,the eyes engaged hers to speak of death. In all her life, 'Hawk had never felt such intense hatred from anyone. Three Eagles was trying to *kill* her.

Locked in a struggle for her life, 'Hawk tried to punch her opponent's ribcage, but the frightening grip around her neck was crushing the air from her lungs and strength from her limbs. Forced by

184

instinct alone, she tried to pry the entwined fingers from her throat. Slowly she managed to grip a thumb and pull it backwards. Her eyes narrowed as she began to answer Cloud's overpowering glare with one of her own. A glare that meant, kill me, asshole, and I'll hunt you down from the grave. And 'Hawk's eyes were supremely capable of making someone believe she could do just that. She pulled harder on Cloud's thumb and began to lean into her attacker.

Cloud saw the look in 'Hawk's eyes. No demon she'd encountered, whether in dream or ritual, *ever* looked like *that*. The demons she knew were benign compared to the otherworldly thing she saw in 'Hawk.

Unaware she had done so, Cloud backed slightly away from the sight, giving 'Hawk the edge she was looking for. She moved her arm upward to break the hold around her neck and whirled away, gasping and heaving, trying to restore her breath. She blocked two more lunges and got in one weak punch before she felt revived.

'Hawk removed her hat and tossed it in the crowd. A hush fell over the gathering. Even Cloud's expression noted a small bit of concern. 'Hawk was mad now. She'd been fighting fair to this point, but most people she fought would have been dispatched by now. Certainly any woman, and most men. 'Hawk seldom encountered people equal to her in strength and ability. Cloud and Tiên Le were the only women 'Hawk had gone out of her way to avoid fighting. She seriously doubted she could defeat her general, and she at least questioned her chances with the Indian. But she'd turned the corner on reason and could see nothing before her except the image of a fallen opponent. Cloud Three Eagles wasn't a person any more; she was the *enemy*.

Cloud's split-second of doubt proved to be her downfall. 'Hawk's fist hit her so hard the power of it snapped her head back. The left fist made contact with Cloud's right eye turning her around. The interlocked fists came down on the back of her neck dropping her to the floor on her knees. A knee cracked her ribs sending her large body sprawling. A boot into her kidney sent sharp pain messages to her brain and dull nausea to her gut. Cloud grabbed herself, coughing deeply, her mind blank.

Six women jumped into the arena to grab 'Hawk and wrestle her away from her helpless victim shouting, "'Hawk, 'Hawk, stop it! Cool it, man!"

Tiên Le clapped her hands together in 'Hawk's face to bring her back to reality like a hypnotist bringing a patient back from a distant world. "It's *over*, 'Hawk," Tiên Le said sharply.

'Hawk focused on her general's serene face and came back to the here and now. Her chest stopped heaving, her muscles relaxed and the blaze in her eyes dimmed.

"Let her go," Tiên Le instructed. The women backed away; someone handed the hat back to the leader.

Cloud's struggle for breath lessened and she sat up. 'Hawk had already put her coat back on and was placing her rings on her fingers. The leader looked like she hadn't done much more than win a game of pool, except her cheek was bleeding and her eye was swelling and her neck was raw.

Cool, unruffled, 'Hawk pulled Lori close. "I think it's about time you found a new bar to make trouble in and a new woman to fuck, Three Eagles." Returning her gun to her holster and knife to her sheath, she ordered condescendingly, "Get her out of here," and took Lori into her apartment locking the door behind them.

Lori's head was spinning. Everything had happened so fast! She had been frightened and worried about both fighters; much too much concerned to realize that the fight had been partially over her. She had frightened herself by standing up to Cloud. She really *did* want to stay with 'Hawk. The past few weeks with the warrior had been excruciatingly pleasurable for her. It had been her own idea to keep working in the bar. She wanted to earn her keep and didn't feel being 'Hawk's bitch exempted her from normal adult responsibilities. There hadn't been much intimacy beyond sexuality but Lori was nothing if not patient. To be the direct focus of 'Hawk's sexuality rather than a convenience had its rewards. Lori had been enjoying the most exciting sex she could have imagined. And 'Hawk really *wanted* her sexually, which was overpowering in itself. Still, all their contact had been in the front room of the apartment or in the bar.

So what was she doing sitting on 'Hawk's bed?

Standing in the light of the kitchen through the doorway, 'Hawk took her heavy jacket off and tossed it on her trunk. The snaps and zippers and chains clattered noisily. She sat on her weight bench to remove her boots and socks, stood to unfasten her studded belt and pants, peeled them off and laid them on the bench. On top of the pants she placed her studded wrist sheath and hat. The calculated striptease held her audience spellbound.

With the greatest care, 'Hawk placed her gun on the nightstand next to her bed and coaxed Lori to lie down on the bed. She moved onto the bed with Lori, stretching her body lengthwise next to her lover. The girl's eyes were soft, expectant, trusting, willing. There was nothing more she could do to prove her worthiness. She'd done it all. It was 'Hawk's turn to show Lori what was in *her* heart.

Her full, dark lips covered Lori's pink mouth. Their first kiss was a tender one. 'Hawk had never closed her eyes when she kissed a woman. She didn't even know they'd been closed with Lori until she opened them. Lori's were still closed, her beautiful lashes lying on her soft cheeks. 'Hawk stroked Lori's smooth face. The eyes came open and smiled at her.

Lori couldn't have dreamed that 'Hawk knew how to look at a woman with softness and caring. The demon eyes seemed incapable of performing such a vulnerable task. Only the truest emotion from 'Hawk's deepest heart could transform the diamond-hard toughness of those eyes. Lori could truly look into them without her heart beating fear through her veins. The contact was brief but meaningful. The kiss that followed was tinged with passion which led to another, colored more deeply.

Both women felt the sharp stabs of want puncturing their affectionate interchange. 'Hawk's tongue pushed open Lori's mouth, diving into its receptive depths. Her hand fell upon Lori's soft breast. She had set out to be gentle with this girl but she couldn't help herself. Her voice was filled with longing when she broke away from the kiss. "I want you so damn much."

"Oh, 'Hawk. Take me. Please, 'Hawk, take me hard," Lori begged hungrily.

'Hawk didn't wait to be asked again. She rolled on top of her plush woman and reached down to guide her dildo into Lori's wet and waiting cunt. She pulled Lori's knees up around her ribs and reopened the mouth with her tongue. Grabbing Lori's shoulders with her massive hands, she braced herself for an untamed, mindless fuck. The bed creaked and shook beneath them. 'Hawk's knees were planted in the mattress to give her hips the leverage to rock and buck with increasing speed as she jabbed Lori's insides over and over.

Lori's eyes rolled inside her head as she absorbed shock after shock after shock. She was senseless with the excitement of inspiring this brutal desire. Being wanted and taken this totally was the divinest of thrills. Feeling 'Hawk's sweat drip on her face to mingle with her own, hearing 'Hawk's moans harmonizing with her own, riding the tide of passion to its crest, Lori had never known such happiness.

When she raised her upper body and thrust the last conquering-jabs through Lori's body, 'Hawk thought her brain was going to explode, so great was the rapture. Her release came upon her like fantastic waves of joy surging through every fiber of her being.

"Ohn, god," she wailed. Collapsing, all 'Hawk could manage to utter was, "You're . . . incredible." Limp and drained she panted long and hard to restore herself. She could only hope Lori could withstand her weight because she *could not move.*

Lori was in heaven and oblivious to her lover's massive weight. This was what her body was made for: sexual pleasure. She was fine.

'Hawk slept for a short time and awoke with a wicked smile on her face. Tantalized by Lori's peaceful, patient expression, 'Hawk raised up, pulling her cock luxuriously and infuriatingly from her partner's cunt. Lori gasped frantically when the gesture re-awakened her unsatisfied need. The warlord pushed the vibrant body further up the bed and lowered her wicked smile to the gaping, creamy, scintillating pussy. The poor, unprotected, helpless clitoris; it didn't even have its own lips to cover it. She couldn't resist tormenting the girl.

"What's this?" she asked pointing to the hard point and fondling the chains that pulled the cunt lips apart to constantly expose the vulnerable spot. Lori's mouth parted, her chest heaved in response to the suggestive question. "Why is it so hard? How come everybody looks at it like they want to play with it? Or better yet: lick it?"

Lori's eyes opened wide with eagerness.

"Oh. You like that idea, eh? Let's see just how *much* you like it." 'Hawk let her tongue glide leisurely over the point. Lori hissed. "I'd say you like it a lot." So did 'Hawk. Teasing this sex object was fun—but so was making it come. Her tongue began to tickle the point with the speed of a furious tap dance. No more than a couple minutes elapsed before the girl doubled up from pleasure, screaming and panting then fainting away entirely.

Lori regained consciousness and found 'Hawk dozing lightly next to her. Now was a perfect time for a seemly exit. She could creep quietly back to her own bed and avoid 'Hawk telling her to leave. She made it around to the foot of the bed when she heard a word that stopped her heart.

"Lori," 'Hawk spoke firmly but tenderly.

Lori turned toward 'Hawk, uncertain what to do.

'Hawk stood, pulled the covers on her bed back closed the door and took Lori by the wrist. She placed Lori in the bed, removed her shoes, then joined her. Gathering her lover into her arms, 'Hawk kissed her sweetly on the mouth. "Go to sleep," she whispered.

The couple drifted into deep, comforting sleep.

THE RAGING PEACE
Vol. 1 Throne Trilogy
by *Artemis OakGrove*

$7.95

"Dykes on the prowl for nighttime reading, THE RAGING PEACE captivates."

—GCN

DREAMS OF VENGEANCE
Vol. 2. Throne Trilogy
by *Artemis OakGrove*

$7.95

"An overwhelming, breathtaking plot filled with revenge, violence and spiritual turmoil . . . far more than just another SM book."

—KSK

THRONE OF COUNCIL
Vol. 3 Throne Trilogy
by *Artemis OakGrove*

$7.95

". . . concludes the compelling fantasy of a love between two women that withstands the passing of centuries, the barriers of time and memory, reincarnation, earthly trials and spirit war."

—Bookpaper

TRAVELS WITH DIANA HUNTER
by *Regine Sands*

$8.95

"From the first innocent nuzzle at the 'neck of nirvana' to the final orgasmic fulfillment, Regine Sands stirs us with her verbal foreplay, tongue in cheek humor and tongue in many other places eroticism."

—Jewelle Gomez

A THIRD STORY
by *Carole Taylor*

$7.95

Ms. Taylor's wonderfully funny novel takes a candid look at university life and explores what can happen when the wrong people discover the heroine is a lesbian.

THE LEADING EDGE
edited by *Lady Winston*
introduction by *Pat Califia*

$9.95

THE LEADING EDGE is the hottest, sexiest book yet from Lace's Lady Winston Series. Journey through time from the world of an ancient-day Queen to a 19th century pirate ship skirting the New Orleans shoreline with a bloodthirsty crew of women bent on revenge to lurking the shadows in a modern-day New York bar in search of the perfect candidate to steal away to a forbidding red planet far from Earth. With contributions from Ann Allen Shockley, Dorothy Allison, Jewelle Gomez, Noretta Koertge, Merril Mushroom, Charlotte Stone, Cheryl Clarke, Artemis OakGrove, C. Bailey, Chocolate Waters and others.

JUST HOLD ME
by *Linda Parks*

$7.95

This romantic novel about women loving women, faith and determination will hold you fast in your favorite reading chair from the intriguing beginning to the hope-filled conclusion.

JOURNEY TO ZELINDAR
by *Diana Rivers*

$9.95

Sair lived a sheltered life in her city, Eezore. Her father kept her innocent of the world and its wicked ways. When this bright innocent young woman had to marry the captain of the Guard, she had no idea what her fate would be when she refused his marital caresses. Given over to the Guard to preserve her husband's injured pride, Sair was raped and tossed aside to die. JOURNEY TO ZELINDAR is Sair's exciting tale of survival, learning and growth from her rescue by the Hadra women to her eventual telling of her tale to the archivist of Zelindar. Travel with Sair across the Red Line to the powerful mysterious world of the Hadra; learn their secrets and dreams that such a world really exists.

ORDER TODAY (clip or photocopy this coupon)

____	Copies of The Raging Peace (Vol. 1)	$7.95 ea. =	____
____	Copies of Dreams of Vengeance (Vol. 2)	$7.95 ea. =	____
____	Copies of Throne of Council (Vol. 3)	$7.95 ea. =	____
____	Copies of Travels With Diana Hunter	$8.95 ea. =	____
____	Copies of A Third Story	$7.95 ea. =	____
____	Copies of The Leading Edge	$9.95 ea. =	____
____	Copies of Just Hold Me	$7.95 ea. =	____
____	Copies of Journey to Zelindar	$9.95 ea. =	____
	Postage and Handling $1.50	=	1.50
	TOTAL*	=	____

____ Enclosed check or money order

____ Charge my MasterCard/VISA

Acct. No. _____

Exp. Date _____

Signature _____

Name _____

Address _____

City, State, Zip _____

Send order form and payment to: Lace Publications, PO Box 10037, Denver, CO 80210-0037

*Colorado residents add 3% tax. Thank you.